Greta and the Goblin King

Greta and the Goblin King

CHLOE JACOBS

Entangled Publishing, LLC
2614 South Timberline Road
Suite 109
Fort Collins, CO 80525
Visit our website at www.entangledpublishing.com.

Edited by Heather Howland
Cover design by Heather Howland

Ebook ISBN   978-1-62061-003-9
Print ISBN   978-1-62061-002-2

Manufactured in the United States of America

First Edition November 2012

For Carlo. Always.

*Mylena's curse will only be broken once the evil
that the disgusting humans sent here is purged from our world.
If we have to align ourselves with that very evil in order
to accomplish this, then so be it.*

- the Goblin King of the Western Counties of Mylena

Chapter One

When she'd set out to track the foul beast hunkered down in the cavern ahead, Greta hadn't counted on gale force winds and an ice storm engulfing three goblin territories descending like a bitter, frozen plague to torture her.

She should have. A blinding blizzard was nothing less than typical Mylean weather, and after spending four years stranded here, she definitely should have expected it. The cold had long ago penetrated her thick coat and the layers of wool and soft cotton, until it seemed more like days than hours since she'd felt the welcome of a roaring fire in the hearth, but her comfort would have to wait a while longer. A young goblin boy had gone missing from his home in the village. She refused to believe he was dead already.

With a weary sigh, she squinted through a break in the canopy of gloomy evergreens, gauging the amount of fury left in the turbulent sky. The shadows falling across the blanket of craptastic white stuff were still long, but at least she could see her hands in front of her face again. She had to have been on the ghoul's trail for at least three hours by now.

Three hours of non-stop fun.

She approached the cave entrance carefully. After scoping it out from a safe distance, she circled back and came at it from the side.

Her stomach twisted as she thought of the kid suffering inside, but the image that came to mind wasn't of a frightened goblin child. Instead, she saw a human boy from another time and place. *Drew.*

Shaking her head, she squared her shoulders and kept moving. Blizzard or not, she needed to bring the goblin home alive if she wanted to get paid, and the creature who took the boy had ensconced itself and its prize deep inside the cave.

A noise. Distinctive from the natural groaning of tree limbs weighed down by snow. A crunch behind her as someone took a step closer.

Damn. She'd miscalculated, assuming no one would have followed *her* while she was following the ghoul.

She spun as a familiar flash of amethyst rushed her in the not-quite dark. Before she could duck and roll, a thick, muscled arm slammed across her chest and shoved her against the cave wall so hard the back of her head scraped rock.

With a speed and strength that had been drilled into her daily for four years, Greta brought her knee up. Her attacker evaded but wasn't quick enough to avoid her headbutt to his lying face.

"Danem Greta, stop." Isaac grunted and frowned down at her. She sneered at his use of the conventional form of Mylean address. Not that she wasn't used to it, but coming from Mylena's shiny new goblin king—who was only a little older than her seventeen years—it felt like a veiled insult instead of an expression of respect.

With a hard swallow, she took in his appearance. His fur-lined cloak gaped open at the throat, and black hair streaked with deep purple curled at his neck. He had a square face and sharp features, although his cheeks were pale and smooth in the dark of the forest.

Like most goblins, he was tall and wide, built like someone had simply chipped away at a hunk of granite. It wasn't hard to imagine him in a fight to the death for the goblin throne, no matter how young he was.

He rubbed his abdomen with a pinched expression. "What did you do that for?"

Because I knew it was you? "Oddly enough, I don't enjoy being attacked from behind by strangers."

His startling violet eyes locked on her. Lying eyes. *Manipulative* eyes. Eyes she'd been seeing in her sleep for too many nights. He chuckled low under his breath. "Ah, but I'm not a stranger to you, am I?"

She fought against the deep cadence of his accented voice and the mischievous grin that curled his lips, reminding herself it was all an act. Their entire relationship was based on tricks and lies, and Greta wasn't going to fall for them again.

"But since you mention it," he continued, "which one of us is out lurking in the *Goblin* Forest in the middle of the worst storm all year?"

She rolled her eyes. Sure, if he wanted to press the issue, this was technically the Goblin Forest and he was technically the goblin king. She was trespassing.

Technically.

Not that she cared about such minor things as legal boundaries. Not when it came to doing her job. Especially in a territory run by an arrogant goblin whose biggest claim to fame was that he happened to be the youngest monarch Mylena had ever seen. "This can't be the worst storm all year," she said. "I'm sure the one that slammed us a fortnight ago was just as bad. Are there ever any conditions in Mylena other than crappy?"

He grinned and his face was transformed. Suddenly, he was the boy she'd met that evening at Maidra's who smiled at her and made her feel accepted for the first time since…well, since she found herself trapped here. As the only human in a world where her kind was reviled and any suggestion of their presence created a furious outcry for blood, acceptance and the possibility of friendship were things she'd never expected to experience.

But she didn't want him to be that boy again. He should go back to being the goblin king. At least then she knew where she stood—as far away as possible.

"I wasn't aware you felt so strongly about the weather, Danem," he teased. "Perhaps it irks you because it is one thing that remains irritatingly beyond your influence."

If the weather really were the only thing out of her control, she wouldn't have much to worry about. But after being torn from her family and everything she knew at the age of thirteen, thrust into a hostile environment where food and warmth were luxuries someone like her could not afford, and forced to hide her true identity, Greta had ended up with a whole host of issues. If she ever made it back home, some lucky shrink was going to have a field day trying to figure her out.

"I have legitimate cause to be here. I'm on a job. Why don't you let me do it?"

With a shove, she tried to get around him but he pushed her back against the rock. Not hard enough to hurt, but enough to make a point. "Unless you want to alert the ghoul in there to our presence, quit fighting me so we can handle the situation together."

"Aren't you too important to be talking to me? Go home. You have a responsibility to stay safe and provide for your people now."

His teeth ground together. "Why don't you let me worry about my people and what they need."

Her shallow breaths exhaled in a fine puff of vapor that twirled around his, becoming one before dissipating into the frigid air. Greta finally nodded and his grip on her arms relaxed. She twisted and knocked her elbow up into his abdomen. A petty move, sure, but she wasn't above immature displays of annoyance when the situation called for it—or maybe even when it didn't.

He grunted as she darted around him and clasped his wrist in a quick twist behind his back. She used the momentum to push him face-first into the rock. In the shadows, his oversized incisors peeked from the corners of his mouth. He twisted his head to the side to look at her.

Her knife was at his throat before he could blink, going a little way towards salvaging the pride that had been damaged when he managed to sneak up on her. "Maybe you've forgotten, but I don't play nicely with others."

His arm tensed under her grip, and his gaze flickered to her mouth almost hesitantly. "On the contrary, I think the two of us would play *very* well together."

The warm rush of mortification flooded her cheeks. "You may think because you can spy on my dreams you have some kind of claim on me, but it's never going to happen," she spat. "Not in any way that counts out here in the *real* world. Let's just get that straight right now."

The light in his eyes flared. "You have such a peculiar way of speaking," he said. "I rarely have any notion what you're talking about, but I could listen to your voice all day long."

She'd adamantly held onto her human expressions and mannerisms over the years. It was a little like hanging off the edge of a cliff, desperately scrabbling for every crumbling handhold. She did it despite knowing it further isolated her in this world, because the longer she stayed here, the more afraid she was of losing herself completely.

It was already happening. She remembered less and less about her life before Luke, one of Mylena's more reclusive wood sprites, had found her in the snow that long-ago night and took her in. The people and places from that former life, even the person she'd been…it had become a foggy blur that slipped away a little more every time she closed her eyes.

Greta lowered her blade and sheathed her dagger in the custom leather sleeve fitted to her forearm. She barely noticed the sleeve anymore. It was simply a part of her, like her freakishly tall body, big nose, and long blond hair—hair she kept plaited to hide her human ears from prying goblin eyes.

Locals in every county liked to gather around their tavern hearths on stormy nights and tell tales about how humans were responsible for the endless winter, and turned the daughters of the Great Mother—Mylena's two moons—against them.

All of it was crazy mythology, of course. But it had forced a young girl who'd found herself stranded in a strange land to hide her true self from everyone.

He straightened with a shrug, reminding her that the goblin king topped her in both height and breadth by several inches. She wasn't small, but next to him, an Amazon would look like a dwarf.

"Have you finished ogling me?"

His audacity made her grumble. "Don't you ever get tired of being so full of yourself?"

"Don't you ever tire of being so contrary?"

"Jerk."

"Interesting sentiment, *sprite*."

Greta barely stopped herself from adjusting her braids over her ears. No, there was no way he could know. She'd be dead by now if he had somehow discovered her secret.

He watched her closely. "As much fun as this has been, you don't want to waste any more valuable time, do you?"

Resigning herself to the fact that he wasn't going to go away, not with one of his own being held inside that cave, she crossed her arms. "Come along, then. As long as you realize the bounty is mine," she added.

His smile disappeared and he looked about as serious as she'd ever seen him. "I don't care about the coin, Danem. I'm only here to make sure the boy gets out alive."

"Let me do my job and he might." She didn't bother telling him that the thought of the helpless goblin child being held by that monster was almost more than she could bear. That it hit too close to home, made her stomach lurch and her head pound, and even if there'd been no reward, she would have still come for him.

"Of course."

His tone hardened with the turn of their discussion and she watched as all the responsibilities of his position fell back onto his shoulders. The night they met, he'd seemed so animated as he shared his passion for inventing gadgets and his dreams of traveling to exciting places. She'd been mesmerized by him, and not only because he was the only boy who'd spoken to her— besides Luke—for what felt like, well…ever.

It was hard to reconcile that spirited boy with this dour person who seemed consumed by obligation and duty. Then again, everything that night had been for show. He'd probably just been laying his trap, setting her up.

She'd fallen for it in a big way.

"Fine. Good," she said, annoyed by the jolt of pain the memory of that night always brought on. "Make sure you don't get in my way."

His lips pressed together in a thin line as he looked her up and down. "Agreed. You are the professional. I will yield to your judgment."

Satisfied the high and mighty lord of the goblin realms would at least *try* to play by her rules, she braced one hand on the cold stone and stepped forward, narrowing her attention on the opening in the cavern wall. She strained to detect the faintest sound, but from their position at the mouth of the cave, she could hear nothing but the intermittent groan and crackle of tree branches bending against the will of the wind, and Isaac's softly measured breaths as he fell into place close behind her.

She gripped the hilt of the sword strapped to her hip, but dared not draw it. Even that slow glide of steel against leather would echo. Any advantage they had would melt away like the snowflakes landing softly on the tip of her chapped nose.

Greta wished for a flashlight as they passed into the full dark of the cave. It wasn't the first time she'd have given her last meal for one of the modern conveniences she'd once taken for granted, and doubted it would be the last either. Oddly enough, the things she found herself wishing for most often included a decent pair of warm gloves and—

Thud. From deep inside the cavern.

A big hand clasped her elbow and squeezed. She nodded and picked up some speed but refused to rush headlong into the dark. Winning the day rarely came down to being stronger or faster or braver than the other guy. Mostly, it came down to being colder, smarter, and more ruthless than the other guy. Luke had taught her that.

The farther she traveled into the dark, airless cave, the easier it was to imagine what torture the poor kid was suffering. It tugged at her control and she had to hold herself back.

When she stopped to look over her shoulder, Greta could no longer see the entrance. The last of the weak light was gone. The goblin king himself was but a hulking shadow, although she felt him poised and ready behind her.

Violence hung in the air like the sticky haze of a muggy day, filled with the thick scent of fresh blood. The sudden unmistakable sound of a pained cry being silenced mid-shout completed the disturbing effect.

He surged past her then, arm brushing her shoulder as he took the lead. She shot forward and tugged him back before he went barreling down the narrow passage like a raging bull. He turned, his chest heaving against hers. She could barely see the pulse in his cheek ticking away.

After a tense moment, he gave in. He let out a silent breath and stood back to let her take the lead again, but Greta wasn't immune to that plaintive cry for help either. She finally drew her sword.

"We go in," she whispered. "You get the boy. I'll handle the ghoul." He clasped her fingers and squeezed his assent, but she wasn't finished. "Then I want you to get out of there. Don't go all heroic, thinking you have to stick around and help—you'll just be in my way. That kid is going to need medical attention. That's your first priority. Got it?"

"Hasn't anyone ever told you it isn't wise to give a king orders?"

She ignored him and turned back around, trailing a hand along the wall of the cave to keep track of her position as she started forward. It annoyed her that the goblin followed with ease, like he had the benefit of night-vision goggles—but something so cool had never existed in Mylena.

After a few hundred feet, a soft glow became visible ahead of her.

Fire.

A sliver of anticipation bloomed, the same pathetic combination of expectancy and defeat that crept past her defenses whenever she came across such a place. With it was the insane hope that, maybe this time, she would find the evil witch who sent her here and could manipulate the fire to open a portal back home.

She was always disappointed. In four years, luck had never been on her side.

She shoved away the foolish feelings. "Follow my lead."

Chapter Two

With adrenaline pushing through her system, Greta adjusted her grip on the hilt of her sword and turned the corner. She wasn't disappointed. What lay in wait was one of Mylena's most monstrous creatures.

Ghoul. A disgusting distortion of life that fed on innocence and purity with a ferocious brutality—and that was its natural phase.

Everything here had a natural phase and a raw—or moon—phase. Most of the reasoned beings like sprites, faeries, and goblins, had evolved to the point of being able to control their shift, but there were situations that could force a transformation, including strong emotions like hunger, fear, and rage. Additionally, all creatures of Mylena felt the pull of their raw phase most strongly during the rare occurrence when the moons came directly in line with either or both of the planet's suns. An eclipse.

And then the whole world went crazy.

Greta had experienced only two eclipses, and both times, she'd spent the couple of days before and after locked behind a reinforced, bolted door hidden in a damp and dark place under the floor of her pater's home. Closed-in, dark places had always been her biggest weakness, and Luke had known it, but he'd still shut her in. All because the strong, protective wood sprite—who had the strength of a steel spike and had never turned in front of her, not even once—had been afraid he would tear her apart during the eclipse.

Through the thick smoke from the bonfire crackling in the middle of the cavern, Greta eyed the gray-skinned, skeletal figure. The fact that it stood approximately eight feet tall, was even uglier than usual, and sported a mouth full of teeth the length of her best dagger proved they were in big trouble.

It had turned.

This was one of the Lost, a being that had given in to its raw form completely and would never revert back to a more civilized one, "civilized" being a term applied loosely when it came to ghouls in any case.

Her entrance had gotten the thing's attention. It crouched on the other side of the flames and faced her with a growl, bulging eyes glowing a sickly yellow in the low light. It pushed forward on all four lanky limbs, readying itself to spring. The horrific sound of its enraged roar bounced off every inch of rock surrounding her until Greta wished her eardrums would explode and end her misery.

The goblin boy huddled in a tight little ball against the cavern wall. He held his right arm close to himself and cringed as far from the nasty creature as he could. Greta paid no heed to his injuries. He was still breathing, which was more than she could have hoped for at this point.

Knowing she had to get the ghoul to come for her, she edged

along the wall in the opposite direction of the cave entrance. She kept her gaze on the creature, trusting that the goblin king would do what she'd said and get the boy to safety.

"Come on, you ugly mother," she muttered.

The ghoul's eyes widened as he charged, leaping over the blazing fire and across the small space in three long strides. Chancing a glance out of the corner of her eye, she watched his highness run for the young goblin and sighed with relief even as she lifted her sword to defend against the ripping talons aimed right at her face.

If they connected, she'd be done for. They would tear her in half. Greta swung her blade and ducked. The claws weren't even her most imperative concern. Ghouls were rabid creatures, desperate to sate their hunger for flesh, blood, and bone. Very strong and super fast, and yet their most dangerous weapon was a poisonous toxin expelled with their saliva that rendered its victim immobile for hours—which was just long enough to be consumed by your worst nightmare, inch by agonizing inch.

A ghoul could shoot a stream of that nastiness with paralyzing accuracy, and her back was up against the wall. Literally. She had nowhere to go, which made her a decent target.

Remaining far enough away to avoid the deadly slice of her blade, the ghoul roared again, opening wide to launch a thick jet of its poison.

She swore between clenched teeth and ducked to the side so it didn't get her full in the face. The fluid struck the rock behind her. It splashed, bounced off, and splattered onto her neck, cheek, and the hand she lifted to protect herself. "Damn it."

She righted herself and quickly jerked out of the way of another swipe of those wicked claws. "Damn. Damn. Da—"

The effect of the poison was practically instantaneous, numbing her hand, cheek, and the exposed skin at the base of her neck. It traveled quickly across her face, down her neck and left shoulder.

Okay, now she was worried.

She told herself the exposure was minimal and probably wouldn't hit her heart, move any farther than her elbow, or inhibit her brain function. *Yeah, right.* The arm was already practically useless, and "damn" was likely to be the last coherent word she would pronounce with her thickened tongue for a while.

It would suck if her last word *ever* was a mumbled "damn." When the time came—hopefully not today—she had hoped to be in a position to impart some profound and meaningful advice—

Another swipe of claws. She barely shifted out of the way in time to prevent her innards from tumbling out onto the dirt floor of the cavern.

Maybe she should think of that meaningful advice real quick.

Glancing up, she realized the goblin king was watching her dodge and parry. His indecision was clear as he paused and hitched the boy up in his arms.

Just what did he think he was going to do?

Worried his royal goblinness was about to attempt something royally stupid, she shook her head and glared at him before twisting her hip and leveling the ghoul in the chest with the heel of her boot. It stumbled back a few steps.

"Go! Get out of here," she shouted. It came out sounding more like *Het ooh a hee* because she couldn't make her lips form the words, but he would get the picture.

He had better get the picture.

Either way, she couldn't afford to wait and see. Ignoring the tingling in her forearm—hell, that stuff was potent—she returned her attention to the ghoul, countering its next attack with a hard, straight jab.

Her blade sank into its shoulder. She pulled back and quickly backed it up with a solid roundhouse to the gut, trying to throw the thing off balance. Knowing she couldn't afford to let up, she struck again with her blade, slicing its chest open from end to end. The creature howled. The sound grated in her ears like metal scraping over metal.

With a relentless lack of mercy or compassion, she advanced again. And again. Looking for the opening, she needed to end this once and for all.

Despite Greta having gained some ground, the ghoul wasn't slowing down, and it wasn't backing down. Its growing rage had only made it more determined. She got the distinct feeling since she had deprived the thing of its dinner, it had decided she should take the boy's place.

She was toast.

Her next strike was deflected and her hand whipped back in a wide arc, her wrist striking rock. She hissed, barely managing to hold onto her weapon. Stumbling, she tried bracing herself against the wall but her arm wouldn't respond and she just leaned against it instead.

The ghoul lunged. Its claws tore into her shoulder, wrenching a scream from her throat. She was thrown back and bit her lip hard. Her head bounced off the wall and she groaned. *Second time today.*

She was going to have a bump—not that a headache would matter much *to a dead person.*

Swallowing the blood in her mouth and fighting off the wave

of nausea that threatened to take her consciousness, she put her back to the wall. How was she still on her feet? *Ah, hell.* She was weakening with every heartbeat, her system shutting down fast in reaction to the always-great combo of rapid blood loss and ghoul poison.

Blinking back the globby dots swimming in her field of vision, she pushed off the wall and skirted to the side in time to avoid another wicked swipe—a close one. Would have taken her head clean off.

The fact that she'd started musing about her imminent death knocked some sense back into her. With a deep breath, she ducked beneath the creature's long arm, the point of her blade puncturing its side again.

Once more, a flash of movement drew her attention from the fight. The goblin king had re-entered the cavern alone, without his heavy outer cloak. He must have left the boy covered up somewhere outside.

Is he completely out of his mind?

Gritting her teeth, she turned her back on him, pissed that he obviously hadn't believed she could handle this creature on her own. Granted, she'd already gotten herself fatally spit on and clawed to ribbons in the space of what couldn't be more than two minutes. Probably closer to one and a half. Still, this was her job. No way was anyone going to interfere.

Duck and roll. When she came back up, it was with a renewed determination and her sword held high. A shout rumbled from deep within her churning belly as she forced her arm down in a sweeping diagonal arc and waited for the ghoul's head to slide off its neck to the ground. Which it did with a satisfying *thunk.*

The rest of its body tumbled over into the dirt a long second later, and Greta herself slumped against the cavern wall. Taking deep breaths, she waited for *her* body to catch up with her brain and realize the fight was over.

Good thing Luke wasn't here to see how badly she'd butchered this job. It was bad enough that it was his voice she heard in her mind, ripe with disappointment, telling her that after the embarrassing way she'd fought, she should be the one lying bloody in the dirt without a head.

No argument there. She hadn't been focused. She'd ignored her pater's teachings, especially the most important of them all: *Always stay in control.*

As much as she hated to admit it, she'd broken that rule today.

And look what had happened.

"Danem Greta." Isaac came forward, reaching for her. She jerked away and pulled a cloth from her pocket, ignoring him as she wiped the ghoul's black blood off her blade and slid it into the sheath at her waist.

Wincing, she unstrapped a leather bag from her belt. It had a thick drawstring and the inside had been oiled to make it resistant to leakage. Whether that would work with corrosive ghoul poison…

Her shoulder screamed with pain until she wanted to scream right along with it, but she'd already let the goblin see more weakness from her than she'd ever shown anyone except for Luke, so she forced herself to bend and grab her prize.

She clutched the ghoul's head by the coarse strands of its dirty, matted hair. Immediately, the disgusting bite of hundreds of tiny crawling parasites stung her hand and arm as they rushed to flee their food source. She stifled an involuntary shudder of disgust.

"Leave that thing be."

The creature's perma-snarl threatened soundlessly up at her as she started to shove it into her bag. As per the terms of the county writ, it wasn't enough to have rescued the boy. She needed proof of the creature's death in order to collect the reward.

"Proof," she said with big, numb lips. *Pooth.*

"You don't need that," he insisted, his mouth curling in revulsion. "I'll make certain you get paid."

She hesitated, contemplating whether she should ignore him out of spite. But she wasn't quite that stubborn. There was a whole mountain of things Greta wouldn't have trusted him with if her life depended on it, but he had no reason to screw her out of this bounty. If she didn't have to carry a dead ghoul's disgusting head on her back all the way to town, so much the better.

"Fine." *Faaa.* With a shrug, she dropped the thing back into the dirt and wiped her hand on her pants. She was going to have to burn these clothes.

Adrenaline and poison pumped hard through her bloodstream. *Deep breaths. Pull yourself together.* With a small shake of her head, she looked at the mess surrounding her. Her job was not over. As much as the entire operation turned her stomach, it wouldn't do to leave without cleaning this up.

"Go. I'll burn the body then put out the fire," she said, carefully forcing the slurred words past her thick tongue. "Get kid…out. Cold. Medical attention. Parents will…want to know."

He just watched her. He didn't answer, didn't mock her pathetic excuse for a rescue attempt, or her garbled words.

And he didn't leave.

She frowned. If that turned out to be pity on his face, she was going to punch—

"Why do you do this?"

His sudden, pointed demand startled her. She forced a snort. *Why indeed?* "What do you think I should do instead?" She pursed her lips, willing the feeling back into them. "Settle down in some pasture with a beefy troll, raising ornery cattle and little munchkins?" *Liddoo mushins?*

He frowned. "I wouldn't have said that. But why *this*?"

Because one of these days it could lead the way out of here. She gazed into the bonfire still blazing in the middle of the cavern. "Why not this? It hasn't gotten me killed yet. The pay is decent. It's as good a career choice as anything else in this ridiculous world."

He tilted his head, studying her.

She bit her tongue. Served her right for letting bitterness seep into her voice. "Now go before that kid freezes to death and costs me my bounty." *Boondee.*

Chapter Three

She came back outside much later. Aching, filthy, exhausted.

Propping her head against the rock wall, she took several deep, cleansing drags of winter air into her lungs. For once, she was grateful for the cold.

Looking up into the late afternoon sky, Greta half-expected to see the goblin king waiting for her. There was nothing but the trees, and a lingering scent of smoke—probably coming off her clothing—but from the looks of it, he hadn't been gone very long. His tracks remained in the snow, illuminated by the soft pink glow of Mylena's two large moons.

She spared a glance down at the massive boot print in front of her before stepping over it back through the woods the way she'd come hours ago.

She trudged along slowly, the wind whipping across her face. "Sand and sp-p-lashing surf." Blinking away the crystals forming on her eyelashes, she glanced up at the evergreens, so wide and tall all around her, they seemed to be closing in. "T-t-tender barbecue chicken." Her teeth chattered together. "T-t-tall, leafy palms. A w-w-warm yellow sun."

After tripping for the third time, she paused. Unfortunately, the cold hadn't yet made her delusional enough to believe the wet stuff filling her boots and trickling down the back of her neck was anything but miserable, icy snow, or that she was anywhere but miserable, far-from-home Mylena.

She breathed heavily from the exertion of pushing herself through the deep drifts, and tried convincing herself—without much luck—that it was good for her.

By the time she made her way to the edge of the woods, she was dead on her feet. She shuddered uncontrollably, but not entirely from cold. The whole left side of her upper body was still numb. Probably a blessing given how the rest of her felt.

Her right shoulder had been sending shooting pain up and down her arm ever since the ghoul clawed it all to hell, and now it also throbbed with a sweeping heat that said a nice infection was setting in. It emanated through the heavy layers of her outerwear, strong enough to convince her foggy brain she just might be close to that tropical paradise she'd been imagining.

Blinking, she forced her leaden legs to carry her onward, muttering aloud to nobody in particular. Luke would have told her to quit complaining. He would have reminded her that tonight's outcome could have been much worse. She could have been killed.

Death might actually be an improvement right about now.

Just a few feet from the road, she tripped over a branch hidden beneath a layer of snow and went down hard. Unable to move quickly enough to brace herself, she caught a face full of the cold stuff and tore her pant leg.

Frigid wetness trickled down her calf into her boot. At least it numbed the sting from whatever rocky outcropping had cut open her shin.

She flopped onto her side.

Waited.

Nope. Still not getting up.

Greta's eyelids drooped and she had to force them open again. Losing consciousness here, now—not a good idea. Chances were she wouldn't ever wake up.

She groaned. "Come on, you great big wimp. On your feet."

Moving slowly, she planted her hand in the deep snow for balance and tried to push herself up. A pathetic little shove. There was nothing left in her body to back up her will—and her will wasn't exactly cooperating anymore, either. Maybe it was the cold, the poison in her system. Perhaps blood loss and exhaustion.

Or, hey, why not all of the above?

Whatever. She was done.

Expelling a slow breath, her eyes fell closed. So tired and weak, she tasted salty tears at the corner of her mouth and realized they tracked down both her cheeks. Her heart ached as badly as her body.

Mama. I want my mama.

She laid her head on her arm, knowing the dreams would come, but without the strength to hold them—or the goblin king— off any longer.

~~~

He was here, sitting in the corner of the noisy taproom, just like he'd been the first time they'd met a fortnight ago. She ignored him now like she should have done then, making her way to the bar through the unusually thick crowd of sprites and goblins and…

whatever the heck that gray guy was.

Dreaming or not, she could still use a drink.

She pulled up an empty stool and sat beside a brawny troll with a scrunched-up face that reminded her of the pit bull that lived in the corner house on the street where she grew up.

Shaking her head of the memory, she waited patiently for Maidra, then ordered a hot linberry tea to stave off the always-present chill that was part and parcel of a world where winter never ended. All the while, she sensed the goblin king watching her, felt the itch of his gaze right between her shoulder blades.

She focused on the swirling tendrils of steam coming from her mug. It seemed to linger, to expand and spread out in front of her until the entire room was shrouded in a light fog.

He was doing it again.

She sighed. This wasn't the first time he'd stolen into her sleep like a thief and manipulated her dreams. Those "interactions" were part of the reason their relationship felt deeper than it should have considering they'd only known each other for two weeks.

Focusing on her reflection in the mirror over the back of the bar, Greta's slim brows lifted in an arch over pale blue eyes, and her lips compressed into a thin, uncompromising line. She wasn't wearing her own clothes—the familiar leather and furs of a bounty hunter—but soft, feminine fabrics similar to what other Mylean girls her age wore. And her blond hair fell loose to her shoulders instead of braided to cover her ears.

She had some control in these dreams, at least. He seemed able to fashion the environment however he chose, but he couldn't really force her to do things. It wasn't like she was stuck playing a part in his own private stage production.

Which made what happened the first time she'd dreamed of

him that much worse.

She blushed whenever she thought about it because, at that point, she hadn't realized what he was doing. Hadn't realized she was no longer alone in her head when she dreamed. She'd let him see the girl she wished she could have been the night they met— free to laugh and flirt with a good looking guy—instead of Greta the bounty hunter, who'd been on guard and unable to show any emotion.

It wasn't hard to guess from the wolfish look in his eyes when she finally figured it out that he was never going to let her live it down.

"Greta."

No polite "danem" this time, huh? The casual trill of her name on his lips was more than a little ironic considering what saying *his* name had cost *her*.

His voice was lower than usual, as if encouraging her to confide in him. Yeah, right. She glanced into the pitted mirror above the bar, and gasped to find him standing only a few feet behind her. When had he gotten up from his seat and crossed the room?

Probably when she was trying so hard to ignore him.

He said it again, her name. More like a whisper, actually. But closer and clearer than it should have been with all the others around them, drinking and laughing…

Except suddenly there was no one else around. She was alone with only him and the mist for company. She whirled around to face him.

"Who are you?" he asked. "Exactly where do you hail from?"

She leaned back as he pushed forward, until the edge of the bar pressed against her spine. Questions. Of course. Luke had warned here there would be questions if she allowed anyone to get too close. Thankfully, her life was a fairly solitary one. Other than Luke, she had few friends. Okay, none. Not that it bothered her. It didn't. The risks of unwittingly revealing her human heritage far outweighed any benefits that might come from having someone to talk to.

Especially if that someone was a hot goblin with a penchant for hijacking dreams, who also just so happened to be the newly minted *king*.

Just thinking about that made her want to break her fist over that square chin of his, and wipe the confident smile from his lips. But this was still just a dream. It wouldn't really be her fist flying and it wouldn't really be his face under her knuckles.

"You know I never answer your questions. Why do you keep asking? Why waste your time in my dreams?"

"You said my name," he answered. He reached out, taking a lock of her hair between his fingers and rolling it as if he was fascinated by its softness. When she self-consciously tugged her bottom lip between her teeth, his eyes flared and his gaze locked on her mouth. "You invited me in. *You* gave me the power."

He touched her cheek with the most feather-light caress, the pad of his thumb following the line of her bottom lip. She swatted his hand away before she did something stupid like lean into his touch. "I didn't know what I was doing."

"How could you not know?"

The implication went unsaid, but it was still there. She should have known because *everyone* knew saying Isaac's name had consequences. Everyone who belonged in Mylena, that is.

Well, she didn't belong in Mylena, and loneliness had gotten the better of her the night they met in Maidra's tavern. When he approached her despite the menacing *keep-away* glare she always wore to protect herself, she'd faltered in the face of his bright smile. Nobody had ever looked at her as if she were beautiful and interesting before.

They'd talked for hours and before she knew it, she'd plummeted into his trap. After she'd broken more of Luke's rules than she thought possible and reluctantly stood up to leave, he'd asked her name. Greta had only reciprocated, thinking nothing of it.

Just call me Isaac.

So she had. Apparently, it didn't matter if you were an ignorant human whom no one had bothered to explain the rules to. She'd been vulnerable to him. Was *still* vulnerable.

"It doesn't matter why I didn't know!" Her hands clenched into fists. "My ignorance didn't give you the right to take advantage of me." Closing her eyes, she tried to remember where she really was, willing her consciousness to get a clue and—

Wake. The hell. Up.

"You only wake when I'm ready to let you go."

"Then what do you want with me?"

His smoldering look went all the way through her. Her stomach fluttered madly and she stepped back, hoping to God she wasn't blushing. "Are you reading my mind?"

He snorted. "I'm *in* your mind, getting to know every part of you."

Her face burned with embarrassment. "You're deluding yourself if you think you can know who I am or what I want from spying on me in my dreams. Therein lies a realm of fantasy, and while it's an interesting place to visit every once in a while, we both have to live in the real world, don't we?"

"You can put up walls, Greta, but sooner or later, I'll break down every last one. There won't be any secret you can keep or any part of you I don't know…" He leaned forward, his voice lowering to a whisper. "Intimately."

Her knees shook at the thought. Intimacy meant weakness. Weakness that he was obviously trying to exploit. She realized it now. His appearances in her dreams…all that talk…craftily designed to subvert her defenses.

He'd implied he never wanted to be the king, but *of course* he wanted to be king. Who wouldn't? He was a power-hungry goblin so full of arrogance she felt like an idiot for not seeing it before it was too late.

She would not—could not—give into the things he made her feel. That way lay disaster, even if part of her was tempted to find out exactly how *intimate* they could get.

Frantically, she plotted. She didn't just need to wake up, she had to find a way to put an end to these visits once and for all before her will to resist was gone. "Why would you even want to? Trust me, I'm not the slightest bit interesting."

"You intrigue me," he said.

Greta huffed. She was nothing. Less than nothing. She had none of the strength of the goblins, none of the beauty of the nymphs, none of the magick of the sprites or the faeries. She downplayed her few curves beneath a hostile scowl and multiple layers of clothing to keep others from looking too closely and wondering if there was a reason why she was so spectacularly unimpressive.

No, he couldn't know her secret. If he did, he would've cut her down out there in the forest by now. And if he didn't want to get his hands dirty with it, not even Luke would be able to protect her from the lynch mob that he would send after her. "Get out of my head."

He smiled. "But I just got here."

"I don't want you here."

His hand lifted back up to her cheek. She flinched, but he only pushed her hair off her cheek. She held her breath. Even knowing his touch wasn't real, tingles danced all the way to her toes.

After what seemed like forever, he dropped his hand, looking thoughtful. "You're so secretive and prickly, Greta. Why is that?"

"None of your business."

"Oh, I think it is. In fact, I think who you are and what you do is very much my business." He stepped closer and she drew back, ready to defend herself if he decided to try "persuading" her to talk. But he only gripped her arms as if to pull her into an embrace.

She tensed and put her hand between them, on his chest. His heart was pounding fast, maybe as fast as hers, and she could almost imagine that this was real. She glanced up to find him looking at her intensely. And then he did pull her closer. Close enough to press his forehead to hers as he whispered, "Reveal yourself to me, Greta. Trust in me. Tell me your secrets, and I can be lenient with you."

She shook her head. Deny, deny, deny. That was standard operating procedure.

The hard look in his eyes returned. He dropped his gaze and let her go. She expelled a long, slow breath, unsure if she was relieved or disappointed.

"We'll discuss this again," he promised. "Now, wake."

❧

She was aware of his presence the moment she took her first

conscious breath. It didn't take much longer to pin down his position. Opening her eyes, she zeroed in on his figure sprawled in a chair in the deep shadows across from the cushy bed—a softer, warmer bed than any other in Mylena, she would bet.

But with no fire in the hearth and only one covered window, the room was cold and dark.

"Where am I?" Her voice was too loud, echoing in the cold room. Shaky and pinched, the hoarse sound threatened to tear her open, expose her to the reality of the cold world when she was still reeling from the dream.

The aches and pains of her battered body settled back in quickly now that she was awake. As much as she wanted to demand some answers and make some threats, Greta's body wasn't quite in sync with the rest of her.

"You're safe. For now." His low-voiced answer came out of the darkness. She still couldn't see his face but his shoulders were hunched, and he sounded tired and tense.

Greta remembered the ghoul. The woods. She remembered being hurt.

Had he come back for her?

She remembered the way he'd looked at her in her dream. He'd wanted to kiss her, she was sure of it. And she would have let him, she was sure of that, too. Her cheeks were burning so hot, he would immediately know what she was thinking. How could she face him?

She decided not to think about it. None of it. At least not until she got out of...wherever she was.

Shifting, she dropped her legs over the side of the bed. The blanket slipped and she shivered from the chill in the air. Her cloak and shirt had been removed. Nothing but thick bandages covered her upper body. Soft white cotton had been wound around her arm from elbow to wrist and over her burned hand. Another wrapped over her shoulder and across her chest.

No, no, no. Please, no. A spike of cold horror arrowed through her, and her fingers tightened in a death grip on the blanket as she jerked it back up to her shoulders and tried not to think about Isaac seeing her naked.

She couldn't bear the thought that he'd been the one to remove her clothes, and clean and bind her wounds. It didn't seem likely, though. He was the goblin king, after all. There had to be a houseful of servants ready and waiting to do his bidding. They were probably standing just outside the door. The thought eased her panic just a bit.

Still. How long had she been unconscious and at his mercy? Taking some small comfort in the fact that she still wore her pants—as crusty and abrasive as they felt against her screamingly tender skin—Greta rolled her shoulder, stifling a wince as sharp pain reverberated down her arm.

"The ghoul's poison worked its way through your system fairly quickly, but your wounds became infected. They are taking a surprisingly long time to heal...for a sprite. You've been out an entire day fighting off fever."

She nodded, taking the news as matter-of-factly as possible given the stunning revelation that she'd been gone for that long. Luke would have started looking for her by now.

Her muscles ached, and beneath the bandages, her upper body felt raw and torn. No doubt it was going to take a few more days for the gashes in her shoulder to heal, and then she'd be left with a whole new set of scars to show for her latest adventure.

She stared into the dark corner where the goblin king

continued to sit and watch. He reminded her of a great cat following its prey's every move, waiting for the perfect moment to strike. His intensity made her nervous. Rattled and sore, she didn't know what she would do if this cozy scene went south.

Finally, he leaned forward into the small shaft of light coming through the window and braced both elbows on his knees. Her mouth went dry as she zeroed in on the thick, corded muscle that defined his wide shoulders, and she had to look away just as fast. But the rest of him didn't help her state of being any. His hair was mussed, standing straight up in places as if he'd been dragging his hands through it. There was a sleepy, softened look to his face that only increased her agitation. He was too appealing like this. Too close.

Deep breaths.

She forced her gaze away and glanced around, pretending to stare at a particularly interesting knot in the wood paneling across the room, the fine pieces of furniture, the smudge of dirt blurring the view out the window…anything to avoid looking at him. "Why did you bring me here? Why didn't you just dump me off at home?"

"And where exactly is home for you?" He watched her with a piercing coldness. "Your *real* home, that is?"

She lifted a hand to the side of her head only to find that her strategically positioned braids were gone. Her hair fell forward, long, pale ends swinging in front of her face. Unbound, it made her feel too soft, too vulnerable.

Over the years, she'd learned all the tricks. Keeping her hair plaited just the right way. Keeping her head down. She knew how to blend in, become just another face in the crowd. She could fudge some of the other inconsistencies, but her lack of faerie points was the one overt physical feature that proved she wasn't who she'd been saying she was. Greta never left her hair down, even when she was certain of being alone. The chance that someone could get a glimpse of her rounded human ears was too great.

She remembered the way he had touched her hair and caressed her cheek. If the ice in his glare was any indication…

Her stomach hollowed out and her heart pounded too fast. How long had he known? Did he discover the truth *before* invading her mind, or was it the dreams themselves that had betrayed her? And which dream? Thinking back to his words and actions, it was obvious that he'd known the truth for a while.

But that didn't lessen her fear. What happened now? After uncovering Greta's most vulnerable weakness, what would the goblin king do with the knowledge? And why hadn't he done it already?

She chanced a quick glance at the door, expecting a horde of goblin warriors to barge in at any moment and put her in chains. Her blades were lying atop a tall table on the other side of the room. Too far away. In top form with weapons in hand, she might have been able to take him. *Might.* But half dead and without a shirt? She probably shouldn't try unless it became absolutely necessary.

She lifted her chin and dropped her bandaged arm to her side, slowly pushing herself to her feet and tugging the bed sheet along for cover. "What is this place and why am I here?"

He rose with her, but didn't come any closer. "I saved your life out in the snow and you cannot be bothered to even say thank you?"

She jerked her gaze back to him, surprised. That's what he was worried about? The level of her gratitude? "I'm sorry," she said slowly. "I am grateful for your help, but my pater will be worried about me."

"Your pater is Dolem Lucius, the bounty hunter?"

She nodded. Mylean youth either became farmers like their fathers or were contracted at early ages to skilled masters for training in other fields, depending upon the position and wealth of their families. Trades like iron working and weaving were considered worthy career choices.

Bounty hunter...not so much.

"And how exactly did you become bound to him?"

Gangbusters with the questions again. If he was planning to call her out as a fraud and have her hauled away, he needed to do it already. "There was no contract, if that's what you're asking. He's my father."

After a long moment, he only shook his head. "Your pater is a very reclusive sprite, and nobody knows much about him. I didn't realize he had a daughter until I met a capable new bounty hunter working in goblin territory."

She tried to take a few steps, but her movements were slowed by pain and nausea, making her woozy. She might just throw up on his boots. That would serve him right.

"Well, he does. So if you're finished bombarding me with questions, I'd like to go home and see him now." She started looking for her own boots, hoping he wouldn't push the matter any further.

"Say my name and I might agree to let you go."

She glanced up at him sharply. His eyes were dark, almost black. Dangerous. God, why did that make her heart beat faster? "Now, why would I do something as stupid as that again? You might have fooled me once, but—"

"No games this time."

He sounded so sincere. She wanted to believe him.

That was part of the problem.

She took a deep breath and was flooded with him. The scent of wood smoke and spice, the way his body vibrated with strength and energy. His vitality overwhelmed her.

No games, he said. What a joke. Between the two of them, it was nothing *but* games. Even if he hadn't been a conniving jerk, there could never be anything else between them. There were so many reasons why it was impossible, why she wouldn't let herself fall for him.

"What do you get out of it?" she grumbled.

"I like hearing my name from your irreverent lips."

Pressing her eyes shut, she shook her head. "We don't always get what we want."

"And what is it that *you* want?"

A vision formed in her head. A bright kitchen. Long rays of sunshine coming through the flawless window, bouncing off the polished chrome handle of a refrigerator door. A woman opened it and pulled out a carton of juice. It was one of Greta's only memories of home where all of the details remained absolutely clear as crystal in her head.

Except for the fact that she could no longer see her mother's face.

Something in his expression altered as he continued to stare at her with that unwavering intensity. He was just waiting for her to slip up and reveal too much, wasn't he?

"Nothing. I don't want anything at all. Especially not from you." She abruptly made a beeline for her clothes, gritting her teeth against the physical discomfort.

"I don't believe you," he pushed, coming up behind her before she could reach for her shirt. "Everybody wants something and you're no exception. I can see it in your eyes."

She didn't know if that was true or not, but if she didn't turn around, he couldn't confirm anything, could he? "Yeah? And you're going to give me what I want, is that it?"

"It's what I do now." She felt him standing behind her, the hitch in his breathing as he hesitated. Finally, his hands fell on her bare shoulders.

She tensed, little electrical tingles tripping down her arms to her fingertips, which curled tighter into the sheet she held wrapped around her.

With a hint of pressure, he urged her to turn back around. "But you have to ask me."

"When hell freezes over." The familiar ache of loss stung. It was a damn lie anyway. He couldn't give her what she truly wanted, nobody could. And she hated that he brought to the surface all the emotions she had worked so hard to keep hidden.

Need to get out. She tried to shrug out of his grasp and snarled when he didn't budge. "Right now, what I want most involves a certain goblin king's dismemberment and eternal suffering. Shall I demand that you honor my wish?"

He didn't respond to her angry sarcasm except to lift an imperious brow.

"And if I did ask for something, the only cost would be my soul, is that it?"

"It wouldn't have to be like that, not in the way you think. We would be bound together." He paused, his gaze straying to his hands still on her shoulders. "Would it be so horrible to belong to me, Greta? To give yourself into my keeping and trust me to take control of your happiness?"

"What the hell does that even mean? Do you get to dance through all of their heads as well? Doesn't that make for a busy night?"

He frowned. "The ability to penetrate dreams has always been a curse, but the obligation to grant my people's wishes came with the mantle of king."

"I'm not one of your people," she said. Is that how he saw her? She should have known better to believe she might be special to him. "How many others are 'bound' to your keeping?"

"Those who wish to barter with me for their deepest desires do so of their own free will, with full knowledge of the payment required." The dark slash of his brows came together in a stormy frown and he stepped back, dropping his hands to his sides. "Sometimes I wish I could turn them away, but just as the sprites are bound to the earth, air, fire, or water, the goblin king is bound to his people."

Her chest constricted, as if the bandages around her were being wound tighter. She tamped down on the feelings with a ruthless frown. She refused to feel sorry for him—that was exactly what he wanted. "This bartering of yours…what do you do, wave your magic goblin wand and presto—wishes granted?"

"You wouldn't understand."

She rolled her eyes.

"I'm linked to every person under my care, it doesn't matter where I reside, they can reach me. I cannot ignore an honest and direct call for help. And yes, once I grant a wish made from the soul, that soul belongs to me because I have assumed responsibility for his or her future happiness."

What he was talking about reminded her of an old Chinese

proverb: *Save a life and it's yours forever.* Taken literally, that could get complicated. It sounded like a nightmare...maybe for him as much as for the ones who paid his price.

It also sounded like a load of crap. The goblin boy she'd met at Maidra's hadn't said anything about responsibility, or being a caretaker of his people's souls. *That* boy wouldn't have accepted the kingship if it had been handed over to him on a silver platter.

And yet here they were, proving she'd been a gullible idiot when it came to him.

"So all those plans you told me, about the things you want to do, and the places you want to see—that was just a game to make me like you and say your name?"

He rubbed the back of his neck. "At first it may have been a *challenge*," he finally admitted. "But I didn't lie to you."

"Then what changed? Why am I talking to a king now, when a fortnight ago I was just talking to a cool goblin boy?"

He clammed up and looked away.

"Fine, it doesn't matter. I wouldn't believe you anyway." Besides, he wasn't the only one who hadn't been completely forthcoming when it came to their identities that night. She swung around and tenderly pulled her shirt on while he wasn't watching before letting the sheet drop. "But I'm never going to make a wish, Isaac."

A big, satisfied grin transformed his face as she turned back to face him. Oh, hell. She'd gone and said his name again.

"Does this mean I can leave?" She tented her hands on her hips, daring him to say no.

"Where do you plan to go?"

"Back home."

He raised a brow. "And where is home, really?"

"Didn't we just go over this?" She still couldn't decide what his game was. If he knew she was human, he wouldn't be talking about letting her go, right?

He sighed. "All right, I'll take you."

Everything still hurt, but a couple hours walking in discomfort was a better alternative than spending any more time alone with him. "That's not necessary. I'm used to walking."

"Yes, it is necessary. You're in no condition to make it to Dolem Lucius's home from here, on your own."

"And where is here?" she asked again.

"My home, on the outer eastern circle of goblin lands."

She groaned. That put her almost a full day's travel if she went on foot. "Then I'd appreciate a ride if you can spare one of your royal minions to take me in your carriage."

"I don't have anyone here who can take you. I will take you myself."

"What do you mean? Where are they?"

"Where are who?"

"Your servants?"

He shook his head. "I don't keep servants with me."

"*What?*" If that was the truth, then he'd *definitely* been the one to undress her. How could she ever look him in the eye again without thinking that he was picturing her naked? "Why not?"

He only shrugged.

"As quiet and cozy as this place seems"—she threw a glance at the stone cold hearth—"I can't picture the king of the goblins without a slew of slobbering servants and pack followers hanging around all the time."

"I like my privacy."

"Privacy I can understand, but this is more like self-inflicted banishment. Doesn't that make it a little difficult to do your kingly duty?"

"I didn't ask to be the damn king. I didn't ask for any of—" He stopped. A veil dropped over his face.

"You went to a lot of trouble to get something you didn't want." She shook her head. "It's too late now, *your highness*. You can't make me believe you're anything but an arrogant, power-hungry liar."

His lips pressed together in a line, but he didn't try to plead his case anymore. It was just as well. Greta did *not* want to know what made Isaac tick. She didn't care why he would bother lying about his reasons for taking the goblin throne, why he would rather invade her dreams than have real people around him, or why he would suffer a cold, empty house when he could have his choice of female companionship.

Caring was a luxury she couldn't afford in Mylena.

"Now get out of here so I can get dressed. I still have a bounty to claim."

Chapter Four

Greta tried rolling her stiff shoulders, but the wheels of the carriage hit another rut. She bit off a low groan as she was thrown against the side yet again.

"Are you *aiming* for every ditch and hollow in the road?"

"Just be glad you aren't walking."

"I said I was fine walking," she muttered, but her head pounded and her body ached, and he was right when he'd said she would never have made it on foot. A gust of wind could have pushed her over.

She glanced at him. While wood sprites like Lucius were expected to be reclusive tree huggers who lived in the forest because of their strong connection to the Great Mother, most gnomes and goblins lived on top of each other in the city, or on farms with large families. It was strange that Isaac chose to live out in the middle of nowhere, unless…what if he truly hadn't wanted to be the goblin king and wasn't digging the responsibilities that came with it?

No. If the rumors were true, he'd gone way too far to get his hands on the throne not to have wanted it in the first place.

As they rounded the turn that would put her in view of the tiny cottage, Greta strained to see if Luke was waiting for her out on the front porch. It was kind of a tradition. Whenever she'd been out on a job, she would round the last corner and there he'd be, waiting to welcome her back safe and sound.

As a young bounty hunter determined to prove herself to her mentor, it had bugged the crap out of her. But at some point that had changed, and it was now an expected and necessary part of coming home.

Home.

The word brought on a whole host of conflicting feelings. As much as Greta constantly told herself that home and family were elsewhere, the memories of that place were fuzzy and vague, like a half-remembered dream. She still went through the motions of searching for a portal, but her hope was fading.

When Luke said she was ready to hunt solo, she'd been relieved because it meant she could give him something in return for her room and board. She could never make enough to repay him for *everything* he'd done for her, but it felt good being able to contribute. Almost as if she had a purpose.

At the same time, she doubted this was the life her mother and father had planned for her when she was just a little girl playing with her dollies. Putting aside the whole living in another dimension thing, they wouldn't have wanted to know the person she'd become—a quick, ruthless killer. It would have destroyed them.

What is with you today? She shook off the dreary, pointless mood, and squinted against the sunshine reflecting off the high snow banks.

Isaac had been tight-lipped during the long carriage ride. They seemed to have agreed to a moratorium on uncomfortable, probing questions, but he was still watching her much too closely. The sooner she could get away from him, the better.

She still didn't see Luke. Beyond the jingling and clomping sounds of the moving carriage, the thick woods surrounding the small cottage were too quiet.

At the narrow drive, Isaac pulled back on the reins and slowed down, but she was already jumping into the snow. The horse looked over its shoulder, eyeing her as if she might be a tasty treat. Mylean horses actually bore very little resemblance to the horses she remembered from back home, except that they had four cloven hoofs and a long snout.

She danced out of reach before it could take a chomp out of her. "Thank you for the ride."

"Would you like me to wait?"

Was it so obvious that she was worried? "I'm home now. You can go." *Please go.*

She walked away without saying goodbye, not bothering to have the "stay out of my dreams" discussion with him again, because it would take too long. Despite her racing heart and the almost painful feeling foreboding, she was still surprised when she reached the familiar—but empty—front porch.

She tried telling herself she was being ridiculous. He was probably just busy inside. Cooking. Maybe sleeping. Or in the back shed. "Luke!"

Greta tromped up the plank board steps just as the suns were starting to dip down to the horizon, but rushed forward when she saw the door was hanging open an inch. The gloom within the cottage was oppressive, impenetrable by any light that might have tried to follow her inside. A dank smell that she didn't want to identify had already made itself at home.

Her stomach dropped and cold settled over her heart. "Lucius?"

Trying not to panic as she took in the broken crockery and torn linens strewn over the floor, the upended furniture and the cold, gray hearth, Greta looked for signs that something other than wanton destruction of property had taken place.

Signs of blood.

The place looked like an ogre with a bee up its nose had been trapped in here. But maybe Luke hadn't been. Maybe he was out on a job and didn't even know the place had been ransacked.

The optimistic thought didn't have time to root. She felt and heard the sorrow of the forest. As a wood sprite, Luke had a connection to the land that ran deep. Being human, Greta couldn't understand it completely, but she had learned to listen and respect it, and right now every leaf on every tree—the very ground itself—was weeping.

She forced her feet forward, making her way through the destruction of Luke's normally pristine home, tasting the bitterness of fear. "Luke, please." She tried swallowing the lump that was lodged in her gullet like a ticking grenade. *Be alive. Be alive. Be alive.*

Lifting her gaze from the splinters of wood that used to be a chair, a wave of panic threatened to drown her. "Damn it, Luke. Where are you?"

"*Here.*" Barely audible, the pained whisper was the most welcome sound ever uttered. She spun around, her breath coming out in a jerky rush of relief, and dashed into the bedroom.

At first she didn't see him.

But then she saw the blood.

"Oh my God." It was *everywhere*. Soaking the single white sheet crumpled on the bed. Covering the walls in long slashes. Pooling in dark burgundy splotches on the floor. "Oh no."

Frantic, she searched the room. Now she hoped she'd been wrong in what she'd heard. She didn't want to find Luke here. He needed to be anywhere *but* here.

Her gaze landed on a bare foot peeking out from the other side of the bed and she hurried over, sliding to the floor as she reached his side. Her knees skidded in blood, but she barely noticed it.

"Luke?" She reached for him, running her hands over his chest and down his arms, searching for the source of the blood. She didn't know where to start. God, there was so much of it, from so many cuts and slashes and punctures.

"Who did this to you? Luke, please talk to me." His eyes remained closed. "Come on! Wake up and look at me."

Her voice shook as badly as her hands. His body shuddered through some kind of spasm and she moaned with him, moisture blurring her vision.

One particularly gaping wound in his chest was seeping steadily. She planted her palm over it in a lame attempt to stem the flow, eliciting a hoarse cough from her mentor. "We have to get this bleeding stopped."

"Greta," he whispered. His eyes fluttered and he struggled, like he wanted to say something to her, but when he opened his mouth and hacked weakly, blood bubbled from between his lips.

She blinked back tears, refusing to dishonor him with weakness. "Shh. It's okay. Don't talk. Just…just let me fix this." Her gaze darted over him as she tried to decide what to do first.

"No, I have to… You have to know…"

Greta shook her head, but he only tried harder to get the words out and the blood splattered from his mouth onto her arms and hands. "Damn you, shut up," she said. "Luke, *please*. You can't—"

"*Gretel*." She stilled at the stern tone she knew so well. "Stop… and listen."

Impatient and scared to death, she took a deep breath, aware of the blood streaming between the seams of her fingers as she continued to press against his chest wound.

His expression was one of sadness and defeat before he seized the fabric of her sleeve. "You have to leave…find a way to go back. He knows. The key… Greta, he *knows*."

She had no idea what he was talking about. "I will. No problem. I'll do whatever you want once you're better. Just let me get you some help first."

"Hurry. They'll be coming for you." He struggled to continue. "Can't let Agramon…"

"*Never mind that now*," she said, becoming more desperate as his color turned from chalky white to all out ghostly. "Luke—"

At the sound of a booted foot at the door, Greta swung around with a snarl, hand going to her sword. She released a harsh sob when she saw who it was.

"Oh, thank God." She didn't even bother trying to hide her relief. "Help us. Lucius…he…I need help," she said. "Please… Isaac, he's hurt. And I…I don't know what to do."

He took in the scene and was at her side in less than a heartbeat. Thankfully, he was thinking more clearly than she was, reaching for the cotton sheet from the bed and dragging it down to press it to Luke's chest. He held it in place while he carefully assessed the rest of the damage.

"His wounds are extensive. He's lost a lot of blood."

The finality in his voice was unmistakable. Everything in her railed against it. "I know, but it's going to be okay," she insisted, even as darkness clawed its way into her heart. "He'll be fine. We just…we need to get him outside and into the ground. He'll heal better there."

Isaac looked into her eyes. Just when she thought he was going to tell her it was too late, he nodded. "All right. Keep pressing this over his wound while I lift him."

She did as he asked, silent while Isaac gathered Luke into his arms.

As quickly as they could, they carried him out of the cottage and down the three wooden steps. "Over there," she said, gesturing with a tilt of her head to a tall thicket of very old trees a few hundred feet from the house.

When they reached the copse, Isaac turned sideways to step between two tall tree trunks acting as twin guards at the entrance of the sacred circle. Within it, no snow had gathered and the grass was lush and green.

Greta couldn't go any further. She was forced to let go of Luke and stand waiting beyond the circle's boundary while Isaac carried him through. He turned around, but she waved him on. "Hurry," she said, motioning him on. "Get him in there."

As much as Luke had taken her in and treated her as his own, Greta was no wood sprite and controlled no magick, so she couldn't enter a sprite's sacred circle. She hadn't even been certain Isaac would be able to, but thank the Great Mother, he crossed the boundary without any trouble. "You have to lay him down in the middle of the circle."

"I know," he answered, his voice calm. Even. Greta took some comfort from his competence and the gentle way he released

Luke to the earth.

Without waiting for her instructions, Isaac reached over and quickly started digging a shallow trench in the grass all around the body with cupped fingers. When it was done, he tilted his head to the sky. Her lips moved with him as he said the sacred words, praying for the ground to open and enfold the wood sprite in its healing, mineral-rich earth.

Nothing happened.

"Why isn't it working?" Her fingers dug into the rough bark of the trees that acted as the circle's silent guardians. She met Isaac's gaze, unable to hide her desperation and fear. "Do something," she begged. "Isaac, please. You've got to do something else."

He only shook his head, his eyes solemn and dark. "I'm sorry. There's nothing more to be done. The Great Mother—"

Suddenly, Greta felt a pop. A release. She pitched forward, one foot landing inside the circle. The invisible shield was gone. The magick had winked out of existence.

"No! Oh God, no."

She dove through the stand of trees and pushed past Isaac, falling to her knees in the grass. "No, no, no. Luke, don't you dare!" She bracketed her hands on either side of his face and pulled him into her arms, rocking him sharply. "Wake up."

The tears started coming. She couldn't hold them in. "Wake up. You've got to wake up!"

He was so still.

"No, you can't do this," she sobbed. "Don't go. Don't you go and leave me here." Taking the sprite's already cool hand between hers, she clutched it close to her chest, dropping her forehead to his. "I'm so sorry."

At first, she didn't notice that Isaac's arms had come around her and he was patting her shoulder, his big hand landing in heavy thumps that jolted her out of her sorrow. She fell silent, pushing against his loose hold until he let her go.

He took her hands, tugging them away from the blood-stiffened fabric of Luke's shirt. She curled in on herself, but he stayed with her, saying something in a low voice. She didn't know what. It didn't even matter. It was his voice she needed. That hypnotic, soothing voice that seemed to numb some of the pain.

After a long time, he pulled her up and started to lead her out of the circle. The weight of her sorrow pushed on her chest, making it so hard to breathe. "No, I can't go. I can't leave him there all by himself."

"I think your pater would want to rest here in the woods. He is one with the Great Mother now, and will never be alone." He paused and squeezed her hand. "I can take care of him for you, but maybe you should wait in the carriage."

She shook her head and worked to pull the world back into focus, determined to get control of herself. "No, I can handle it. Staying with him until the end—it's the least I can do."

He looked at her for a moment before nodding. "All right. I'll go to the house and get a spade. Don't go anywhere."

Where am I going to go?

When Isaac left, Greta made her way back to Luke's side. Seeing the dark stains marring his face, she grabbed a clean edge of the sheet and wiped off the blood as best she could, but it was mostly dry now, caked on like a dark birthmark.

Isaac returned and insisted on doing the digging. He stopped only once to peel off his heavy cloak and roll up the sleeves of his white lawn shirt, despite the cold winter air. When the hole was deep enough, he lifted Luke's body and laid it in the fresh grave.

She pushed to her shaking feet and walked across the grass—already turning brown and crispy now that the magick that had kept it alive through the perpetual Mylean winter was gone. When the last shovelful of dirt locked her mentor into his grave, she stumbled back to the edge of the circle and darted into the trees.

She made it maybe a hundred yards before falling to her knees and glaring up into the night, drawing great gulping breaths into her lungs. The skyline was a black shadow unmarked by endless power lines or the jagged blight of a thousand skyscrapers. Flora that would just as easily kill as nourish. Mountains which refused to bend to any force but that which came from the Great Mother herself. Everything about this place was hard. Merciless.

She swiped her sleeve across her eyes and took a deep breath. Luke had been trying to tell her something before he died.

Agramon.

Chapter Five

Agramon.

What did that mean? Person, place, or thing? Had Luke been trying to name his killer or pass along some last bit of fatherly wisdom that she didn't get because she hadn't been in her right mind while he was losing his lifeblood all over her?

Isaac came up behind her. "Are you all right?"

Greta shook her head, knowing if she spoke, she'd lose control again, and forced herself to go back inside the cottage. *Treat this like any other job. You're hunting a monster. It's exactly what Luke trained you for.*

"There's nothing here for you."

"I can't leave yet. There must be *something* here that will tell me who did this to him."

He stood behind her, smelling warm and alive, of fresh earth and sweat. "Anyone could have gotten in here," he said, touching her shoulder. "One of the Lost. Or drifters perhaps."

"I don't think so." The blood on the floor was drying to round black blots that would leave a telling stain in the natural wood grain.

No creature of the Lost could have done this. It all felt much too methodical. "I think Lucius knew who it was. He was trying to tell me when I found him. He said *Agramon*." She turned around to look up at Isaac with a frown. "Do you know what that means?"

Isaac's eyes widened. Before she could ask what he knew, he took her hand and started pulling her towards the door, his brows drawn together. "Hurry, come with me."

"What is it?"

"It isn't safe here. If he finds you…"

So Agramon was a person. She jerked out of his grasp. "What do you know about him?"

"I know that he will come for you."

She stiffened. "*Me*? Why me? Did this guy kill Lucius because of me? How do you know this?"

He rubbed his neck and glared at her as if trying to decide whether he'd be able to throw her over his shoulder. "He sent his gnomes to do it for him. And more will be on their way."

"Gnomes?" She curled her fingers into her palms to keep from reaching out and shaking him, her insides crawling with too many emotions. "*How do you know this*?"

His lips pressed together in a pained expression, but he refused to say anything else.

"It doesn't matter," she said. "I'll save him the trouble of putting together a posse by finding him first."

"Don't be ridiculous." A sharp glower twisted his face. "You have no notion of what you're dealing with."

She shrugged and turned away, hiding her fear and despair. "I'll figure it out, won't I?"

"So stubborn," he said behind her. "Is that a *human* trait?"

"*What?*" She gasped and swung back around.

"Are you going to deny it?" His flinty stare dared her to try.

"Listen." She'd figured out that he knew the truth after their conversation in his house, but the way he spat "human" like the very word left a rancid taste on his tongue hurt. "I'm just going to leave. I think it's best if—"

Isaac stepped between her and the door. She could see the condemnation in his stiff stance, the wariness in his hard gaze. He seemed to be waiting for her to do something revolting and thereby prove that humans were as horrible as he'd been told.

"Why should I let you go?" he asked. "You are the very reason my world was cursed, and you're the only way for us to be free of it."

Her mouth dropped open. "Whoa. I know you people have thought up some paranoid crap about humans, but let's not get carried away. You don't actually believe all those crazy stories?"

"Humans brought a monster to Mylena that remains to this day. It has leeched into the very ground we live off, the lakes we drink from, the air we breathe, and infected us all. Only by exterminating humans from our land will we be able to find prosperity once more."

Greta didn't like the sanctimonious tone of his voice. "That's bull—"

"Quiet," he snapped, his inscrutable expression causing her muscles to tighten in readiness. "Who are you?"

She bit her lip. "No one. I'm not a threat to you or anyone else. I'm just a girl, not some harbinger of great evil. Really. Please Isaac, just let it go. Let *me* go."

His eyes narrowed at the sound of his name coming as a plea from her lips. "You're not going anywhere until we have a talk."

She crossed her arms and glared at him. "I don't have time for this."

He laughed at her. *Laughed.* The jerk. "At least now I understand where your impertinence comes from. Humans are notoriously irritating and troublesome, are you not?"

And how would he know what humans were like? "You're no walk in the park yourself," she snapped. "Arrogant, manipulative smartass."

He ignored her jab. "Gather whatever you think you might need and meet me at the carriage. You have two minutes. No longer."

Isaac might not be the biggest, strongest, most menacing thing walking—yet—but the potential was there. He was better suited to his new position than he let on. He already spoke with the unshakable confidence of a male used to getting his way, used to the privilege of his position. Another couple years and he'd be completely intolerable.

Her jaw ached from clenching her teeth so tightly together, but she didn't say anything. In this world, his will would always be upheld over her own. If he decided to assert his authority, there would be no one to stand up for her.

She found a lantern that had survived the carnage. Needing some matches, she headed for the cupboard across the room. The twin doors of the supply cabinet stood open, one of them hanging drunkenly by only one hinge. The few contents within had been wiped from the shelving and strewn over the floor, but she was able to find a box of matchsticks to light the lantern.

With a soft glow illuminating a small circle of space around her, she pulled out the two empty shelves from the cupboard and turned a hidden latch. The back wall of the unit swung out on a hidden joint, revealing a secret compartment.

She surveyed the selection of weapons still resting neatly in their places upon the high shelf. Knives and daggers. A sword and an axe. A quiver of arrows and a short bow to go along with it, along with a few other fun things. She got what she wanted, and then headed back into Luke's room.

He'd taken Greta in and protected her when anyone else on this damn planet would have gutted her like a pig and set her rotting head up on a spike. She never figured out why, although at times she thought he'd decided to kill her with exhaustion. He'd tortured her with hunting lessons, weapons drills, and survival training every day until she couldn't move, but at least it had kept her from giving in to despair when she realized going home was not an option.

No matter how harsh he'd sometimes been, Luke became her friend. He was also a father and a teacher to her. Now he was dead. Now she was alone. She needed to remember this moment. Not the fear or the loneliness—although those feelings were strong enough to tear her apart inside—but the anger. That was something she could use, it would give her strength.

"You are taking too long," Isaac called from outside.

She gnashed her teeth and left the room, veering into her own small sleeping area. It was just an alcove Luke had set aside for her, with a heavy curtain to give her some privacy.

She grabbed her tiny gold locket and a walnut from the rickety table beside her cot. While she was there, she figured she could use her comb and a change of clothes, so she stuffed them in a bag and walked out without looking back.

On the front porch, she paused. A fairy tale-like crystal coating of snow shimmered over everything, glinting pink in the soft light of Mylena's low-hanging moons. It was difficult to make out Isaac's expression in the darkness. She didn't know what was going on inside his head, but she also didn't care as long as he let her leave.

She went around him and down the porch steps, away from the post where he'd tied his carriage. Before she took two steps further, he was standing in her path.

Tired, she sighed. "I'm not going with you."

"And where will you go?" he asked, glaring down at her.

Hell if she knew. It was all catching up with her again. The despair and loneliness. She really didn't have anywhere to go. Anyone she could trust. Soon, she would break from the strain. She could feel it riding up on her, and couldn't let it happen here in front of him. "What business is it of yours?"

"As you well know, everything that runs, walks, or crawls in this county is my business."

Yes, the cool boy from her dreams was definitely gone, and the goblin king had returned. "Is under your thumb, don't you mean?"

"If that's the way I want it," he ground out in a stubborn growl. "Especially when I have to deal with a reckless, bullheaded human with an irrational death wish, stupid enough to take off after forces she should never attempt to face alone."

"Reckless and stupid? No wonder you live alone—the pretty flattery never stops," she said. "And there's nothing reckless about my running down this Agramon monster. I was trained by the best hunter in this entire frozen wasteland."

"This is different," he insisted. "This is no common ghoul which has succumbed to the moons. You're human. You don't have the slightest chance against one such as Agramon."

"And what do you know about it?" She waited, but he still

refused to answer. She snorted and tried to get around him again.

"Scoff all you want, but you need my protection."

"*You're* going to protect me?" She laughed. "Shouldn't you be leading the lynch mob out to get me?" Greta's stomach lurched at the thought. "It'll be a cold day in hell before I look to you for protection."

"While I don't doubt you can take care of yourself against an ogre or two, what are you going to do against an entire army?"

"Start a conga line?"

He sneered. "Always you make ill-bred jokes."

"That's me. The lowbrow human. How can you even stand to speak to me? Oh wait, because you don't speak to me. You manipulate me. You order me around. You lie to me—"

"Enough! Tell me where the other renegade humans are hiding and I might be persuaded to keep your secret. I could help you."

Renegades?

"There aren't any renegades. No other humans at all," she answered truthfully. "As far as I know, I'm the only one."

He regarded her for long moment. "You aren't the only one."

"You've seen others?" She'd heard tales, but they were old stories and always began with the nasty humans being birthed from a cloud of black magick and set upon Mylena like a plague of locusts, ending with her kind being murdered for the good of everyone, usually by fire or beheading. She stepped forward. "When did you see them? Where?"

Isaac stood his ground. A frown furrowed his heavy brow. "More than a fortnight past, a couple of humans were found poaching in Leander's county."

Leander was a powerful gnome king whose county included

Rhazua, the largest Mylean city, and the lands bordering Isaac's territory to the south. She didn't take jobs in that county often, but if something had gone down, she should have heard about it.

"Even if they were human—which is doubtful—they were probably just trying to find food and shelter."

He shrugged. "I don't know, and it didn't matter. We hunted them down."

"If this happened on Leander's lands, why did *you* have to deal with them?"

"The humans disappeared into the Goblin Forest. The gnome king asked for my help, so I took a contingent of hunters out searching for them. We found the first male hiding deep inside the brimstone caves. He seemed no older than the goblin boy we rescued from the ghoul, but he was a mad creature. His fingers were scraped raw and bloodied, as if he'd been trying to dig through the rock with his bare hands."

Had the boy guessed—like she did—that fire was the key to the elusive portals connecting the dimensions, and tried to get to the molten lava that flowed beneath the surface of the caves?

Greta closed her eyes. Four years ago when she'd awakened on a dirt floor in the dark, it had been in the brimstone caves located deep in the mountains bordering faerie lands. Since then she'd been all over those caves, but found no way home.

Shivering, she thought how easily that poor boy could have been her. If not for Luke, she would have been all alone, maybe driven to insanity by the shock of this alternate world.

"Despite his crimes, we wanted to capture the boy without further injury. We were going to use him to lure the second human out of hiding."

The unemotional premeditation of his admission sent a chill

up her spine, until she thought of all the Lost she had systematically hunted down and executed. Was she just the same? As coldly calculating and without mercy? "What happened?"

"He tried to run and slipped on the rocks. He fell over the edge of a cliff. The second boy arrived just as the other fell, and attacked us as well."

"You killed him."

He flinched. "He forced me to cut him down."

"And how exactly did he force you?" She sneered. "Was he armed to the teeth, threatening your life as you threatened his, or just a nuisance you swatted away like a fly?"

Isaac sputtered, indignant. "I wouldn't have killed him. I wounded him, yes, and I would have taken him to Leander for sentencing, but he managed to escape."

"So he's probably dead now, too, and I *am* the only one." Tears burned behind her eyes, but she shook them away.

"In our search for the two criminals, we found evidence of more humans hiding in the forest."

She'd never come across even a hint of other humans in Mylena. In fact, she still wasn't certain she believed Isaac's story. She made a beeline for the tree line at the opposite end of the path, but once again, he stopped her.

"Use some sense, if you have any." He sighed as she tried to shove past him. "First of all, it's dark and cold."

"I've been colder," she said stubbornly.

"As the king, I have every right to hold you until you give me what I want. But I find I'm less interested in forcing you than I am in making you see that you can trust me."

She pulled up short. Trust? Between the two of them? She trusted Isaac about as much as she trusted a hungry black wolf when both of the moons were full. And she knew he didn't trust her either. Whatever his game, she wasn't interested in playing.

"If you aren't keeping me against my will, then I'm leaving. I've been patient because you helped me with Lucius. But if you have any idea where this demon is, you'd better tell me."

"As you say, Greta…forget it."

The wave of frustration and anger consumed her, and before she'd even thought about it, she kicked him in the shin. He jerked back and glared at her. "Why you vicious, ungrateful…" She suddenly noticed how long and sharp his claws had gotten.

The points of Isaac's incisors had lengthened as well, protruding from his mouth in a snarl, and his eyes glowed darkly. He took a halting step away from her.

He's going to turn.

No, wait. His whole body was stiff, as if he was holding onto control by the skin of his teeth, but he *was* in control. As she watched, the claws retracted and his eyes lost that feral glaze.

"What the hell was that?" she asked.

He let out a guttural growl and shook his head. Had she really pushed him *that* far? She'd been much more aggravating than this and no one had ever never lost it before.

"The eclipse is close." He was still taking deep breaths, the shirt beneath his open cloak stretched tight across his heaving chest. Veins stood out in his neck, and his square jaw was clenched tightly.

"Just how close are we talking?" Luke had warned her only a few moons ago that it would be soon, but she'd avoided thinking about the event for as long as possible because it would mean being shut away for the duration. Now she regretted putting those blinders on. An imminent eclipse certainly explained the added hike in her encounters with the Lost.

"Seven days." He wiped a hand over his brow.

"You're certain?"

His expression didn't change.

"Okay, okay. So you're certain." She shrugged. *Seven days?* A heavy ball of dread settled over her chest as she remembered the horror of the damp, dark pit Luke had locked her in during the last two eclipses.

She had gone willingly the first time, but the pitch black did something to her. Last time she argued that it wasn't necessary, that she could take care of herself. She'd even been ready to fight him on it, but he hadn't given her the chance. One morning she'd simply woken up with the dirt floor under her, trapped in the darkness.

No way was she doing that again. A scary thought suddenly occurred to her. "You're old enough now, aren't you? You're going to turn when the eclipse hits."

He swallowed hard. "I don't know."

He's lying. She crossed her arms over her midsection. "Fine, don't tell me."

He groaned. "I think I will turn, yes. I could feel it last time, crawling beneath my skin, but I was still too young. I think this is the year."

The bleak look in his face sent a stab of sympathy through her. She hated the idea of Isaac caught up in the madness of an eclipse. She could imagine just how much he would hate the loss of control.

Don't waste your time worrying about Isaac. Worry about your own damn self.

That got her moving. She hiked her pack high on her good

shoulder. "Good luck with that."

He stopped her again. This time, he looked nothing like a manipulative and dangerous goblin on the edge of transformation. Just a boy who was already tired of all the crap that had been shoved onto his shoulders. "What if I...*ask* you not to go?"

Her feet froze to the spot. "Is that what you're doing?"

"Well...if I was? Would you stay?"

Greta swiped her palms over her hips and ducked her head. "I can't. There are things I have to do."

The vulnerability in his expression vanished, replaced by the arrogant goblin king she'd grown to hate. Lips pressed together, he turned and started to walk away from *her*.

It must be a trick. He wouldn't just let a known human roam free. "What are you going to do? Are you going to tell—?"

"Your secret is safe." He looked back over his shoulder. There was just enough moonlight shining on his face for her to see the frown crinkling his forehead. "For now."

"For now? What is that supposed to mean?"

"I don't know." He ran a hand through his hair absently. "Go if that's what you want, but you know you can't hide from me if I decide to find you."

Chapter Six

According to every piece of Mylean lore passed down through the generations or put to parchment, she was the very thing Isaac should hate, and yet he'd let her go free.

Which worried her.

He'd said he could always find her, though, and maybe that was true unless she found a way to lock the door on her dreams again—at the top of her list of annoying problems to deal with—but it still didn't make sense. It was like she'd become a pawn in some game, but didn't know who had the next move—or what the board even looked like.

She'd spent two days asking everyone she came across about Agramon while trying to remain inconspicuous. As far as she could tell, the demon was a myth, or at best, a phantom. Still, she kept searching. There was nowhere for her to go now anyway. Without Luke, she didn't have a home. She didn't have anything.

Blinking back tears that would only freeze on her cheeks if she let them fall, she turned off the lane and stomped toward the only public house to be found anywhere this side of Rhazua.

What she wouldn't give for a freak heat wave the likes of which Mylena had never known. She'd once asked Luke how it was possible for a planet to orbit two suns but have no summer, and he had countered by asking if Earth had been a paradise. She'd described the big golden sun and its radiant warmth, told him of spending long summer days at the beach where she and her brother Drew had splashed around in nothing but bathing suits because it was hot enough to fry eggs on the pavement.

She stuck her hand in her pocket and closed her fingers around the walnut she'd taken from Luke's place. Such a silly little thing to keep, but it was all she had that mattered besides her locket. More tears blurred her vision. Angry, she swiped at her eyes and took a deep breath.

As always, the front entrance of Maidra's Place was shut against the perpetual chill, but the inn itself never actually closed, except maybe during an eclipse.

As she approached, warm golden light spilled from the crack beneath the door and through the single heavy-paned window beside it. How long before Isaac found her here? She hadn't caught him snooping around in her dreams. Then again, she hadn't slept longer than an hour or two at a time, for just that reason.

Was he looking for her, or had he finally decided she wasn't worth the trouble?

Didn't matter. Greta only needed an hour here, maybe less. Enough time to ask a few questions, get a few answers. And then she would be on her way.

Maidra's monopoly over the county's supply of cheap spirits meant the small tavern attracted a wide variety of visitors and the atmosphere could turn ugly in the blink of an eye. Before she walked up the steps, Greta double-checked her braids, pulled her hood down low over her eyes, and patted the blade on her hip. *Ready as I'll ever be.*

The door swung open before she reached it, releasing a cacophony of merry sounds to the early evening air. A female goblin tripped out, a brawny male trailing eagerly in her wake. Greta didn't recognize him, but there was no doubt he was a fire sprite. Lanky and tall, his hair was so vibrant it shone red with the light from the tavern behind him. And his eyes glowed. Greta dismissed him.

The goblin was another story. Now *her*, she recognized.

Siona was a hunter and, like every other goblin she'd met, including Isaac, a pain in the ass. She'd stolen a few bounties out from under Greta's nose, but Greta had done the same to Siona often enough that it sort of evened out. She had no real issue with the female goblin on a personal level—not that there *was* anything personal between them. Greta didn't do personal with anyone, Isaac apparently being the exception.

And look where that's gotten you.

Siona was also beautiful for a goblin. *Too* beautiful. She lacked the thick-boned bulk and sharp features that categorized the species, making Greta think there was a juicy scandal somewhere. They'd never been close enough for her to ask, but the female's tall, slim build reminded Greta of the reclusive faeries. She had long, shiny black hair and big amethyst-colored eyes, though. Just like Isaac.

The pair was about to step aside and let her pass, but Siona glanced up at the last minute. "Danem Greta, is that you?" She peered closer as if trying to see beneath the layers of winter gear Greta wore. "It is, isn't it?"

Siona's own sleek ankle-length leather coat hung open despite the weather. The gauzy blouse and skin-tight pants beneath couldn't have provided her with much protection against the cold, but at least her knee high boots looked furry and warm. She carried a long sword at her waist.

For a flickering heartbeat, Greta envied the young female who pulled off sexy, graceful, *and* deadly in a way she couldn't begin to match. They were about the same height and age, but Greta had never owned clothing that would be considered frivolous or decorative, and couldn't remember what it was like to do something just for fun.

She stepped to the side to encourage the couple to pass her. "Good evening, Danem Siona. Excuse me."

"I heard about Dolem Lucius's death," Siona said, staying right where she was. "I'm sorry for your loss."

Anger bubbled up anew. "Please let me pass," she said carefully. "I would hate to interrupt your evening."

Siona pulled her companion close and whispered in his ear, but her eyes remained fixed on Greta. Whatever she said didn't seem to go over very well. The sprite gave Greta a fiery glare before stalking past them down the lane.

Greta settled her hand on her waist, very close to the sword strapped to her hip. "What is it you want, Danem Siona?"

"Out of professional courtesy, I thought I would try to warn you," she answered, grim lines pulling her forehead tight. "There are a lot of interested parties looking for you right now. In fact, I could earn a nice bag of coin if I turned you in myself."

"Turn me in? Are you saying there's a bounty out on me? On *my* head?" Greta barked out a surprised laugh. "On whose authority? What are the trumped-up charges?"

"The writ stipulates that you be taken alive for the murder of

Dolem Lucius."

Her stomach lurched. "Why would I have killed my own pater? And who is telling such lies?"

She shook her head. "Don't know. Anonymous bounty."

"Someone had to have proof in order to push it through. A bounty is never completely anonymous."

She nodded. "You're right. There are rumors that King Leander of the southern counties put up the guineas for the writ."

Leander again? What was up with that guy? Greta had never been to Rhazua, never had a job go bad, or clashed with the gnome king or any of his people. At least that she could remember. Why would the death of a wood sprite in another territory matter to him one way or the other?

Unless maybe someone had put him up to it.

"Whatever he has is crap."

Siona cocked her hip and pulled her coat together as a gust of icy wind blew between them. "It seems to have been enough to convince the Council. He's also taken great pains to make it a cross-border writ."

Greta snorted.

"This is no joke, Danem. Hunters from every county have come out of the woodwork, looking to bring you down." The goblin's eyes gleamed, her lips twisting in a bemused smile. "And a lot of them aren't even in it for the money."

Greta waved that away. "We've all stolen bounties from each other. I lost one to you last fortnight. First in, first out, first to get paid."

The goblin's smile faded as she looked over her shoulder at the closed tavern door. "But the secret is out that the late Dolem Lucius's ward is not quite who she says she is," she said in a low voice. "For them, it's no longer just a matter of being bested by another hunter…"

Greta stepped back. *Isaac?* She didn't want to believe that he'd orchestrated this…but how else? His promise that her secret was safe "for now" apparently had a pretty tight time limit. Or maybe *this* was how he intended to find her.

Her shoulders slumped, but she forced herself to throw off her disappointment. "Why are you telling me all this? You would have had a better chance collecting the bounty if you hadn't just spilled the beans and put me on guard."

"And you think I won't be able to take you in? Puny little *human* that you are?"

Greta forced a laugh. "Don't forget, this puny little human is still the same person who had to pull your sorry ass out of that wraith's den in Eyna's Falls."

"You have nothing to worry about," the goblin finally said, sliding her fingers through her long black hair. "At least not from me."

Greta's grip on the hilt of her sword relaxed a bit. "Why not? Shouldn't you be spitting on me in disgust, hauling me away as a threat to society?"

"You weren't a threat to society yesterday." Siona's sculpted brows lifted. "Are you saying you're a threat today?"

"No more than you are, but that's not the point, is it? You don't care what happens to me, so don't pretend otherwise. Why wouldn't you cash in on that bounty and rid Mylena of an undesirable at the same time?"

She only shrugged. "I've got other orders."

Suddenly Greta knew *exactly* who had given the hunter a side job. "So that's the real reason you're here? You've been staking the place out, waiting for me to show up because *he* asked you to? Well, run along." She waved in the direction the fire sprite had gone. "You've seen me, and now you can tell him I'm done with his damn games. Ogres will wear bikinis before he comes anywhere near me again, and I don't appreciate him keeping tabs on me."

Siona looked a little baffled. "I believe he actually fears for you."

"If he's so concerned, why isn't he here himself?"

"His people need him." Was there a note of censure in her tone? "There was some trouble with a pack of gnomes. Hordes of them have flooded into our county from the outlands, terrorizing villages. They seem to be looking for something." She paused. "Or perhaps some*one*."

Sadly, there was no need to guess who that might be. She only wondered if the gnomes were responding to the writ, or working for Agramon like Isaac had said.

"For some reason he seems to think you are a bad influence on his duty." Siona frowned and accessed Greta's appearance, looking less than impressed. "I can only imagine why."

"If you think I believe for one minute that he can't trust himself to be near me—"

She tilted her head and narrowed her gaze. "I agree. I don't get it either."

"Gee, thanks," she said with a hint of sarcasm before realizing she sounded offended.

"This is made even worse with the eclipse fast approaching."

Greta barely smothered her gasp. The eclipse. Had she really almost forgotten something so catastrophic? Isaac had nearly changed in front of her the last time they were together. She remembered the look in his eyes, and the way he'd struggled to pull himself back. He was so strong, it scared her and excited her at the same time.

Siona seemed to study her face, her eyes lingering on Greta's heated cheeks. Great.

"I'll give my cousin your message," the goblin said, "if only because I get so few opportunities to torture him and I'm going to enjoy watching the two of you play off each other."

Cousins? Greta would've never guessed. Aside from the violet eyes and thick black hair, they didn't look much alike.

"A most unlikely pair you make, and I'm not sure I understand what he sees in you."

"Yeah, you already said that." Greta didn't know whether to agree with her or kick her ass. "So get going already."

"Eventually," she said. "Although I cherish the chance to torment my *cousin*, my *king* wants me to keep an eye on you, and his will must be obeyed."

"His will be damned," she snapped. "Isaac is not *my* king and as far as I'm concerned, he has no right to follow me or sic his cheap flunkies on me."

Siona's gaze turned sharp with warning. "Beware of using that particular goblin's given name so casually, Danem."

Why couldn't she have mentioned that *before* Greta met Isaac? At the limit of her already strained reserves of patience, she groaned. "Listen, I'm looking for some information about a demon named Agramon. I need to know where to find him, and so far no one's talking."

To her frustration, the goblin was already shaking her head. "For good reason, Danem. Don't go looking for more trouble than has already set itself in your path. That would be very dangerous."

"Since when do you give a crap about my 'path,' hunter? You

and I both know I can take care of myself. And if I should fail… well, then I guess you'll just have less competition for the next bounty, won't you?"

Siona's eyes filled with something that looked a lot like sorrow. "I understand your anger and pain, Danem Greta. I too have felt the kind of loss you are suffering now."

"I doubt it." Siona was from Mylena. She may have lost someone before, but she still had family. Greta forced a hard swallow past the thick ball lodged in her throat. "I don't need your understanding, Siona. What I need are answers."

"This path can only lead to disaster, and I can't be the one to take you there."

"Then, if you'll excuse me…" She moved past the other female toward the door.

"You really should not go inside." She took Greta's arm, her nails biting into Greta's skin. "There are two hunters within. Ogres from Florin's county. They've been lying in wait, assuming you would show up here eventually."

She hated to be so predictable, but it didn't change her mind. "Then I guess this is going to be their lucky night."

"You realize that if you insist on this, I'll have to come in with you."

"No you don't. You're off the hook." Greta had been trained for this. Nothing was in there that she couldn't handle. Not to mention, it was cold and she needed to get feeling back into her fingers and toes. "Who's to say you even saw me here?"

Siona leveled her with a haughty gaze and released Greta's arm. "Nice try, but it doesn't work like that. Not with me."

"Fine. Have it your way." Greta shrugged and opened the door.

Chapter Seven

The blessed heat was the first thing to hit her. Greta's extremities didn't remember what it was like to be warm, and the ache that accompanied their return to life shocked a groan out of her that she couldn't quite muffle.

Truthfully, as much as she might be an idiot for walking into what was probably an ambush, she didn't have any other choice. With another storm on the horizon, there was nowhere else to go, and especially now that every hunter was on her ass, the only person who might still help was Maidra.

She wanted to make a beeline for the fire and strip off her heavy gear, but didn't dare, having already picked out the two hunters Siona had mentioned. They were so obvious, their gazes following her from the moment the door had opened.

Pretending not to notice, she unbuttoned her coat, moving to a free spot along the stained and pock-marked bar. She took a seat, waiting for Maidra to be finished with her other customer. When the sprite saw her, trepidation rolled across the old crone's face before she took a fortifying breath and came forward.

"Danem Greta." Maidra's low voice was devoid of its usual warmth as she absently swiped her cloth over a wet ring in front of Greta, then twisted the fabric tightly in her fists. "You shouldn't be here."

"Good evening to you too, Maidra. Some of your hot tea would be wonderful, thank you." Wondering if she was going to be tossed out, Greta simply waited. Finally, Maidra huffed and turned her ample girth around to fetch a mug.

Gaze lowered, hands on the counter, Greta was aware of everybody in the room.

Out of the corner of her eye, she watched a pair of goblins looking nervously at each other. One of them jerked his tankard to his lips and swallowed a large gulp of ale, chugging it down quickly before they both got up and made a break for the exit. They had the right idea and she hoped others followed their example. The less people in the way when trouble went down, the better.

And Greta had no doubt there would be trouble.

Maidra's daughter, a buxomy water sprite who liked to flit from one male to another, perched stiffly on the lap of her current partner and stared at Greta, showing none of the lithe grace that normally oozed from her pores.

Siona had moved off to the far side of the room by the hearth. Maybe so she'd have a good seat for the show. The goblin could say what she wanted, but Greta didn't believe she'd stick around when this went bad.

So far, the two patrons who interested her the most weren't making a move. She sized them up through the mirror hanging on the back wall of the bar. Definitely ogres. Oversized bodies with mallets for hands. Huge cauliflower noses. Slobbery expressions.

They betrayed their inexperience in their very obviousness,

showing none of the constant awareness of seasoned hunters, or the careful motions of fighters ready to surge into battle from any position. Yes, they were big physically—holy hell, look at those tree trunks for thighs—but still just babies.

She didn't think she'd met either of these particular winners before, but after one glance, she knew she'd be able to take them both, although she hoped it didn't come to that. It went against the grain to destroy such youngsters. What she wanted to do was send them back to their pater for more training.

Maidra returned with tea. Setting it down quickly, she jerked her hand back from the cup before Greta could reach for it. Shifting in her seat, she only sighed, knowing the slight could have been worse.

She grasped the mug between her palms, and brought it to her lips for a sip. Despite the tension vibrating from every corner of the room, she couldn't help but take a moment to savor its warm, tart taste. "Thank you, Maidra. This is just what I needed," she said with a polite nod and a small smile for the female bartender who had comp'd her late-night beverages more than once to thank her for breaking up the occasional bar fight.

When Maidra still said nothing, Greta leaned forward. "Nothing about me has changed, you know. I'm still the same person you've known for years."

She tried to take Maidra's hand, but the female gasped and pulled out of reach, staring at Greta as if she'd grown a huge wart on her nose, or another head, which probably would have been more acceptable in the eyes of the old sprite than becoming human overnight.

"All right, fine. I understand."

Maidra glanced up over Greta's shoulder. "I think you should leave, Danem," she croaked.

"Listen, I won't stay long," she protested, "but I have to ask a few questions. I'm looking for—"

"No. No questions."

"Maidra," she warned. "I watched my pater die this week. You better believe I didn't come here just for the tea, and I'm not leaving until I have the answers I need."

Her eyes widened and a whimper escaped her compressed lips as she shook her head with agitated vigor.

"Tell me what I want to know and I'll go," Greta pressed. "I'll leave and never come back if that's what would make you happy."

"What do you want to know?"

Obviously, Greta had used just the right sort of threat to open the floodgates. "Agramon. Where can I find him?"

"No one speaks of the demon."

"Well, someone had better, or I'm going to get cranky. You think you hate me now…" Biting back frustration and impatience, she turned from the sprite and slowly rose from the bar to face the company at large. "So, who's going to give me the information I want?"

If it was possible, the silence got heavier, until a few stools screeched back and the more intelligent half of Maidra's clientele hurried to file out of the tavern through the closest door. The rest of them looked a little bit like cattle separated from the herd, skittish and lost.

The two newbie hunters finally stepped up to the plate, but she had a feeling it wasn't to give her answers. Greta glanced over at Siona—whose nonchalant posture up against the wall was suddenly looking a lot stiffer—before she took in the ogres standing before her.

Each of them was easily the same mass as a small island, taller than some decent-sized trees. And probably just as thick in the head, although she shouldn't make assumptions. That was one of Luke's first rules of combat. Never underestimate your opponent. Or, in this case, opponents.

With her elbows braced casually on the bar's countertop behind her, she looked back and forth between them. They weren't particularly scary looking, but there was never any guarantee that she'd come out of a fight alive. Shit happened. Bad, unpredictable shit. Recent events were proof of that.

Behind the ogres, the door whooshed open, letting in a blast of frigid air.

Greta didn't have to see who was coming to know the arrival didn't bode well for her already dicey situation. She could have blamed the arctic chill racing up her spine on the cold wind and snow blowing into the tavern with the newcomer, but she'd learned to trust her instincts, and right now, they were screaming at her to be wary of more than just the weather.

A faerie stepped into the open doorway.

Nobody dared yell at him to shut the door. In fact, no one dared say anything at all, or even breathe too loudly. From the edge of her field of vision, she saw Siona step away from the wall. A worried look settled on her face as she pushed the flap of her coat behind the hilt of her sword.

While Greta wasn't intimidated by the pair of ogres, she couldn't say the same about this guy. She had a strong suspicion the faerie hadn't stopped in for a friendly round of drinks with the locals. Faeries hated the locals. In fact, faeries hated pretty much everyone, even their own kind.

Which made him another hunter. But not just any hunter. The

only faerie bounty hunter. Lazarus. She'd never met him in person, but his notoriety surpassed even Luke's impressive reputation.

The way he looked at her, there was no doubt in her mind what he was here for.

Lazarus didn't bother to wipe the snow from his shoulders or stomp the ice off his boots. He only pushed back the hood of his thin cloak.

Growing up, Greta had shot up in height before everyone else. She vaguely remembered being ridiculed by the boys—probably because they didn't like having to look up at a girl—but in Mylena the things that used to make her feel awkward quickly turned into strengths. She'd been able to stand her ground against creatures who would have pummeled a smaller, frailer breed of human into the frozen tundra.

But this guy… He stood taller than her five-eleven by at least another foot and a half. Even with the winter wear covering him from head to toe, she could tell he was wiry thin, the kind of thin that hid a core of relentless steel, with sleek muscles that would be dangerously deceptive in their strength. And in contrast to his white skin and pale blond hair, Lazarus's eyes shone black and empty.

He'd been a bounty hunter longer than there'd been bounties to collect, but nobody could really say how old he was. In theory, faeries could live the equivalent of ten goblin lifetimes, which was something like twenty-five human lives, but at some point, most of their race had withdrawn deep into the mountains, refusing to have anything to do with all other Mylean species. Nobody knew whether the ancient ones still lived or not.

Combine that with the fact that faerie clans were always at war, killing each other off for some reason or another, and the likelihood of coming across a thousand-year-old faerie by random chance was quite slim.

Of course, random didn't enter into the equation. Not for this guy.

"Place is closed for the night," she said, nodding toward the door and indicating he could march himself right back through it. "Private party."

Glancing left, she saw Siona's mouth drawn tight. Worry lines etched her perfect brow even as she widened her stance.

Lazarus remained still and silent, taking in the ogres without blinking. There was no doubt that he was a true creature of Mylena, exemplifying the land in every way. Impenetrable, like the Mists of Luna. Desolate, like the barren plains in the west. And frozen, like everything else. He was exactly what a hunter should be, and no doubt more of a hunter than Greta would *ever* be unless she let go her grip on that one last sliver of human vulnerability—a pesky penchant for mercy.

She tightened her grip on her sword to keep her hands from shaking as Lazarus turned to face her. The weapon would be useless against a faerie of his age and experience. She'd never get close enough to use it.

"*Human.*" He sneered, imbuing so much malice and disgust into his expression, Greta felt like a nasty slug at the bottom of an oily sludge pit in the roasting depths of the brimstone caves.

"Look buddy, if you want a piece of me, you better come back tomorrow and get in line. I'm all booked up for tonight." She feigned a cavalier look of contempt, but it was probably as effective as the looks the two ogres had tried with her just minutes ago.

Ogre number one—Wart Nose, she decided—was getting

antsy. Definitely ready to leave. She couldn't blame him. If he'd
been outmatched against *her*, it didn't take a genius to calculate
the winner of a fight between the ogres and the faerie.

With ogre number two at his back, Wart Nose roared and
nervously went to push past Lazarus.

Oh, crap.

The faerie moved so fast, she didn't even see what he did to
Ogre number two, but the big guy crashed to the floor with a high
wail that was cut off when his head smacked the plank board floors.

Wart Nose cried out.

Blood splattered.

Lazarus was a blur of pale skin and hair, steel and...something
else. It was as if he drew the very air around him into a whirling
vortex. Anything caught within it was trapped, at his mercy, sliced
to ribbons—and right now, that was Wart Nose and his cohort.

With a shout, Greta jumped forward to intercede, but Siona
was at her side. She slapped the flat of Greta's blade down and
shoved her back. "Don't be ridiculous. You can't help them. You
have to get out of here." Her voice was changing, deepening.
"Hurry, Danem. Run. *Run now!*"

Greta could see the moon in Siona's eyes. She was turning.
Claws and teeth had elongated and become sharp. Her skin was
darkening, her profile filling out. The way Siona threw herself
into the change, it was obvious that it wasn't her first time. Since
Myleans only changed with the eclipse or when emotions ran
extremely ragged, Greta had to wonder what tragedy the goblin
female had suffered—and how she hadn't ended up one of the
Lost.

With another hard shove, Siona spun away, her echoing howl
confident and fierce, a challenge Lazarus wouldn't be able to

ignore. As expected, he turned to her and dropped what was left of Wart Nose to the floor at his feet. Greta groaned. The faerie had begun to change, too, the fire of battle and the pull of the moons turning his eyes icy silver as they filled with dark magick.

"Siona, don't," Greta cried out. She didn't have a chance. That faerie was going to mutilate the goblin, tear her apart piece by piece.

This was all her fault.

No. This was *Isaac's* fault.

"Go." Siona snarled, baring her teeth. "Before the change is complete and I forget I'm protecting you instead of hunting you down."

Greta wasn't about to let her face him alone. They might have a chance if both of them bolted out of here and ran deep into the woods. It was a long shot because Lazarus was going to be very close behind, but if they could lose him, faeries weren't as good at tracking as some of the other species. They didn't have the same ingrained animal instincts.

When she reached out to hold Siona back, the goblin spun around and, suddenly, Greta was flying across the room. She landed hard in a tangle of arms and legs, the air knocked out of her as she choked out a shout of pained surprise.

Siona came after her before Greta could jump to her feet, mouth full of crazy sharp teeth and claws extended right for her throat. Good God, she was barely recognizable from the surprisingly honorable goblin who'd been teasing her about Isaac and promising to watch out for her such a short time ago.

The faerie surged forward, attacking from behind. The thing that had been Siona snarled as she whipped around and scored a long gash down Lazarus's chest. Like the rest of Mylena, the faerie's moon form was a baser manifestation of his more civilized self. Raw and primal. But in this case, maybe because their kind had mastered the ancient magicks long before Mylena's curse had befallen them, even Lazarus's raw form seemed highly evolved— if devastatingly vicious.

As much as she wanted to help Siona, it was too late. Greta scrambled backward, fingers grazing the sword she'd lost on her trip through the air. She grabbed it before pushing to her feet and launching herself over the bar. Crunching down onto a scattering of broken glass, she was surprised to see Maidra still cowering by the door to the kitchen, breathing heavily like she might pass out.

"What are you doing here?" Grasping the crazy female's forearm, she pulled her along through the door, but came to a halt when the old sprite stopped and refused to move another step. "Danem, hurry."

Maidra shook her head. "I won't go with you."

Greta groaned, impatience and irritation scraping her raw. "Maidra. Do I really look like such a big freaking threat to you?"

"You don't understand."

"You're damn right I don't." Something in the other room yelped in pain. *Ah, God. Siona.* Time had just run out. "We have to get out of here."

Maidra's arms crossed over her ample chest. "Go, human. This isn't where you belong."

No, really?

The old sprite wasn't going to budge. Greta was batting zero today.

She swore, but there was nothing more she could do. "May the Great Mother keep you safe then, Maidra," she said, then slipped out the door.

Chapter Eight

Greta was still running long after both the moons had set and Mylena's distant suns were well on their way to rising.

Fear and urgency had kept her other emotions at bay as branches scratched her cheeks and caught in her hair. She stumbled over roots and rocks, trying to steer clear of anything that made a noise—above and beyond the inescapable sound of her own heavy breathing. And still, it eventually all caught up with her.

Damn this place.

Damn Isaac.

Even if the bounty on her head had been issued by the gnome king, Leander couldn't have known she was human. Not unless his fellow royalness and altogether good neighbor had ratted her out in the interest of "public safety" or some other pathetic excuse.

But then why pretend otherwise? Why not make more of an effort to keep her under lock and key when he had the chance? And why sic Siona on her with instructions to keep her safe, instead of adding the other bounty hunter to the posse already after her?

The only thing that made sense was that it was all still part of some game he was playing.

She finally came to a halt in a small copse of trees and bent over with her hands on her knees, sucking in deep breaths. She blinked up at the morning's soft sunlight. As tired as she felt, she was glad there'd been no opportunity for sleep. No way could she have dealt with Isaac on top of everything else, even if it meant keeling over from exhaustion now.

"Damn goblin," she muttered, taking deep drags of the cold air.

Where to go next? The most logical place would be Rhazua. As much as the gnome city would be filled with Myleans who would kill her on sight if they recognized her for what she was, Isaac would never expect her to go there. She might be able to evade him a while longer.

Then again, staying in the forest gave her an element of control. She knew these woods, and she'd still feel close to Luke.

Neither option would keep her safe more than a couple of days, not with the eclipse dogging everyone's heels.

She unbuckled the scabbard from around her waist. Leaning against a tree trunk, she let her legs collapse and followed the thick bark all the way down to the cold ground. She tried not to think about anything as she clutched her weapon in her lap and closed her eyes. Not Siona or Maidra. Not Luke or Isaac. Not Agramon, or what she would do to him when she finally tracked him down.

The high-pitched screech of her sneakers on the smooth yellow linoleum echoed in the empty hallway. The place was completely empty, which made sense because nobody wanted to stay late on the last day of school. But then, why was she still here?

Better get out to the parking lot. Mom said she'd be waiting to pick her up as soon as the bell rang so they could finish packing and get to the airport. She and dad had been acting like three weeks in Germany, visiting a nasty old man she'd only ever met once before, was the type of summer vacation every thirteen-year-old girl should be excited for. If Grandpa wanted to see them, why couldn't he come here instead?

The strap of her backpack was slipping. She squeezed it and hitched it up on her shoulder. The thing suddenly weighed a ton, as if the books were multiplying just by thinking about them.

And they didn't feel like books. Bowling balls maybe.

Or heads. Two of them. Maybe a pair of ogre heads in fact.

She stopped in her tracks. *Damn it. No, not here.*

She flung the pack off her shoulder, eyeing it at arm's length for the dark blood she was sure would be seeping through the thin canvas bottom, but there was nothing. It was just a pink and white checkered backpack. Perfect for a teenage girl who had once loved pretty colors, pretty clothes, and pretty bags…

This *wasn't* the last day of school, and she *wasn't* thirteen years old anymore.

None of this is real.

She dropped her arm and let the bag drag on the floor, looking down at herself. Jeans, t-shirt, sneakers. Yep, typical middle school uniform, but with one major difference: the girl filling those clothes was about four years north of thirteen, and it showed.

Spinning in a circle, she took in the scene with new awareness.

Definitely Lincoln Heights Middle School. The lockers were a boring shade of army green, and the long fluorescent lights in the ceiling flickered randomly. She remembered that the janitor had forever been up on his ladder changing those long thin light bulbs, but the flickering always came back.

She glanced to the right, through the small square window in the door of her old science classroom.

There he was.

Isaac was too wide and too tall for middle school. He looked out of place dressed in his heavy winter cloak, perched on a stool at one of the lab benches with his long legs crammed beneath it. He hunched over and squinted into the eyepiece of a microscope.

Barreling forward with gritted teeth, she shoved the door open with her fist, still clutching the ridiculous backpack. She drew back and threw it at him. He looked up just in time to dodge the oversized missile, and actually *smiled* at her.

"How dare you," she hissed, even as his smile disarmed her. It wasn't calculating or filled with irony, but honest and open like it had been that first night, and the sight of it tugged at her heart.

It's a dream. Only a dream. Not real.

"How dare you show your face in my dreams again after—"

"I was not the one who told Leander about your true origins. Do you really believe that I would do that?"

Yes. No. Maybe? His denial took the wind out of her sails, and she sagged. "You're the only one who knew."

"Not the only one. Leander has long been an ally of Agramon. He is the one you should be afraid of."

"And you were aware of this?"

He paused. "Yes."

More lies! "What else haven't you told me?"

He deliberately ignored her and pointed to the microscope.

"This machine is for looking at things very closely, isn't it? What kinds of things, do you think?" Then he pointed at something over her shoulder. "And what is that contraption over there?"

She glanced at the telephone hanging on the wall by the doorway. It was supposed to be for reaching the main office in an emergency, but she remembered her social studies teacher using it to call his wife at home so he could ask what they were having for supper.

Isaac got up and moved to one of the large windows overlooking the schoolyard and the road. "And that? It has wheels. How does it move?"

She winced at the sight of the crisp green lawn outside the window and the way the sunshine glinted off the shiny steel roof of the city bus parked across the street. It was the bus she used to take home from school every day.

There was a billboard for acne cream sticking up over the buildings across the street, and the flowers in the garden along the boulevard were a mixture of pansies and daisies. Greta never would have believed all this detail had been locked away in her brain. Isaac's ability was definitely torture, but given the right circumstances, maybe it could also be a gift.

"If you're manufacturing my dreams, how did you know—?"

"I don't create the dream, I only unlock the right doors in your mind to let you release the things I need to see."

"And what makes you think you need to see my old school?"

"I'm interested in the place you call home. This is where you would prefer to be, is it not?" He pointed out the window at a car in the parking lot. "Is that a carriage? In your world, would it move without horses? Are there any horses in your world at all?"

"Yes," she answered, taken aback by his excitement. "We have horses, but they're not like the ones in Mylena."

"When we were younger, Siona and I were both fascinated by the idea that heat and steam might one day be harnessed as a source of power. Once, she and I even designed a carriage that would use such power to turn its wheels without the need for a horse to pull it. We'd both been snapped at one too many times by the ill-natured beasts, you see," he continued with a chuckle. Something wistful passed across his face. "I suppose I will have to leave the invention of such things to others now."

It was his own fault. If he hadn't fought to be the goblin king, maybe he'd still be able to do stuff like that. Even so, she found herself feeling sorry for him, and shoved her hands in her pockets. Time for a change of subject. "Siona is alive? She's okay?"

He paused. "It was close. She was hurt very badly."

Greta pressed her fingers to her lips, her stomach plummeting.

"But she heals quickly," he reassured her. "She will be fine, and she took great delight in torturing me with all the trouble you caused at Maidra's."

She let out a long breath, but the tight, cramped feeling in her belly wouldn't go away. How many more people were going to suffer because of her? "I'm glad your cousin torments you. Someone should." She ducked her head and watched the toe of her sneaker digging at the floor. "I felt bad about leaving her."

"She lives, but so does Lazarus. Siona tried to track him down before her injuries became too much, but the faerie is still hard on your trail—and he's not the only one. Tell me where you are, Greta, so I can protect you."

She laughed. "Yeah, like that's going to happen."

"I think she likes you."

"Who? *Siona?* No way. She—"

"Not everyone in Mylena must be your enemy," he interrupted. "Not everyone wants you dead. Despite her grumbling, Siona has expressed a desire to be your friend."

A friend in Mylena? As unlikely as it seemed, Greta thought she would like to have the strong female goblin as a friend. "And what does that make us?"

"A king doesn't have friends." His tone had turned flat.

"Why did you kill your father and your uncle? That night when we met, you talked about so many things, but being king wasn't one of them."

He stiffened sharply, hands curling tight over the window ledge. "Do you care, or are you simply curious?"

Her mouth fell open. She hesitated, but he'd been there for her when Luke died. He deserved the truth, even if they still had things to work out before she could think about trusting him. "I probably shouldn't because I'm sure it will only come back to haunt me, but yes, I care."

He let out a long breath and nodded. "I didn't kill my father."

"But you *did* kill your uncle?" She raised an eyebrow. "Why? What happened?"

"*You* happened. The night we met, I entered your dreams and discovered your secret."

Surprised he'd actually told her the truth, she glared at him. "Just how many times did you spy on me without my knowledge?"

"It didn't take more than once to suspect the truth, and not more than twice to be absolutely certain. Although, there were more times…they were just for fun." He grinned as she blushed, as if he knew she was remembering the way she'd flirted with him. "Your dreams are like none I've ever visited."

"Should I feel flattered?"

"Perhaps. They are certainly unique. You don't always dream about this world," he lifted an arm to encompass the classroom, "but your identity is in every move you make. Now that I know who you are, I don't know how anyone could *miss* it."

She pushed a hand through her loose hair. "Because I obviously can't seem to remember to do up my braids in my dreams?"

"It's more than that." He raised his hand to her face. She thought he would push her hair behind her ears again to check, but he only drew a smooth line high on her cheek with his thumb.

"The truth is right here," he murmured. Before she could react, he leaned forward and pressed a kiss to each of her eyelids.

She gasped, but he wasn't finished. His hand moved lower and flattened on her chest, right over her heart. "And here," he murmured.

Clearing her throat, she straightened her quivering legs, and tamped down on the ache in her chest, but she couldn't stop her racing heart. She pulled away slowly. "So, um, what does that have to do with you becoming the king?"

Isaac cleared his throat and stepped back. "After talking with you, and watching you in your dreams, I was…confused. I told my father about you. My uncle overheard and threatened to give you up to Agramon. I defended you, so my father defended me…and he was killed."

There was no more sign of the smiling, keen goblin. He opened his hands and turned them over before clenching them into fists. "I had to challenge my uncle to avenge my father's death, but also to protect you. If he had lived long enough to become the new goblin king, you would be dead by now."

She struggled to speak, but what could she say in response to that when she'd done nothing but doubt him and call him a manipulative jerk?

Stunned, she blinked and shook her head. "But why? Why would you do something like that for me?"

She drew in a sharp breath as his fingers caressed her cheek, his thumb grazing her bottom lip. He leaned in and her heart pounded hard against the wall of her chest. "Isn't it obvious?"

Her eyes fluttered shut as his mouth covered hers in a gentle whisper of touch. Warm and softer than she would have imagined. She didn't even have time to adjust to the feel of it before it was over, and her whole body swayed forward as he straightened away from her.

Her protest came out as a jittery croak as she tried to get back on track, but he wouldn't let her back away completely. Brows furrowed, he took her hand.

"What does this Agramon guy want from me, to make both Leander and your uncle willing to turn me over?" she asked, captivated by his touch. "If he's locked away and his evil can't touch anyone anymore, how is he getting everyone to do his bidding?"

He dropped his gaze and watched their entwined fingers. She thought he'd brush off her questions, but he only shook his head. "Your people are the reason my world is in chaos, and you are also the only cure for it."

She'd heard that before and still didn't understand it, but a stab of sympathy went through her as his shoulders slumped. He was being pulled in too many directions. He may not have wanted to be king, but once he took on that responsibility he didn't seem like the kind of person who could disregard the demands of his people—and all of them seemed to want her blood.

He would have to make a choice sooner or later—his people or Greta—and she wasn't naïve enough to believe he would choose her, even if she was the reason he'd become king. She tugged her hand back and stuffed both deep in the pockets of her dream-conjured jeans.

His gaze followed her, slowly traveling up her torso and chest until they were staring into each other's eyes. She swallowed past the dryness in her mouth as the air sizzled between them. She thought he would take her hand again, pull her closer, taste her— hopefully more deeply than last time. She wanted him to so badly, it was an ache low in her belly.

He didn't do any of that. His gaze fell and he took a deep breath, as if he needed to regain his equilibrium as much as she did. After a long moment, he said, "There was a time when Mylena and all its creatures lived together harmoniously. The land was fruitful and green. We shared a bond with the Great Mother, and in return she provided us with everything we could ever want or need."

"Sounds like my world's creation story and probably a hundred thousand other ones. This is where you tell me the part about the deadly apple and the naughty snake, isn't it?"

Isaac frowned. "It was a paradise, until a demon defiled our world with his evil."

"Just like I said…naughty snake."

"This snake was called Agramon. He destroyed everything within his reach until the Great Mother was forced to retaliate in the only way she could; with ice and snow. And still, the demon wreaked havoc for centuries. He was eventually driven deep into the mountains and imprisoned with magick, but the land was already tainted, and the Great Mother's daughters—the two moons—punished the Mylean people for failing to protect her."

Luke had told her a long time ago that the people of Mylena

hadn't always been slaves to its moons, and that the curse of the eclipse was a punishment. "Why should I believe this is anything but mythology?"

"There is truth in every mythology. Agramon was originally from *your* world. He came through the portals between our worlds."

She stifled a shiver. "All of this was eons ago. Even if humans were originally responsible for letting this phantom menace of yours loose, *I* didn't—"

"No phantom," he said. "Flesh and blood, and very powerful. It is said that only when humans are held accountable for their betrayal will the demon leave our world, and Mylena's bond with the Great Mother can be restored."

"What?" He had to stop talking in fairy-tale speak.

"It's *you*," he said. "You're the one that releases Agramon. The demon's followers are scouring *my* land as we speak, putting *my* people in danger, all because he wants *you*. And I can't afford to waste time chasing you across three counties." He sounded impatient. "You will tell me where you are so that you can be protected."

He still hadn't said how or why or what the demon needed her for. And apparently, he wasn't going to. "Nobody asked you to protect me, Isaac. I've been taking care of myself for a long time."

Her stomach clenched painfully at the look in his face, but she shook it off. Even though her heart ached and her lips still tingled from her first-ever kiss, nothing she'd just learned changed anything between them. She would never be accepted in his world, and he couldn't serve his people if he had to waste all his energy protecting her.

The last spark of hope she hadn't even realized she'd been

harboring died, leaving her feeling bereft and hollow.

"Greta."

"Forget it, Isaac." Crossing her arms in front of her, she forced a cool laugh. "Just leave me alone. You go your way, I'll go mine."

He flinched as if she'd hauled back and slapped him. His mouth opened and closed. "You haven't listened to anything I've said."

She couldn't make eye contact. "And why should I? You haven't said anything I need to hear yet."

"I can't afford to waste time arguing with you. Just—"

"Then by all means…" She extended her arm and raised her brows. "I believe you know the way out."

She came awake with a start, jerking forward and taking deep breaths. The cold had seeped through her clothes and put an uncomfortable ache in her bones, although from the position of the suns in the sky she couldn't have been out very long.

"Goodbye," she whispered with a sigh. She didn't want it to be this way—especially after all she'd learned—but it was for the best.

Blinking, she stretched her neck from side to side and reached for her sword.

It was gone.

Chapter Nine

She jumped to her feet and reeled around. There were fresh tracks in the snow, but they'd been laid over top of hers, following right up behind the tree she'd been sitting against and then around. Whoever it was had turned to face her then. Good God, had she really slept so deeply she hadn't even been aware of the threat?

"Looking for something?"

She spun towards the source of an unfamiliar male voice. A figure stepped from the relative protection of a tall, needly shrub. A large hood obscured his face, making it difficult to determine the extent of the trouble she was in. He was too wide for a faerie and too tall for a sprite, but short for anything else. Greta calculated that he only topped her by an inch or two, if that.

Her hand clenched into a fist at her side as she saw her blade in his hands. How had he gotten that without waking her?

And she called herself a professional?

Self-disgust twisted her lips as the male swung her sword in front of him, casually testing its weight as if inspecting the wares of a street vendor. "This is a nice weapon. Lightweight. Balanced.

Custom, right? Probably worth a couple of guineas."

There was something about that voice…

"It's not really your color," she said. *Remain calm.* Bending slightly, she casually wiped the snow from her butt and legs, her eyes on the shadowed face peering back at her. "Why don't you hand it over and I'll give you the name of my smith," she said. "Then we can talk about how rude it is to sneak up on people."

Something about his deep chuckle made her pause, but she still couldn't decide what it was about him that set her instincts bouncing up and down in a frenzy of warnings.

"I wish I could say I *had* been sneaking up on you instead of stumbling over you by accident. The premeditation would certainly be better for my reputation."

"What kind of reputation is that?" she asked.

"Oh, nothing so lofty as your own, I imagine."

She stifled a shiver. She didn't know what to make of the stranger. His voice wasn't familiar, and yet it was. Almost. There was something off about the accent, and she didn't recognize his face. But what she could see hinted at a square chin and high cheekbones that made him look as if he hadn't eaten a decent meal in a long time.

Was he another hunter after the bounty on her head? Greta didn't think so. He didn't stand like a hunter, and having plenty of experience with the type, she could usually pick them out from a mile away.

"And what do you know of my reputation?" She raised a brow and rolled her shoulders to work out the stiffness. She might have to thank Isaac for terminating her dream, otherwise who knows what might have happened while she lay asleep and vulnerable.

She didn't like that he had her sword. It made her feel naked.

"Well?" she prompted. "Are you planning to hold onto this stalemate thing much longer, or are you going to give me back my property and tell me who you are?"

"Actually, I'm thinking of keeping it." Watching him lift the sword and point it right at her as he stared down the length of the blade set Greta's teeth clenching so tightly she worried about cracking a molar—always a concern considering modern dentistry didn't exist in Mylena.

"After all, it might be my only defense if things get rough between us," he added.

"If you hand it over now, I promise I won't gut you with it."

"That's real sporting of you, bounty hunter. It really is. But under the circumstances, I think my odds are better if I keep this, don't you?"

So he *did* know a thing or two about her reputation.

Well, he didn't know everything, or he wouldn't be standing there smiling.

In a fast, fluid move, Greta's dagger went from the sheath on her arm to her hand and into the air, flipping end over end right for him in a blur of flashing steel.

He shouldn't have seen it coming, but surprisingly, he shifted at the last minute. Instead of lodging in his shoulder, Greta's dagger sliced through the arm of his coat.

At least the result was what she intended. Her sword fell into the snow just as she leaped forward to close the distance between them. He made a grab for it but she was there, holding her third blade to his throat.

"You didn't really think that was my only weapon, did you?"

With a sigh, he put his hands up in surrender and she shoved him upright to look into his face.

What she saw surprised her.

He had a thin, scruffy face. Brownish hair. Deep brown eyes.

Human eyes.

Her mouth fell open. She glanced over at the clean slice she'd put in his jacket. She had drawn a thin line of bright red blood. Could it be that she had drawn *human* blood?

His gaze flicked upward over her shoulder and then he smiled. A broad, dazzling smile full of mischief that stopped her breath.

"You didn't really think I was alone, did you?"

Chapter Ten

Jerking the man's body in front of her as a shield, Greta yanked them around and watched as his companions crept out of the protection of the surrounding foliage until they were completely surrounded.

She couldn't believe what she was seeing.

Isaac or Siona. Ogres or gnomes. Those she could have handled. These were just boys. Humans, all of them.

But only children.

Human cheeks gaunt with hunger. Human eyes staring out at her from dirty human faces set in human expressions of caution and mistrust. Human hands clutching makeshift spears and stones—all aimed at Greta's head. Most of them were wearing threadbare Mylean garb that had probably been stolen, but one of the younger boys was actually wearing denim, and another had a pair of tennis shoes on his feet.

Now she knew why his accent had sounded unusual, but familiar.

"You're human," she whispered, needing to hear it out loud.

"All of you. You're really human."

Assuming there weren't any more hiding in the woods, Greta counted six bodies. All boys, all of varying ages, but none over twenty. In fact, the oldest—the one who'd lifted her sword in the first place—was maybe only a year older than she was.

"Who are you?" she demanded, tightening her hold and digging the point of her blade a little deeper into the guy's neck. "Where did you come from?"

The boys watched her with mixed expressions of fear, awe, and even what was clearly aggression. Great. As if she didn't have enough people looking to carve interesting patterns into her hide.

"She's not one of us," piped up one of the oldest. She could hear the sneer in his tone. "She's one of them."

Wow. He made *them* sound about as appealing as a hall full of gnomish tax collectors. Greta eyed the grumpy-looking one. The boy wasn't holding a gnarly stick shaved to a point or a heavy rock to brain her with. No, this kid had already slickly commandeered the dagger she'd thrown.

He looked to be about sixteen, although it was hard to tell through the large hood that obscured his face.

"I told you this was a bad idea," he continued with a voice full of anger, addressing the one with her blade still at his throat. "I don't think she looks anything like a human."

It was good to know her disguise was still fooling *someone*.

Two of the older boys nodded their heads in agreement, while one particularly little guy took the opportunity to pull off his threadbare mitten and pick an obviously bothersome booger from his nose.

Granted, it wasn't ghoul poison or anything, but still… *Ew*.

"Oh, I don't know…" Her captive shrugged as if she wasn't

this close to cutting his throat. "She looks human enough to me."

Shocked and confused by his cavalier attitude, Greta hissed. "Listen to me, all of you. I don't know what this is about, but everybody except me is going to drop their weapon right now." She held her hard gaze on each boy in turn, feeling rather like a mean-tempered schoolteacher with a group of unruly students. "Unless you all want to be missing limbs."

The thief lifted his hand to the blade she held at his throat. "Would you really harm a group of little kids?"

Greta didn't know what she would do. In fact, she might be too stunned to react at all—and that meant she had to take back control immediately.

"Just a group of little kids, huh? Little kids who happen to be aiming spears at me all Lord of the Flies-ish?" She snorted. "Absolutely, I would."

"She must be human," he called out to the other boys as if she wasn't threatening to spill his very red blood on the pure white snow. "She's read William Golding."

Greta drew a hard breath. "Buddy, considering the position you're in right now, what the deadly bounty hunter holding a knife to your throat has or hasn't read should be the last thing on your mind. What you need to be thinking about are answers to my questions."

He sighed. "Can't we *all* lose the weapons and talk like reasonable people?"

She wanted to trust him. *Humans in Mylena.* Could they possibly know how to find a portal home?

Finally, she nodded. She had to take the chance. "Agreed," she said. "If everyone drops their sticks and stones, I'll put away the knife."

The little ones eagerly threw their makeshift weapons into the snow. Some of the older boys grumbled a bit, but eventually they did the same.

Only when Grumpy had added Greta's other dagger to the pile did she release their leader and push him clear of her.

Replacing her knife in its sheath, she put her hands on her hips and took a closer look at the boys. They gathered together behind the older one and as she watched, the smallest reached for his hand, crowding into his side as if for protection.

God, they were so young.

"Who are you? How did you get here?" She bent to retrieve the last dagger, as well as her sword and scabbard, strapping it around her waist before returning the full weight of her gaze to the guy who'd stolen it right out from under her. Greta had to admit, that had been a pretty ballsy move.

"I'm Wyatt Castle," he offered. "Formerly of a little nowhere place in North Dakota." He rubbed a hand over the small scrape in his neck, but Greta only crossed her arms and waited. He wasn't going to get any sympathy after sneaking up on her like that.

"This is Ranier, but everyone calls him Ray." He nodded at Grumpy. "We've also got Charlie, Jack, and Sloane...and the mean little guy here is Jacob." He paused to muss the hair of the boy huddled up to his side who stood looking at Greta with a wide grin that showcased the equally wide space where his two bottom teeth had been until probably just a few days ago.

Greta had a sudden vision of purple flannel pajamas, a pink stuffed elephant, and her larger-than-life father putting her own tiny molar into an empty candy tin and slipping it under her pillow before pressing a kiss to her forehead.

She couldn't remember exactly what he looked like, or how

he smelled, and she couldn't remember the timbre of his voice, but she remembered his promise that the tooth fairy would come and leave her a dollar. He must have told her he loved her. Told her to sleep tight. Said he'd see her in the morning, but she couldn't remember that either.

She shoved aside thoughts of all the nights she'd gone to bed without those words since, all the mornings she'd wakened and he hadn't been there. Instead, she wondered how many other mothers and fathers had been left wondering, waiting, but may never know what had happened to their children. These children.

Had they accepted their losses and moved on? Or were they still waiting? Still searching? Had her own family given up? Probably. And why not? It had been four years for her. They had to give up sometime…and so did she.

Her hand went to the chain around her neck. Inside was a tiny photograph of her parents, the only thing she had. She thought it was probably the only reason her memories hadn't completely faded. At least she had this, whereas these boys had nothing.

There was no defense against the sudden sharp tug on her heart as she blinked and turned her focus back to the children. How hard it must be for the little ones to be separated from the people who loved them, the people who were supposed to guide them through the time honored rituals, traditions, and trials of childhood. Lost teeth. Bad dreams. Learning to ride a bicycle. The first day of school.

"It's…um…nice to meet all of you." Greta winced. God, how ridiculous that sounded coming from her, especially when she had threatened all their lives and held a knife to Wyatt's throat only a few short minutes ago. "I'm—"

"We know who you are." The sullen one, Ray, was still glaring at her as if he carried a very personal grudge.

"Oh?" She raised a brow. "And what is it you think you know about me?"

"We only know *of* you." Wyatt put his hand on Ray's shoulder. To Greta's surprise, the kid visibly reigned in his hostility enough to keep his mouth shut, although those blue eyes continued to shoot daggers.

"Greta the Bounty Hunter," Wyatt continued. "We know that you're one of Mylena's best…and obviously its best kept secret as well."

Not anymore. "At this point, the cat is out of the bag when it comes to most of my secrets," she answered with a grimace. "But how is it that none of you have come up on anyone's radar? How long have you been out here in the forest?"

A rustle of needles in the tree limbs hanging over them captured her attention. Her instincts kicked into high gear and she spun around in time to see a timber cat leaping from its hiding place in the tall limbs of the trees right at Jacob.

Before its claws could put one scratch on the little boy, she was between them and slammed it into the ground.

It yelped, but quickly staggered back to its feet.

Wyatt yelled to the others as he pulled Jacob against his chest, turned his back, and hunched over him. When Ray tried to dart in front of them, Wyatt grabbed his arm, forcing him to hang back, despite the young man's loud and vehement objection.

Thankfully, the others scattered like fleas off a dying ogre, but Greta didn't think they went very far, which was also good. She didn't want them taking off alone out of fear, only to get caught in a similar situation, but without anyone to protect them.

Greta put herself between the humans and the deadly cat. It

snarled at her, but she kept her cool.

"Today is not your day, my friend," she said, swaying slowly from side to side to keep its attention fixed on her. "Why don't you accept defeat? Put that tail between your legs and get out of here, so I don't have to hurt you?"

The beast started to pace back and forth in front of her, eyeing the dagger in Greta's hand and growling as it looked for the weak spot in her defense. Long tendrils of foamy white slobber hung from its jaws.

She swung her blade in a wide circle, forcing the cat back a step. It hissed at her, furious.

"Go on," she yelled, stomping her foot hard into the ground, trying to startle it into dashing back into the woods. "Go! Get lost."

It should have worked. Timber cats were usually pretty skittish, preferring to hide high in the trees rather than come down to the ground where they were vulnerable to larger, meaner predators.

Apparently not today.

Behind her little Jacob let out a hiccup and a sniffle, drawing the creature's attention. When its eyes flicked back to Greta, it growled again, understanding perfectly that *she* was the threat standing between it and its dinner.

"Oh yeah. You know it." She jabbed with her knife, but it jumped back. "You know there's no way in hell you're getting past me today, so let's not even try."

Unwilling to bow out, the cat coiled back on its haunches like a winding spring. The muscles over its spine twitched in fitful spasms.

The look in its eyes gave her only a fraction of a second to predict the long leap for her throat before it was flying through the air.

Her quick reflexes saved her a nasty gash—like she needed another scar—but the timber cat was not so lucky. The slender animal collapsed at her feet, her blade stuck in its chest. All that fire and hunger gone in a final leap. Gone in one choked, desperate rush of breath.

"Crap." Greta resented being forced to take a life when it shouldn't have been necessary. With a hard lump in her throat, she slowly went to her knee and pulled her dagger, then wiped it in the snow to clean off the blood.

Little Jacob stopped at her side, looking sad. "Poor kitty. Why was it angry at us?"

Wyatt took the boy's hand and pulled him a few steps away. "That wasn't normal," he said. "That cat was more likely to hide from us than attack us. There was no reason for it to turn. The species isn't usually feral and eats mostly rodents…never short in supply, so it couldn't have been starving."

She rose to stand beside Wyatt. "On a good day, sure, it wouldn't have bothered," she said. "But the moons are too close now. What, with the eclipse in only a few more nights, nothing is what it should be."

"Eclipse?"

He didn't know? "How long have you been in Mylena?"

"It's been two years." He paused, his hand tightening over Jacob's protectively. "I think. My memory holes are getting bigger, and it's hard to keep track of the time…"

"Memory holes? You too? I have a hard time remembering things from…before…but I thought maybe I was blocking it out just to keep myself sane, you know?"

He nodded. "I think it's a side effect of the portal. We've all experienced it to some degree, but it seems like it hits the younger ones harder and faster."

Jacob reached up and pulled on her arm. "I'm five," he said.

She looked down and spared a small smile for the little guy until the pain in her chest became too much for her to bear. Closing her eyes, she remembered Drew looking up at her in just the same way, with an endearing smile and bright blue eyes amazingly like Jacob's.

"Jacob has only been with us for a few months," Wyatt continued, "and he says he doesn't remember anything from before, but some of the older boys have been in Mylena as long as I have or longer, yet they still have some memories."

It didn't seem fair that they had lost so much, and would eventually lose all memory of their families as well.

Greta blinked and took a quick inventory. It looked like the boys were all accounted for and no one had been hurt. And at least Ray had stopped looking at her as if he wanted to stick her with her own dagger.

"I've been here one year," he admitted with a grunt. There was a darkness in his eyes that was all too familiar. Greta thought she understood where it came from, but it was still disconcerting. For the first time she was on the other side of that darkness, looking into it.

His obvious pain made a person want to reach out to him, but the hard set of his mouth warned her not to try it…and Greta understood that, too.

She turned to Wyatt. "How?" she asked. "How have you all survived?" How could there be so many of them? She knew this area backwards and forwards and she'd never felt an inkling of their presence before today. "How did you get here? Was it the Lamia—the witch? Do you know where I can find her?"

Wyatt turned his back on her to say something to the boys in a low voice. A few of them shot quick looks at her over his shoulder, but most were nodding.

Finally, he turned back around. "We think you should come with us," he said. "It seems there's a lot we can learn from each other."

❦

As Greta followed Wyatt and the others through the woods, she quickly learned why none of them had turned up on her radar before.

They were all freaking ninjas.

The way they moved through the trees—without any sound, blending into the scenery and leaving as little imprint as possible, even when the world was covered in white. It was simply amazing.

Wyatt had Jacob perched on his shoulders. The boy wrapped little arms around his neck and laid his cheek on top of Wyatt's head as if he could easily fall asleep like that.

The other boys fell into step behind, all of them watchful, careful. Ray took the rear with Greta. As they ghosted over rocky patches and between trees, they effectively formed a train, with the two oldest on the ends and the younger boys protected between.

After about twenty minutes, as they passed a section of forest she knew they'd already come through, Greta guessed what was going on. "Are you hoping I'll get dizzy from all these twists and turns, enough not to remember how to find you again? Maybe you're worried I'll rat you out and lead the hordes of other hunters to your door?"

Wyatt stopped and turned around. Jacob had indeed fallen

asleep. Those little baby eyelids fluttered open once at the sound of her voice, and then closed again.

He smiled without apology. "We've got to protect the only home we have. Everyone knows never to approach camp without making absolutely certain he hasn't been followed."

Camp.

"That's very…Boy Scouts of America of you."

He held two fingers to his forehead in a mock salute. "Be prepared."

Greta found herself smiling. "I guess I can't argue with that." The pithy motto wasn't only a popular human one, it had been Luke's favorite saying as well. "Please." She swallowed hard and gestured him forward as she fought the renewed surge of sorrow. "Go ahead and lead us all in another circle. I promise not to pay any attention to where we're going."

He bent his head to her in a gracious nod before glancing at Ray. The two of them had a silent communication thing going on, like parents who'd learned to have entire conversations over the heads of their children without ever voicing a word aloud.

Just what was their story? After four years, many of her memories had gone fuzzy, but some of them were still clear. Sharp. Deep. Painful. Like those of little Drew running ahead of her as they walked through the forest—the Black Forest. Greta hadn't wanted to go on the ridiculous trip to visit a grandfather she barely knew, especially when it had meant three whole weeks away from her friends during the heart of summer vacation.

Greta, hurry. Come here. It smells so yummy. He'd been standing before the mouth of a cave. He took a deep sniff and giggled, his little-boy laugh echoing as he stepped forward. *It smells like… Mmm. Oh, like candy, and mama's cookies baking in the oven!*

She was still too far away to grab him when he disappeared inside, swallowed up by the shadows. Greta called out for the little bugger to stop. He was going to be in trouble if he fell in the dark and put holes in the knees of his new pants.

Only a few feet away, the witch's terrible cackle came to her from deep inside the cave. She remembered shouting Drew's name frantically, fear choking her as she started to run.

The scent of gingerbread had clogged her nostrils and clouded her senses. Now, anything even remotely resembling the smell of spicy cloves, cinnamon, and nutmeg made her sick to her stomach. But not then. Then it had made her feel kind of high and breathless, excited.

She'd raced into the cave, wondering how Drew could have gotten so far ahead of her in such a short time and feeling a deep certainty that she was going to be too late.

And then there had been her brother's terrified scream.

"We're here. This is it."

With a shake of her head, she stopped behind Ray and watched as the boys disappeared one after the other through a practically invisible break in an especially dense section of bush.

"After you." He gestured for her to precede him, but she got the distinct impression he didn't offer out of simple politeness. After all, in front of him, she was less likely to stab him in the back…he could stab her instead.

They watched each other carefully. Finally, her lips twitched, and she ducked to slip through the opening.

Straightening on the other side, she found herself standing at the entrance to a large sheltered area with several small, tent-like structures arranged in a regimented circle around a cold fire pit.

"My God." She looked around in amazement. "I had no idea this was here. It's off the beaten track a bit, but I'm sure I must have walked right past it a hundred times and not even seen it. How did you find this? How have you kept everyone else from finding it?"

Wyatt lifted the sleeping Jacob from his shoulders, handing the little one off with care to one of the older boys—she thought his name was Sloane—who headed in the direction of a large tent, while the others went over to a large bucket of water and washed up.

Greta followed Wyatt as he and Ray showed her around. She asked where they got the water, since the sight of the bucket had started her skin itching and she remembered it had been days since she'd been able to take a bath.

"We have to stay a safe distance away from the river or risk being discovered, but every morning a couple of us head out to bring back the day's supply." Wyatt looked her up and down. "You're welcome to use the 'bath house' if you want to."

Scratching self-consciously at a disgustingly crusty patch on her neck, she nodded. "That would be great, thanks."

She met three more boys—no girls—who'd stayed behind as sentries while the rest had gone hunting. Neither Carter, Leo, or Niall could have been older than eleven or twelve, but like the rest of the kids, their eyes watched her with careful curiosity. It didn't matter how young they were, it was clear they'd seen too much, learned too much, suffered too much.

"We call it the Dugout," Wyatt was saying as they continued to the middle of the camp. "Of course, it wasn't always this sheltered. When we found it, the glade was naturally protected from sight, but we worked hard to make sure it was virtually invisible to anyone and anything outside of our 'walls.'"

Ray nodded. "But we still don't light the fire unless it's full dark. In clear daylight, the line of smoke rising through the canopy would be a flashing beacon announcing our location to every hungry ogre and eager hunter in Mylena."

Greta paused. She wasn't imagining it. His voice turned brittle and angry every time he mentioned *hunters*. "What happened between you and the other hunter, Ray?"

His glare was full of brilliant blue ice shards, and she wasn't really surprised when he turned from her without a word and walked away, shoving back the flap of a nearby tent and disappearing inside it.

"I'm sorry about that," Wyatt said.

Greta shook her head. Ray was defensive, hurt, angry, and there was no doubt in her mind that this place was the cause of it. She couldn't very well hold a grudge against someone who reminded her so much of herself.

"You know, I heard a story recently about two humans being hunted down on the gnome king's orders not too long ago. One of them died in the forest, and it was assumed the other one was captured and dealt with, but I'm thinking now the second human got away, didn't he?"

"Yes, he got away," Wyatt murmured. "But like you said, his brother didn't."

⟡

For the first time in days, Greta was clean and warm, and it felt great. She sat cross-legged inside a small tent on top of a pallet covered with a warm fur blanket. She'd have to thank whoever donated it, because this was definitely more comfortable than planting her butt in the snow and sleeping against a tree trunk.

Examining the shelter more closely, she noticed the tent had been made by stretching stitched-together, cured animal hides over sturdy branches framed with crude twine that looked like it had been stiffened into place with wax. It was impressive work for a bunch of kids left to fend for themselves.

In fact, as tough as she believed herself to be, she never would have managed half the stuff Wyatt and the boys had put together to keep themselves alive. If not for Luke…

She dropped her chin to her chest and closed her eyes, taking several deep breaths.

God, she was tired. More than that. Exhausted. Pure mechanical survival instinct was the only thing keeping her going now. Without any real food in the last two days, no uninterrupted sleep in about as long, and enough shocks to keep her nerves wound tight as a spring, it was no wonder she was running on empty.

Or at least, that's what she was blaming the sudden rush of tears on.

A twitch throbbed in her cheek just beneath her eye, and her hands shook. The strain was starting to show in a big way. Wyatt hadn't even pressed her for information after showing her around the camp, just said there was time for her to rest before they needed to talk.

Part of her had wanted to warn these kids about the coming eclipse and move along. The idea of staying and taking on even a shred of responsibility for them sucked the air from her lungs and gave her the shakes. Trouble was, she hadn't been able to look at little Jacob without imagining the rabid beasts that would be hunting him down in a matter of days. In the end, she'd reluctantly agreed to stay just for the night. Long enough to explain about the eclipse and offer a few suggestions.

She shrugged out of her coat and pulled off her thick wool sweater, leaving only a thinner undershirt. She opened her bag and dug around inside until she grasped the handle of her comb. There was a sharp rap on the outside of the tent flap as she lifted her arms to unbraid her hair.

"Come in."

Wyatt poked his head in just as Greta winced at the stab of pain shooting down her arm. "What's the matter?" he asked.

"It's nothing." She grimaced. "I got clawed and spat on by a ghoul a few days ago, and it's taking longer than I'd like to heal."

He stepped inside the tent, crouching so his head wouldn't hit the roof. He'd removed his winter gear, and yet his presence overwhelmed the space, making the snug enclosure feel too small for the two of them to occupy together.

Her grip on the handle of the comb tightened when Wyatt moved to sit in a matching cross-legged position in front of her. She noticed then that his brown hair had silky blond streaks. It curled over his ears and at the nape of his neck.

His knees knocked hers and she shifted. There were dimples in his cheeks as he looked back at her. She forced a small cough and dropped her gaze, but there was a sudden roaring in her ears.

"...help with that?"

She cleared her throat. "Sorry, what?" she asked, feeling the flush rise in her face.

"Do you want me to help you brush out your hair?"

"My hair? Oh, no of course not. No, that's okay. I can do it. You don't have to—"

"I don't mind." He motioned for her to turn around. "It's been a long time since I've brushed out a girl's hair."

"So you've done this before?"

"I used to brush my kid sister's hair for her because our mother left early in the morning for work. It was my job to get the two of us up and ready for school."

She hesitated.

"Come on, I know you're tired." He gestured for her to turn around.

She thought about refusing—for maybe half a second. But the temptation to have someone else do the chore and save her shoulder the aching strain swayed her. She repositioned herself so her back was to him. She felt him move closer and tensed. He took the beginning of her braid at the base of her head and ran the length of it through his closed fist gently, as if testing its thickness.

"Uh, so…you have a sister?"

"Her name's Danicka. She was my parents' mid-life crisis, coming along when I considered myself much too old for a new sister. I thought I was too good to babysit and play Barbie, or for brushing little girls' hair."

"But you did it anyway."

"Yeah." He untied the strip of cloth holding her hair, and pushed his fingers into the braid to pull it apart. "She would be seven now, I guess."

She half-turned to look back at him. "Where did you live in North Dakota?"

"What does it matter?" He shrugged. "A place called Corbin. It was small. Just a crossroads in the middle of nowhere. There was a bar on one side of the street and a gas station on the other. Our school was beside the church at the next intersection, with a bunch of old houses in between. Most of the kids were bused in from farms and rural villages, but there were probably less than two hundred students any given year."

"You miss it," she said, turning back around.

"I bet it's already been swallowed up to make way for a new highway or something. The school is probably a shopping mall now." Wyatt actually sounded as if he'd accepted his fate.

"You must miss your family."

"Yeah."

Finally, he stretched his arm around her and opened his hand for her comb. She gave it to him. "I still remember the last time I spoke to her," he said. "It was the weekend of her fifth birthday and she was upset because I was going away with my Scouts troop."

"Be prepared?"

He chuckled. "You got it."

"So, what happened?"

"I went with the group on an overnight hiking trip. We left after school on Friday and headed to the nature reserve. By the time we backpacked in and got set up at the site, it was almost dark."

He paused. "The campfire was crackling nicely and the sun had started to go down when I noticed one of the boys—Jason—was missing. I was the oldest in the group, but I still never should have left the supervisors. I thought he'd be just outside camp looking at toadstools or something, so I started walking a perimeter, circling farther and farther outward, trying to find him. I didn't realize how far I'd gone looking for him until I blinked and it was almost full dark."

Behind her, Wyatt dragged the comb through her hair. One careful pass, stopping about halfway down to pick at a knot, then continuing to the bottom. He followed this with the weight of his palm on her head, smoothing all the way to the ends. And then the process was repeated. It felt so good, so relaxing, she could have fallen right to sleep.

"Why did he take off?" she asked, thinking of Drew and the way he'd stubbornly dashed ahead of her that day, as if something had been calling him. As if he'd fallen under a spell.

"At first I didn't understand what could have gotten into him," he said. "Kid was decent. I wouldn't have pegged him as the type to up and leave the group like that. But then I caught this scent. It was amazing, like my mom had just pulled one of her blueberry pies from the oven and put it out on a windowsill somewhere so the breeze could take the smell right to me."

She winced and closed her eyes. "For me it was gingerbread," she whispered. "The gooey, spicy, warm smell of fresh gingerbread used to be my most favorite thing in the world."

"That's how she lures them," Wyatt said. "With something they won't be able to resist." He took a shuddering breath. "And once the scent was in my system, before I knew it I was heading straight for a break in the cliff face that I hadn't even noticed before."

"Was Jason there?" Greta knew what the answer would be. She could see the scene vividly in her mind already. The fire. The cage.

"Yes, she'd lured him in just as she was luring me. Locked him in a cage sitting against the wall of the cave. I was so surprised, before I understood what was happening she had me locked up in the thing, too."

"What did you do?"

"Waited. Once she was done preparing her spell, she came back and tried to pull Jason out of the cage, but I rushed her."

"You stopped her?"

He shook his head. "God, I tried. But I wasn't fast enough or strong enough. She threw Jason in the fire and I remember shouting. I jumped forward, trying to catch him. He was screaming. Instead of closing my hands around hot, burning flesh, I got... nothing. The screams just stopped, and he was gone."

Gone.

Greta swallowed as her own memories cascaded hard and fast over her vision, a horror movie on a loop—playing again and again.

"She pushed you in, too?"

He nodded. "Before I could turn around."

At least Greta had saved Drew. At least the witch hadn't gotten her brother.

Wyatt pulled at another knot before digging his fingers into her hair, and finally fanning the length over her shoulders.

His voice sounded thicker, as if it was hard for him to get the words out. "It happened so damn fast. I could see the flames licking all around me, but they didn't burn. For a long minute, it was as if everything *but* me had been engulfed by the blaze. Like I was cocooned in a bubble while the whole world burned."

He reached around her waist to return her comb. She took it and drew her knees around so she could turn to face him again.

"When I came to, I was here." His face twisted into a wry mask. "Well, not right *here*, but in Mylena."

"What about the Lamia?" she asked. Greta was close. After all these years, she was closing in on the elusive creature. One break. That's all she needed was one freaking break.

"Nowhere. I never saw the witch again."

Crap.

"But I know she isn't the only one. There are others."

"How do you know? Where are they?"

"They hide out in the deepest caves of the Mylean mountains. The one stealing human children is Agramon's personal pet, but there are others."

"Agramon? You know of him? He controls the witch? Are you sure?" Greta rambled as her heart hammered in her chest. "Do all the witches have the same power to open portals? Would they help us?"

"I don't know the answer to any of that," he said. "The source was sketchy, since I was eavesdropping on a conversation between a couple gnomes while trying to make sure they didn't notice me. I haven't been able to confirm or deny what they said, but ever since I told Ray, he's been itching to head out and find the witches."

"Why haven't you?"

"They're supposed to be deep in the bowels of those mountains. The terrain is impossible to cross, and with a bunch of little kids in tow…" His lips pressed together tightly. "I just can't risk taking everyone into that kind of danger. Not until we're able to gather enough supplies, and not without being absolutely certain where we're headed."

A scream of frustration crawled up her throat. It forced her to close her eyes and take deep breaths. The disappointment was crushing, but she focused on the bright spot. Wyatt had given her some important information—more than she'd been able to gather on her own in four years.

"What about a different way home?" she asked. "Have you ever heard of anyone else finding a portal and going through *without* the Lamia?"

He shook his head. His gaze was heavy, sad. "No. I'm sorry."

Clenching her fists in her lap, she nodded. "I'm sorry, too," she whispered.

"We looked for a little while. Scoured every cave and hollow in the forest. But after Ray's brother was killed by hunters, I just couldn't put the boys out there anymore. It was too dangerous." The frown creasing his forehead made him look older than he was. Older than dirt. He took on so much responsibility. How did he manage without it crushing him? Didn't it ever get to be too much?

She shivered. "What did you do?"

"That's when we set up camp here. For the sake of all our lives, we had to accept that this is where fate had delivered us. My job is to keep these kids alive and give them some kind of a life. Some kind of stability, maybe even…family."

"What about your own family? Don't you want to see them again? Don't you miss them?"

"Of course. Every day. But I think this is where I was meant to be."

"What? Why?"

He looked down, staring at her hands. She tried to untwist them, keep them still.

"Because they need *someone*. Half of them wouldn't be alive if I hadn't gotten them out of that place, and brought them here."

Greta shivered, feeling as if the temperature had suddenly dropped. "Got them out of what place?"

"You don't know?"

She shook her head. From the look on his face, she wasn't going to like what was coming next.

"I must have lost consciousness on the way through that portal. When I came to I was in a dungeon with three other human boys I'd never met before, locked up in the dark."

This was the first part of Wyatt's story that felt completely unfamiliar. The rest she could have guessed from her own experience, but not this. "Where?"

"At first I had no idea. I couldn't see a foot in front of my face, but I could hear the others. The place echoed with the sobs and screams of more captives. They were all around me. Caverns and caverns filled with them."

Her stomach dropped. "All *human*?"

"Goblins. Faeries. Ghouls. Ogres. And yes, human boys. All of them imprisoned in the dark like me."

Greta's throat clenched. "Oh, God."

Wyatt nodded. "Agramon's lair. He gives the Lamia orders to bring human boys to Mylena. To him."

"For what purpose? And how come only boys?"

"I spent days locked up in that pit, confused and scared out of my wits. When I was finally let out of my cell, it was pretty obvious. We were being put to work, and I can only assume Agramon wanted boys because he thought they were better equipped for the heavy lifting. He's building a chamber of some kind, in the mountains—I think it's almost finished—and he's using humans as his free labor force."

Wyatt's hand tightened into a fist in his lap. "The gnome guards responsible for keeping us in line had a special affinity for whips. Whenever one of the boys stumbled under the weight of the stone we lugged and shaped and stacked all day, every day, he would be lashed to within an inch of his life. Some of those boys were so young, Greta. I couldn't—" His shoulders tightened. She wondered just how many lives he'd saved by putting himself beneath the whip in place of the other children.

She now had yet another reason to hunt this Agramon bastard down. "What is it all for?"

"I 'don't know, but Agramon couldn't use Mylean slaves to build it for him because they turned too quickly. And when that happened, they'd be lost to the moons and he wasn't able to control them anymore. The wildness of their raw forms made them too unpredictable, not to mention violent."

"How did you escape?"

"That would be thanks in part to our resident juvenile delinquent, Ray, who I don't doubt was no stranger to bars and armed guards before he arrived here, even at the bullheaded age of fifteen. When he and his younger brother showed up in Agramon's dungeons, Ray immediately started plotting. It didn't take him long. After only a few months, he was picking a fight with one of the gnomes while his brother slipped the keys off a guard and tossed them to me to start freeing the others."

Wyatt smiled but it was a tight smile reflecting an ocean of bitterness. "Unfortunately, that's about as far as their planning went. Between blows to his ribs and head, Ray looked right at me and begged me to take his brother out of there. But while he was getting his stubborn ass kicked, the guards were onto us before I'd opened three cells. We made a desperate run for our lives. I got ten boys out, including Ray's brother." He shook his head, his voice lowering. "We had to leave the rest."

It wasn't hard to see that the decision Wyatt had been forced to make still bothered him. "I can still hear them screaming at me not to leave them." He gazed off into nothing. She didn't know what to say.

After a long moment, he looked back at her and shrugged. "How Ray, the stubborn fool, managed not only to stay alive, but get away and follow us out of Agramon's lair in the shape he was in… I still haven't got a clue. But, God, when he found us two days later, I will never forget the way he looked. The beating that guy took, willingly, to free his brother… But then to lose the kid so soon after…"

She shuddered. *He's safe. Drew is safe.*

Greta didn't realize Wyatt had stopped talking. She glanced up to find him watching her with a dark intensity. "Are you okay?"

She jerked back, not ready to reveal her own scars, talk of her own journey.

"Where was Jason, the boy you followed through the fire?" She clasped her fingers together tightly in her lap. "What happened to him?" Jason was one name she hadn't heard in the introductions earlier.

Wyatt frowned. "I don't know. I never saw him after he fell through that portal in the fire back home. I spent over a year in Agramon's dungeon before Ray arrived and we escaped. I looked for Jason's face, but it was like I had imagined him. I started to tell myself that he was safe at home after all, but couldn't quite believe it. There were rumors, you see. Rumors that some of the boys the Lamia brings to Agramon are destined for another purpose. That they're being kept separate from the rest."

"Do you know where? Why?"

"No."

A tense silence fell between them. She ran her hands through her smooth hair, and tossed the length back over her shoulder.

Wyatt continued to watch her. She suddenly felt self-conscious. Was there something on her face? Dirt, or— Oh God, had she been walking around all this time with ogre blood all over her? She swiped at her cheek, but realized it was pointless and forced herself to stop.

"Um, thanks."

"For what?"

She grimaced as she separated her hair into thick sections to re-braid it. "Not taking advantage of my weakness today out in the woods? Trusting me with the location of your camp? Giving me a place to rest—"

"Not to mention, I'm not holding a grudge even though you threatened to slit my throat and maim my boys."

"Yeah." She chuckled. "That, too."

"No problem."

Oddly enough, Greta was calmer than she'd been in days. Tired, but safe and warm. She took a deep breath and the reality of her situation came crashing in on her all at once. Not like an avalanche that destroyed everything in its path. More like a sudden shower on a blistering August day. She remembered days like that, when the humidity was so high that when the storm finally came, she and Drew would rush outside together, lift their laughing faces to the sky, and wait for the water to crash down in sheets that washed away the grime.

She wasn't alone anymore. She was surrounded by people who knew what she was.

And they didn't hate her. They actually understood.

The shadows in the already dark tent lengthened the hollows beneath Wyatt's eyes and cheekbones, making him look older and tougher than he was. At the same time, a hank of hair had fallen over his left brow, making him seem just as young and vulnerable as the others.

His thin nose wanted to be snooty but didn't quite make it because of the peach fuzz coating his cheeks and the sincerity of his quick smile.

She averted her gaze as she finished tying off her first braid and started on the other.

He kept watching her as if the silence between them was completely natural, but inside her stomach flip-flopped. A dark feeling stirred. The feeling had intense amethyst eyes. It taunted her in a husky voice, telling her that she was deluding herself if she thought she had anything in common with this guy just because he was human. That she could barely be called human herself anymore. Humanity was more than a fact of biology, it was a state of being—and while Wyatt and the boys had managed to hold onto theirs by holding onto each other, she hadn't had the benefit of their support to keep her grounded.

"I'm sorry," he said.

She jerked back to him and dropped her braid. She tried hiding her shaking hands under her butt. He searched her expression with a small frown.

"For what?" She laughed, not actually wanting an answer.

"For whatever it is that makes you look so sad."

"Hey, I'm just tired. And hungry. How do I get a bite to eat around here?"

He let out a breath and shifted backward. "Food. Sure, of course. It won't be fancy, but I can get you something warm and filling."

Getting to his feet, he backed up to the tent flap, shoulders bent. "Why don't you rest for a while and I'll have Jacob come and get you when it's ready."

"Oh, no. I could help." She moved to get up with him, but Wyatt put a hand on her shoulder and forcibly pushed her back into the pile of animal skins and thick blankets.

"No you don't. Anyone who could fall asleep sitting in the snow with her back up against a tree, and not hear *my* heavy footfalls coming up right behind her"—Greta groaned again and shook her head, but he only grinned—"deserves at least an hour's rest before the horde descends."

She gladly relented. "Okay, thanks. An hour should be good."

"I wish it could be more, but I think that's about as long as I can keep everyone else from mobbing you. Some of them haven't seen a girl in so long, they've forgotten what one looks like. I think the younger boys are hoping you'll be a suitable replacement for the mothers and sisters they left behind. And unfortunately, some are entering that oh-so-much-fun stage called puberty."

She ducked her head, feeling the heat rise in her cheeks. "Ah, well…aren't I lucky?"

"I think showing off your sword might distract them from the fact that you have breasts…at least for a little while."

She choked, her mouth falling open in shock. "Gee, thanks. Do you think so?"

He grinned and waggled his eyebrows. "It distracted me for, oh…at least a full minute."

Greta laughed as she realized he was joking, but a subtle tension crossed his face before he turned to go. Greta told herself it had been her imagination.

Chapter Eleven

She woke to the rhythmic in and out of a soft snore and the sensation of a small head shoved into her armpit. With her eyes closed, she confirmed by smell and by feel that the solid little person cozied up to her side giving off enough heat to keep an entire village warm, was none other than Jacob.

He had slipped into her tent a little while earlier with all the stealth of a baby elephant, stumbled over her feet and crawled under the blankets to curl into her side. Greta hadn't been able to bring herself to sit up and tell the little booger picker that she was already awake, so she'd lain there quietly, soaking in his warmth, breathing in his little-boy scent, and doing her best not to think of Drew.

Eventually, she must have fallen asleep. Luckily, she couldn't remember dreaming.

Opening her eyes made no difference in what she could see—which was absolutely nothing. Her stomach grumbled, reminding her that she'd been hungry before falling asleep, and that hadn't changed.

She'd been out long enough for the suns to set. Greta didn't want to think about what the same darkness would bring in just another couple of days, when the eclipse turned every native creature into a maddened beast whose only instinct was to hunt and kill, but she had to think about it so the boys could prepare.

Which reminded her that she'd forgotten to explain what was going to happen when she and Wyatt talked earlier.

Careful not to wake Jacob, she eased her arm from beneath his slim shoulders and carefully slipped out of the pallet. She reached blindly to the left for her coat, and found it lying where she'd left it folded atop her pack. She would have patted around for her sword, too, but she had a feeling it was on the other side of the kid.

Deciding that the one dagger still strapped to her ankle would have to do, she carefully pulled on the coat and crawled over Jacob to duck out of the tent.

The afternoon had been clear and bright, which meant the night was clear and cold. Not too late yet, but the harsh bite in the air nipped at Greta's nose as she gazed up at Mylena's large moons and the constellation of stars that circled them.

It always surprised her how different the sky was. Sometimes, especially if she was out hunting deep in the forest where the trees looked the same as home, the snow felt the same, and the air smelled the same…Greta could almost believe she *was* home. Until she looked up, and all her illusions were shattered once again.

Blinking, she folded her arms and held herself tightly. The shelter Wyatt had let her use was on the outer edges of the circle. She assumed that was because the youngest boys bunked down in tents closer to the center of the camp, while the older ones formed a protective wall around them. It's the way she would have arranged them if it had been up to her.

A fire burned low a few feet away, and she walked toward it. Three boys huddled together on one side of the campfire, while Wyatt and Ray sat on the other side, talking quietly.

Wyatt looked up at her approach. "Hey, I thought maybe you were done for the night."

She smiled. "Someone snores."

He chuckled. "Yeah, and for such a tiny kid, he's a little oven. I bet it was like a sauna in there." Shifting, he patted a spot between him and Ray. "But you look cold now. Come sit. We have to keep the fire low so it's not detectible outside of the camp, but it's still warm."

"Thanks." She glanced sideways at Ray. He'd shifted a few inches away and turned to the fire, engrossed in poking at it with a long stick. The same couldn't be said for the three boys across from them, who were staring with rapt attention.

She took a seat, rubbing her arms up and down briskly.

"Are you hungry?" Wyatt asked.

"Yes, but only if it's not too much trouble."

Ray got to his feet. "We saved you some dinner. I'll get it." With a dark scowl creasing his brow, he turned and walked away.

"Is he okay?" she asked Wyatt.

He paused, looking at the three boys still watching with avid interest. "Time's up, guys. Get on to bed."

Surprisingly, none of them voiced any complaint, although there were a few disappointed looks back and forth. Greta nodded as they said their goodnights and trundled off together. She imagined they would be whispering in their tent about her late into the night.

Wyatt braced an arm on his knee, leaning closer to the fire.

"Since we rescued Jacob, Ray has been anxious. He thinks Agramon's thugs have decided we might somehow be a threat, and that they're actively looking for us instead of hoping we'll just waste away from the cold and hunger."

Gazing into the flames, Greta thought of the bounty on her head, and a fresh wave of bitterness washed through her. "It's entirely possible," she said. "How did you manage to rescue Jacob?"

Wyatt sighed. "Once every few weeks Ray hikes back to the edges of Agramon's fortress for a little recon work."

Greta's head jerked up at that. "It's close by?"

"Far enough that he's usually gone overnight. Ray and I have debated the wisdom of packing up and moving farther away, maybe to the anonymity of a big city, but Rhazua would be the only realistic choice, and that's out of the question."

Since Greta had discarded the idea of going to Rhazua herself, she understood completely. "Because of the gnome influence. It would be like begging them to bring you right back to Agramon."

"Right."

"But isn't it dangerous for Ray to go out—?"

"Very."

"And you still let him do it?"

The answer came from behind her in a clipped, defensive voice. "I'm not a child. I don't need anyone's permission."

Turning, Greta grasped the makeshift bowl Ray thrust into her chest. It looked as if it had been made from a smooth, hollowed-out piece of thick tree bark.

"Thanks," she said.

After sending a warning look in Ray's direction, Wyatt continued. "Yes, it's dangerous, but we both agreed months ago that no matter the risk, we couldn't just leave the rest of those kids to rot under the demon's thumb. We've been trying to put together a plan to free them."

Greta's mouth dropped open. She looked back and forth between the two boys—who had obviously *lost their minds*.

Ray interrupted before she could put the words together to tell them so. "No other human in Mylena has the kind of freedom you've enjoyed," he snarled. "While you were out there working for the very creatures who would like to see your own kind dead or in chains—"

"That's not true. They're not all bad, and…" She stopped. "I didn't know there was anyone else."

"And that's supposed to make it all better?"

Wyatt glared at him. "Ray, shove it."

Greta kept her eyes on Ray. "No, he's entitled to his anger. We've all done what we felt was necessary to survive."

"That's easy for you to say when you aren't the one trapped in chains as a slave in the darkest, dankest dungeon in Mylena. Or forced to run for your life like an animal."

That may have been true once, but not anymore. She was running just as fast as everyone else. She looked into the bowl of hearty-smelling stew and began eating, but she didn't taste much. "Maybe you're right," she said after forcing herself to swallow. "So what would you have me do about it now?"

He hesitated, looking back at her.

"Stay with us," Wyatt said.

"Help us free the boys from Agramon," Ray added.

Greta couldn't bear to see the cautious hope behind Ray's scowl. He was serious.

He was also crazy.

Someone had to be the voice of reason.

Someone like you? What you're planning is just as crazy, maybe more so.

At least she was planning to go after Agramon alone, not risk the lives of a bunch of little kids.

"Let's say you even stood a chance against this particular breed of badass, even though everything I've heard says you wouldn't last ten minutes. What then?" She hated playing devil's advocate, but it was the only way Wyatt and Ray—especially Ray—were going to realize the depth of the danger they were talking about getting themselves into.

Ray got to his feet, his face twisting in anger. "I knew she wouldn't help us."

Greta slammed her bowl on the log beside her and rose as well. They stood nose to nose. She put her hands on her hips.

There was no point telling him that she was planning to go after Agramon herself—he would only insist on coming along—but someone had to force him to see that he would need more than just anger, determination, and balls in order to make something like this work. He needed an actual plan, something she still hadn't figured out for herself, damn it. "What are you going to do with all those kids, even if you manage to get them free of the dungeons?"

"What do you mean?" he demanded.

"You know exactly what I mean. How many *children* are we talking here, besides the ones already bunked up together in these tiny little tents?" She gestured at the entire camp.

"At least twenty or thirty," Wyatt said, still sitting on the log. "Could be more than that by now."

"What does it matter if there are a hundred, or just one?" Ray's voice rose with his temper as he looked between them. "It doesn't change their suffering. It doesn't change anything."

"No, it doesn't change their suffering," she agreed. "And it doesn't change how you feel about having to leave them there. But it changes everything else, Ray. You have to see that."

He was looking down his nose at her now as if she'd turned into something he wouldn't even tolerate on the bottom of his shoe. "What do I have to see?"

Wyatt stood beside her. "The same thing I've been trying to pound into your thick skull for months."

He looked at Wyatt as if he'd been betrayed by his own brother.

"Even if you could free them," she repeated patiently, trying to keep everyone on point. "The eclipse is in just a few days."

"You mentioned that before," Wyatt said. "I take it this is a big deal?"

"If you consider everyone in Mylena going moon phase all at once a big deal, then yeah it's very big. Huge."

"What do you mean?" Ray asked. "Are you talking about the Lost?"

She shook her head. "The Lost are creatures that succumb to the normal pull of the moons because of weakness in spirit or body, and aren't strong enough to come back from it. But an eclipse is different. The eclipse forces the moon phase on every creature in Mylena. At the same time."

Ray gasped. "*Everyone?*"

She raised her hand. "Well, most. All the ones who've reached physical maturity."

"So you're saying we're going to be overrun by an army of rabid nutcases once this thing starts?"

"Something like that. Animals, ghouls, ogres, sprites, gnomes, faeries…goblins. They're all going to turn. It's going to be a free-for-all across every inch of this place."

Greta focused on Ray. "If you thought bounty hunters were bad, what are you going to do when this whole county is hunting us?"

"They don't know we're here."

"They'll smell you out, don't doubt it. This little oasis won't protect you. It won't be big enough, or safe enough, or hidden enough."

Wyatt raked his hands through his hair. "Jesus, Ray. No matter how much we want to help the others, this is beyond what we can handle."

"Be smart, Ray. Use your head." Greta locked gazes with the passionate teen. She felt as if she had just channeled a little piece of Luke, who'd drilled her constantly to leave her emotions out of any battle she actually wanted to win. It was ironic, considering she was after revenge—a course driven largely by emotion—on the person responsible for his death.

Ray seethed for a long moment. She could practically see the steam coming out his ears and sighed, knowing they hadn't gotten through to him. But finally, he gave them a sharp nod.

"All right. Smart I can agree with. I know we'll need a plan— not only for rescuing the others, but for getting all of us out of Mylena afterward—hopefully before the eclipse turns this place into a war zone. But we already know generally where the other Lamia are. It can't be that hard to find them. And once we're in the mountains, there are plenty of caves to wait out the eclipse in."

Hell, he hadn't understood a word she said. "That's not a plan, Ray. For something like this, you'd need a miracle. What you're proposing is impossible, especially given the timeframe."

"Not impossible," he said defensively. "Difficult, yes. But I think we can do it. Wyatt and I aren't experts, but we've become comfortable enough with our weapons, and a few of the boys are old enough now…"

"Damn it. No. That I won't allow," Wyatt said in a clipped voice.

Ray frowned. The suggestion that they put weapons in the hands of those children left a bad taste in all of their mouths—as it should. And yet after a moment he squared his jaw and continued. "Wyatt, whether we go after the others or wait out the eclipse, they'll need to learn. Some of them *are* ready," he insisted. "This could be our only chance. I know my way around Agramon's fortress like nobody else. If I can get us inside, we'll be able to get those kids out, I'm certain of it."

"How many?" Wyatt stood to face Ray with his hands fisted at his sides. "How many will die in the process? How many will have to be left behind again?"

"I won't let—"

"You won't let what? You won't let yourself be killed? You barely made it out of there the last time."

"I can do it, Wyatt. You know I can," he said.

"What about the rest?" Greta hated ganging up on Ray, but he had to see how doomed this was. "The mountains are treacherous, and we don't know what kinds of things lurk in those caves you talk about hiding in. And do you honestly think I'd still be here if the Lamia was so easy to find, if portals to earth just popped open whenever you needed one? Like I said, it's going to take a miracle to accomplish—"

His eyes glowed with the light of the fire. "Well then, isn't it lucky for us that we found our very own bounty hunter out in the woods today to even out the odds?"

Wyatt stepped between them, eyeing them both warily. "Come

on, Ray. Not now."

"Why *not* now?" His voice broke on a high note, betraying the depth of his emotion.

Wyatt sighed. "It's getting late."

"Listen," Greta said. "Why don't I try to give the older boys some weapons training tomorrow? I can't promise anything, but it might give you guys a better chance when the eclipse comes."

It was the wrong thing to say. The renewed spark in Ray's eyes caused the ball of dread in the pit of her stomach to get bigger. She snapped her mouth shut as soon as the words came out, but it was too late.

"Don't you get your hopes up, Ray. I still haven't agreed to your plan." Wyatt turned to her. "But if you're willing to give them some pointers, I'll start packing up camp tomorrow so we can leave the glade and find somewhere safer to hunker down. Go on," Wyatt said to Ray. "Why don't you get a few hours of sleep and you can take the second watch later on."

Ray finally nodded. Smart move. The guy had pushed enough buttons for one night.

After he left, Wyatt groaned and rubbed both hands over his face before looking at her. "Do you want to go for a walk? I need to check some things out."

"Okay, sure." She shoved her hands in her pockets and shrugged. It was dark, but the sky was clear and the moons were bright. They fell into step beside each other. When they passed by her tent, she stopped. "Do you mind if I grab a few things? I might be able to set some snares. If we're lucky we'd get a nice surprise for breakfast."

"Sure, that sounds good."

She ducked back into the tent without waking Jacob and

carefully grabbed her pack and her sword.

"Ready?"

She nodded.

They walked together in silence, stopping every once in a while to set a snare, which wasn't easy in the dark. Greta started to feel self-conscious when he hadn't said anything in a long time, so she asked, "Does Jacob play musical sleeping bags with everyone?"

Wyatt chuckled. "He does have a habit of crawling into bed with whoever he's spent the majority of the day with. Most of the time, that's Sloane. Don't worry, I'll grab him when we go back. He'll have a hissy fit when he sees boring old Sloane sleeping beside him in the morning."

Just thinking about it made her smile. He was too cute, that kid.

"You're real pretty when you smile, you know that?"

She stopped in her tracks and glanced away, uncertain how to respond. Maybe he would think she was scoping out the forest floor for a good place to plant the last snare.

"But I guess 'pretty' doesn't matter much to a bounty hunter, does it?"

Wyatt was blushing when she looked back up. She noticed the flecks of gold in his warm brown eyes—so different from Isaac's bolder, violet stare. She couldn't help comparing the two of them. Both of them were strong. Both of them seemed chained to their obligations. But where one was darkly intense and went out of his way to push every button she had, the other was easygoing and so sweet it made her chest ache.

"Um, no. I'm not pretty." Her voice was barely audible. Embarrassed, she thought about the dozens of scars that proved it and started walking again, a little faster. In a louder, breezy voice, she said, "And you're right, it doesn't really matter."

He took a few long steps to catch up with her, hands stuffed in his pockets as he looked down at the ground in front of them.

She took a deep breath. "I shouldn't be allowed back inside your camp, Wyatt. There are so many things after me right now, I'm only putting you and everyone else in danger."

"I think we both know there's a more pressing danger on the horizon, and you're our best hope of staying clear of it."

She stopped and faced him, shaking her head. "You don't even know me. Just because I'm human doesn't make me a good person, doesn't mean you should trust me."

"I understand."

"No, you don't. You *can't*," she said. "I heard stories about other humans in Mylena, but I never looked very hard for them. You want to know why?"

"You don't have to explain."

"Because it was easier. Even if I suspected the truth, I was more worried about myself than any of you."

"That's nothing to be ashamed of. You didn't know anything for sure. Your first priority was to survive."

"You don't get it. Nothing's changed. I can't stay. I have to—"

He grabbed her shoulders and squeezed. "Hey. We did okay on our own. And although I'm glad you're here now, I promise not to ask for more than you can give. Whenever you need to go, just…go."

She didn't know what to say. He was the embodiment of patience and honor. Greta didn't want to be there when she failed him and that patience turned to hate and disgust. She blew out a breath and pretended to pick at a smudge of dirt on her coat.

Wyatt took pity on her and stepped away. "You haven't said

how you got stuck here. How did you become a bounty hunter?"

He deserved to hear her story after he had told her his own. She opened her mouth, but nothing came out.

"Never mind," he said, letting her off the hook. "It's okay, I understand."

That only made her feel worse. "No," she rushed to say, grabbing his sleeve. "It's just…I don't think I've ever told anyone the whole story before. I mean…Luke, but—"

"Luke?"

"He found me." It was as good a place as any to start. "I fell through the portal when I tried to save my little brother from the witch—and in that at least, I succeeded. I remember pushing him out of the way just in time, although I don't remember much else. I think I blacked out."

"That would make sense."

"When I came to, it was dark and cold. I was alone. I didn't notice the snow at first, just stumbled out of a cave. It wasn't until I looked up at the sky and saw the two moons that I started to get confused." She stopped and looked up. "But I thought I was just imagining things, or it was some trick of the light, like Aurora Borealis. Until morning came and there were also two suns. Even then, I kept expecting to take one more step and look around to find myself on my grandfather's doorstep."

"You weren't greeted by Agramon's welcome wagon and taken to his fortress?"

Greta felt guilty now for having been spared that particular horror when he and all of the rest had suffered under Agramon's thumb for so long—were still suffering.

"I didn't even know there *was* a fortress until you guys mentioned it. I wandered around in the woods for days—I'm not even sure how many. I got so weak and disoriented I could barely walk." She shot him a wry grin. "Sneakers, blue jeans, and a cotton t-shirt had not prepared me for Mylean weather."

"Tell me about it." He chuckled in response. "Luckily, I was wearing hiking boots and some rugged backpacking gear when I came through, but I didn't get to keep them once Agramon's gnomes scoped them out."

She glanced down at Wyatt's all-purpose leather boots. They were the same boots every sensible Mylean wore, although his were practically threadbare, the soles held on with twine wrapped around his feet. "Yeah, there are definitely some things I would have packed along if I'd known where I was going to end up that afternoon."

"So what happened?"

She grimaced. "A wraith happened. I was nearly delirious with hunger and sick with a fever when my wandering took me somewhere I shouldn't have gone. Luke is the reason I survived— and not just because he happened to be on that wraith's trail and was able to get to it before it got to me." She paused, waited for the wave of grief that bubbled to the surface to subside back to a manageable ache. "Afterward, he took me home with him. Got me better…and then he taught me how to survive."

"It sounds like you cared about him."

"Yeah, but…it wasn't easy. He was hard to like. Always pushing. Always telling me how I could do better. How I could be harder. That my human weaknesses would end up being the death of me."

"Harsh. You were just a kid."

"That's what *I* said. There were days when I screamed at him to leave me alone. But that only made him more obnoxious.

Especially when he laughed in my face and taunted me with what would happen if he left me on my own."

"What kinds of things did he teach you?"

"Swords and other weapons. To be stealthy, smart, and strong. And never let emotion be my master." And she was a real pro at that one, wasn't she?

"He's gone now, isn't he? He died?"

She crouched in the snow and fiddled with the last snare, glad he couldn't see her face. When she stood up, it took a few seconds to swallow her frustration.

"It's okay to be angry with him," he said. "He was your family, and then he left you here by yourself."

Family. What a strange word. "It wasn't as if he had a choice." Inside, she seethed. How could he *do* that to her? How could he just give up and let go?

"I don't think it matters what we know. What we *feel* often has no rationality."

She sighed. "How did you get to be so intuitive stuck out here with a bunch of roughneck, hormonal teenage boys?"

He chuckled. "Oh don't worry, I can belch and swear with the best of them, too, although Sloane currently holds the title in foul language. He's been here since he was only eleven, and without any....uh...softening influences. Now he's decided becoming a man means using the most vulgar words as often as possible. Fortunately, while his vocabulary is vast, he doesn't understand what half of it means."

"So who taught him those words in the first place?"

"Who do you think?"

"Ray." She laughed in response to Wyatt's long-suffering look.

"Yeah. Sloane really looks up to him."

They started walking back, but this time the silence was broken more often by comfortable conversation as they questioned each other about little things. Normal things. Things from their past, and also about their time in Mylena.

Talking with Wyatt brought Greta's memories closer to the surface and she found herself reminiscing about things she thought she'd forgotten.

And she only thought about Isaac, oh…every *other* minute.

Chapter Twelve

When Greta and Wyatt got back to the fire, Greta stayed with him until Ray returned to take his turn at watch. He immediately started in on them again. Wyatt still refused to endorse his crazy plans, but Greta had stopped arguing. Either way, she was going after Agramon. If they really insisted on tagging along, who was she to stop them?

Would they be successful? Could they find the reclusive Lamia and get one of the witches to open a portal? She frowned into the dark of her tent. Who knew? Who knew if they would even survive a day, especially once the eclipse was full?

So many uncertainties. Luke would have torn her a new one if she'd come to him with such flawed, nothing plans.

As she lay back and closed her eyes with a sigh—Wyatt having lifted little Jacob from her pallet and carried him to his own tent—Greta turned the situation around and around in her mind, but she just couldn't find a way to make it work.

She was in her room, lying in bed with the covers drawn up to her chin. The small lamp on her bedside table cast a weak circle of light. A book lay open on the same table, spine up. Across the room, three posters papered the wall. Different sizes. Vibrant colors.

The window was open, and the sound of chirping crickets filtered in from outside. She heard the whistle of a train not far away. Once. Twice. And two more long blares to signal it was crossing the intersection on its way through town.

Isaac. Greta would always know when she was having one of *those* dreams. He couldn't trick her anymore because she'd already come to recognize his presence, felt it like a buzzing electrical field that could make her hair stand on end.

"What do you think you're doing?" she called. She couldn't see him—not yet—but he would be able to hear her, of that she had no doubt.

His breath suddenly caressed the side of her neck, warm and soft as if he were lying beside her. Her heartbeat stepped up and her fingers clenched in the crisp cotton sheets that smelled like lemon fabric softener and felt so real.

"Show yourself," she demanded, holding her breath.

I thought you didn't want to see me anymore. His husky voice was a beguiling whisper.

The cocky jerk.

She tossed her head to the side, but couldn't get away from him, and then she felt his soft touch, a finger tracing the line of her jaw, her neck, her shoulder. His undeniable scent filled her lungs, but he was still invisible.

"Stop it," she hissed, her back ramrod straight.

She felt his long sigh, but the pressure eased, then finally lifted.

"First my school, now my bedroom. Why?" She blinked. "Why here?"

*How else am I supposed to get close to you? Besides, I like seeing you this way. You're…*soft *here.*

Angry, she flipped back the blue and orange zigzag patterned comforter and stumbled out of bed to the window where gauzy curtains fluttered lightly in the breeze. She braced her arm against the frame, catching her own flustered reflection in the glass. "You can't keep doing this to me. Leave me alone."

Her voice lacked conviction, and every inch of her body strained for his touch. She should be stronger, but couldn't help it, she was *glad* he was here. There was no use denying it, no matter how foolish that made her. She dropped her forehead to the smooth, cool window. Maybe if she closed her eyes and refused to look at anything she would wake up.

His voice was a tickle in her ear. *Is that really what you want?*

Damn him. This had to stop. He couldn't keep coming to her like this, torturing her with these memories. She couldn't take it anymore. She spun around. "Of course it's what I want!"

Suddenly he was right in front of her, looking down at her.

She couldn't speak. Nothing came out. He was dressed only in loose-fitting pants, without a shirt. She wasn't used to seeing him—in dreams or in person—without the thick, full-length winter cloak. Her jaw dropped to her chest. When she realized it, she snapped her mouth closed so hard her teeth clacked together.

With effort, she dragged her gaze from all that smooth, sculpted skin to his face. His eyes glowed in the soft light, and his hair was mussed as if he'd really been asleep in that bed with her. A knowing smile played across his lips, like he knew exactly what she was thinking. Dangerous. Nobody should look that good.

He seemed relaxed and comfortable, as if his winter cloak held all the responsibilities he usually carried on his shoulders and without it he could be himself. And just who was Isaac when he was being himself? She'd seen glimpses, but there'd been so many games, so many misunderstandings…

With a shiver, she crossed her arms, feeling vulnerable in the soft cotton tank and boxers he'd conjured for her to wear out of the memories in her head. She turned toward the window, pushing the curtain aside to look out at the darkened boulevard. She waited for him to start asking questions. How did the lights work on those poles outside? How could that black box beside the bed keep time?

But he didn't say anything for once, and she found herself oddly disappointed.

The level of detail in her dream's setting, just like last time when he'd conjured up her middle school, was actually pretty amazing. The quiet neighborhood was lit in even sections by the tall streetlights. The old royal blue Honda sitting in her parents' driveway had a dent in the side where she'd run into it with her bike when she was nine, and across the street, the neighbor's drooping basketball net looked like it would fall from its place above the garage any day now.

He came up beside her and looked out. Her body practically hummed in response to his nearness, and when his arm touched hers, tingles ran all the way down her body.

"Where are the forests? The lakes?" He looked at the long line of row houses, each much like the other. "Everything looks so hard and gray. How did you stand to be so disconnected from the Great Mother? From what I can see, this world is close to dying."

"It is… was… I mean—" She shook her head. He almost had

her thinking of this as the real thing. "It wasn't all like this. The city is just…a city. As dull and gray as Rhazua. There's plenty of green in the parks." But, who knew. Maybe the home Isaac pulled up out of her head wasn't even there anymore. Maybe it had been turned into a shopping mall or a turnpike, like Wyatt had suggested. Or maybe her family had moved on.

"Why would you want to go back to this, Greta? What could possibly be there for you?" He took her hand. She glanced down in surprise, but didn't pull away. "Why can't you let it go?"

"Who says I haven't let it go?" she said defensively. "Until you started moonlighting in my dreams, I hadn't given this place a second thought in years."

She could tell from the look in his face that he didn't believe her.

She didn't believe herself.

It was suddenly all too much. The memories, the house, him there in the middle of it all. The comforting setting of her childhood home was a trap. It shimmered around her like a glistening, wet soap bubble that might pop at any moment.

"I want out of here," she demanded, throat closing. Her heart pounded and she felt cold. "Out, Isaac. Get me out now!"

"It's all right," he said, following his words with a soft shush of reassurance. She closed her eyes and swallowed convulsively.

"You can open your eyes again."

When she did, she was relieved to see that the bedroom was gone, like washing away a layer of paint on a canvas only to reveal another painting beneath. Now they stood outside, beneath a canopy of heavy-limbed evergreens covered in snow. It was still a dream, though, because she still wore her human clothing.

"What are we doing here? This isn't what I wanted," she

protested.

"Then what do you want? What do you *really* want? Tell me," he pushed. "Let me grant your wish."

No. No. No.

What did he want from her? If she asked for a pair of decent boots, would that get rid of him, or only bind him to her more tightly?

"I don't want anything. Just leave me alone."

"It seems to me that if you really wanted to be free of me, you could have fought harder."

"Believe me, I'm trying," she insisted. But now she wasn't so sure. Her confidence sounded shaky.

"You want me to let you go?" he repeated, his voice low and deep. "You are already the freest soul in Mylena. You have no emotional ties. You aren't bound to the land or its people, and you aren't subject to the moons and their pull."

Was that jealousy turning his tone sharp? "You make it sound as if I have everything, when in fact, I've got nothing."

"If there were trust between us…" He stopped and took a deep breath. "You could have me."

She gasped. *You could have me.* Every muscle in her body trembled. Hope. Anticipation. Dread. The four words caused a ripple effect of conflicting emotions that she just couldn't deal with now. She'd spent so much time isolating herself from others, protecting herself…she wasn't equipped for anything else.

Coward. That's what she was. Too much of a coward to open herself up and take a chance.

"T-trust?" Her fingers fluttered at her throat. She told herself she was being smart. It was too hard to know what Isaac's end-game was. So hard to know when he was being sincere, and when he was acting in his own best interests. When he was manipulating her, and when he was actually letting her see a genuine emotion.

In reality, she didn't trust herself or her instincts anymore. She'd made so many mistakes already. If she hadn't let Isaac into her head, no one would have discovered her secret and Luke might still be alive. If she hadn't left Siona in the tavern, the pretty goblin wouldn't have gotten hurt. If she'd thought of someone other than herself…oh, *ever*…she might have been able to help the boys before now, when it was probably too late to save them.

"You think I'm going to trust you when you keep digging into my head? When you torment me with memories of the life I'll never get back?" She lifted her chin. "You're only proving that I've been right all along *not* to trust you."

He frowned. It was obvious he'd seen her avoidance for exactly what it was. "After everything I've told you, you should know that I'm not trying to hurt you." He pressed forward once more. He wasn't going to let it go.

She refused to meet his gaze, staring instead at the line of his collarbone, broad shoulders, and the length of his defined torso. She held her breath to keep from moaning. Why did he have to be practically naked on top of it all?

"I only want to show you your past so that you can finally leave it behind and embrace the future, accept the life you've been given, embrace the world you now belong to."

He actually made it sound tempting, but Greta didn't belong in Mylena. Just like she didn't belong in that little-girl room, or back at her old school. She didn't belong anywhere. Especially not with him.

You could have me.

As much as she wanted it to be true…

She shook her head. Sure, Isaac made her feel something. But it wasn't "belonging." If anything, it was curiosity, the thrill of a challenge. Yeah, that was it. Nothing more. Except maybe a greater than average amount of frustration and annoyance.

And fear. Now she felt fear as well. Not only for herself, but for Wyatt and the boys.

She clamped down on everything. Shoved her feelings deep down and prayed like hell he couldn't read what she consciously kept from him. She didn't know what Isaac would do if he learned about Wyatt. Although he may have tried to help her, he'd already admitted he had no problem hunting down other humans, and she didn't know how close he was to finding her.

Where is he? At this moment while his mind was entwined with hers, could he be at their very door? Did he have to be asleep to be with her like this, or could he torment her and hunt her at the same time?

"Did you know about the humans Agramon is holding captive—the *slaves* being worked to death in his fortress?"

He swore.

"You did? You knew?"

His brows scrunched together. He shook his head, but she didn't believe him. "I didn't know anything until Siona told me just this afternoon. She tortured the information out of two gnomes who were apprehended in the goblin forest."

Where in the forest? She didn't ask, afraid he would only lie to her.

"Greta, you must tell me where you are."

"Where are *you*?" She threw back at him. "Right now in this moment, *where are you*?"

"My physical body lies in sleep, as you are asleep."

That's not what she'd asked. "Where?"

He paused, and Greta knew. Maybe not his exact location, but she knew he was closing in on her.

"Don't doubt that I'll find you." His contorted expression betrayed his fierce determination. The lines around his eyes tightened almost imperceptibly, examining her, searching for the information that would damn her.

"Why are you doing this?"

His focused gaze was like a rushing tide over all of her senses. "No matter who you are or where you come from, we're the same. We were meant to be together." He said it with such certainty and finality. "It has been decreed in the stars, and in our blood."

She spun away and clenched her eyes shut, disregarding the answering sigh of her soul to his words. "Tell me something real," she whispered. "Something that isn't a bunch of insane, poetic crap."

"Then how about because you challenge me?" he said. "You provoke me, excite me. Make me think about things I shouldn't think about, want things I thought would be impossible once I became the king."

She glanced back up at him. The low ache in her belly sharpened and twisted. "And how is that a good thing?"

"I don't know," he admitted with a rueful smile. "But you feel it, too. You know what's between us is undeniable and powerful."

"So you're saying you want to be friends?" she asked, already knowing the answer. Isaac would never be her friend. The two of them could easily spend forever fighting tooth and nail. They might eventually find opportunities for laughter, and maybe even come to a certain level of understanding and trust. But it still wouldn't make them friends. He was right about one thing; what they had was too strong, too volatile, for something as simple as friendship.

He closed the distance between them until she had to look up to maintain eye contact. "No." He gave her that devastating smile, the one she couldn't resist. The one that made her melt. "Friendship isn't quite what I had in mind."

"Yeah," she murmured. "That's pretty much what I thought."

Her breathing quickened as he reached for her, his fist curling into her hair at the nape of her neck. Her hands spread flat over his chest before she even realized she'd touched him. It was like connecting with a live wire and she didn't want to pull back.

There was still too much left unresolved between them. Too little trust, too few certainties. Right now, none of that mattered because he'd dipped his head. Only inches away and she could feel his breathing hitch against her cheek. Her heart was pounding in her ears, and the tang of anticipation was sharp on her tongue.

She knew it was coming. Her mouth parted on a gasp as his lips finally pressed against hers. Lighter, and softer than she would have expected given the intensity in his eyes. He hesitated as if he half-expected her to knee him in the groin or bite him.

Instead, her body curved closer. She tilted her head just a little and he took that as permission, spiraling them both deeper. His arm slipped around her waist, pulling her closer to him. She groaned as their bodies came into contact, all hard angles meeting soft curves as his lips slanted across hers.

Is this the way it would feel when she was wide-awake?

A sliver of unease wedged its way between them at the thought. She pushed him back.

"Greta," he murmured, leaving little biting kisses across her jaw.

She shook her head and stepped away, taking several deep

breaths as she thought of some way to guide them both back into less explosive territory. His breathing was just as unsteady, hands trembling slightly before he jammed them into his pockets. "You're not going to lose control and start to turn again, are you?"

His lips curled, the sharp points of his teeth flashing at her. "Would that frighten you?"

She made a show of looking him over carefully as she fought to regain control. "Since you're not really here, I'm not going to worry unless it looks like a problem." And since this wasn't really happening, it probably didn't matter whether his physical self was or wasn't on the verge of transforming with the moons into a wild creature that could rip her to pieces without even trying.

She refused to look into his eyes. Instead, she focused on his square chin, and the telling muscle tapping hard in his jaw. The way each long breath in and out fed his entire body. She ran her gaze over his arms, shoulders, and down, comparing the Isaac in front of her to the goblin she knew from the real world.

"Nothing about this feels like a dream," she mused. "You look so real. The small scar above your eye. The maddening way you tilt your head when you look at me. That…kiss." She realized she was touching her fingers to her lips and quickly dropped her hand.

"What is reality after all, but the process of making connections, forging bonds? Where is it written the only way to do that is skin to skin?"

Forging bonds? She couldn't form bonds. Skin to skin, or otherwise. She had Wyatt and the others to consider now. And she wanted to kill Agramon. She wanted to go home.

He'd distracted her from those goals, but she had to get it together again. This was the first time since falling into Mylena that getting *out* of here felt possible. Did she dare give it up when it was the thing she'd wanted for four years? How could she, when the boys were relying on her to help them too?

Shaking her head, she spun around with her hands over her face, trying to find some control.

When she turned around, Isaac was gone.

"What—?"

Can you deny that what's between us is just as real as the stars that shine above your sleeping body, and the snow that falls around you? Once again, his voice was only a whisper woven into the fabric of her dream. *Can you deny that you're going to remember my touch even after you wake? Long after the dream has faded?*

She shivered, crossing her arms over her chest and closing her eyes. "It's not the same."

The construct of the dream was falling apart around her. As soon as Isaac had left, everything about it immediately became less substantial. She was waking up.

Will you tell me where you're hiding? Let me protect you?

"No." As much she wanted to believe he wouldn't hurt her if he found her, she knew she couldn't trust him with the lives of Wyatt and the boys, and she couldn't trust him to let her hunt Agramon, and find the Lamia without interference.

Greta, please. The longer it takes to find you, the more danger you're in. The call of the moons grows stronger.

"All the more reason for you to stay away from me." Her head swam, as if her conscious mind had decided it was time to awaken but Isaac was still trying to hold her in the dream.

You'll have more than me to worry about if I can't get you someplace safe before the moons turn all of Mylena against you.

She could just imagine his idea of a safe place. Of course, it would have to be secure enough so that no creature could get in, which also meant there would be no way out. And what would happen to her once he had her again? He was the king, yes, but a young king whose people wanted her dead or in chains. How could he possibly hold out against them?

A chill eased down her spine. "All of Mylena is already against me. I won't let you lock me up, Isaac. Not for any reason. I'll take care of myself."

Stubborn human. I will find you.

"Arrogant goblin. I dare you."

Find a safe place, then. Because I won't be the only one coming for you.

Chapter Thirteen

She awoke feeling surprisingly rested despite the flood of irritation as Isaac's last warnings echoed in her head. She almost expected to find herself lying in a bed in her childhood home, but of course, none of that had been real.

Or had it?

She opened her eyes and blinked until the ceiling of the tent came into focus. The lines between reality and fantasy were too close, blurring until she couldn't be certain of anything anymore.

Did it count as a kiss if her body hadn't been touched, even though her lips remembered the shape of him, the taste of him? Greta didn't know, and she wasn't going to think about it. She had let it happen. She had *encouraged* it to happen, but it couldn't happen again. So that was that.

Thankfully, the crunch of snow outside her tent distracted her from thoughts of Isaac's mouth, and a moment later, someone rapped on the tent frame.

"I'm coming," she called, immediately guilty. She should have been up much earlier. If nothing else, she could have been checking her snares to see if they'd caught anything interesting for the morning meal.

When she ducked outside with her coat over her arm, strapping her sword to her waist, Sloane was waiting. He honed in on her weapon with big blue eyes.

"Good morning," she said.

"Uh, hi," he stammered, jerking his head up. "Did you want some tea? Wyatt makes it with leaves and tree bark." His lip curled, leaving no doubt as to what he thought of this concoction. "It tastes like crap, but it's warm."

Greta choked at the description. "Thanks. I'll give it a shot after I check the snares I laid last night."

"Snares?" He looked like he was going to ask her a question, but after a moment's hesitation he only nodded and turned to go.

"Hey. Would you like to come with me?" The invitation sounded stilted and overly formal, making her wince. He probably had duties in the camp. Maybe he just didn't want to get stuck with her—

His expression went from guarded to excited in the span of a heartbeat. He actually rubbed his hands together—although that might have been out of cold, the morning was certainly brisk. "Can I show you the snares I've been making, and maybe you can help me figure out why I never trap anything?"

She let out a breath and smiled. "Yeah, of course."

With a grin, he ran off to get his gear. "Don't leave without me," he said.

She pulled on her coat and waited dutifully, waving to Wyatt when she saw him standing by the gently smoking fire pit. He bent down and picked something up, then started walking toward her.

"Good morning," he said, handing her a steaming cup.

"Is this your tea?" she asked, bringing it to her face and breathing deeply. "Sloane says it's really good."

"You're a horrible liar," he said with a laugh. "But it won't kill you, and after last night, it'll help."

"Help with what?"

"You weren't freezing? Even under the fur I gave you, it had to be pretty cold."

"Oh." She blushed and dipped her head. "Well, I sleep pretty hard. And ah, I'm used to the cold." She was *not* admitting that a blizzard could have dumped on her last night and she probably wouldn't have noticed.

She took a small sip of tea and paused, wondering what she could say about a cup of melted snow, twigs, and bark. She decided to fall back on Sloane's less inflammatory description. "It's… warm."

"That bad?"

She laughed, looking at him over the thick rim of the dented metal cup. "You sound pissed."

"I am. No matter what I put in there, it just tastes like…"

"Dirt?"

He glowered at her, but his eyes sparkled. "Not helping."

"Sorry." She gave it another chance and gulped some more. Maybe if she didn't breathe, it wouldn't be so bad. But after swishing it in her mouth a few seconds, she still couldn't swallow. It really was awful. "Um, have you tried linberries? You could steep them with the bark and leaves for a little flavor," she said, thinking of the tea at Maidra's place. "I'm going to go check on those snares we set up last night, so if you want I can try to find some."

"Okay, thanks."

She gave him back the mug as Sloane loped over to stand

beside them.

"I'm going with Greta to check the snares." He spoke confidently, but when he glanced up at Wyatt, he paused. "Okay?"

Feeling a rush of guilt, she hurried to apologize. "I hope it's no problem taking him along. I should have asked you first."

"No, it's fine." He turned to her and instead of the irritation she'd been expecting, there was something like relief in his expression. "If you can teach him something to help him stay alive…"

Her hand fell to the hilt of her sword, fingers curling around it tightly. She cleared her throat and nodded as the mantle of responsibility settled over her. Is this what Isaac and Wyatt felt every day?

She cleared her throat. "I don't know about that, but I can teach him how to set a proper snare, at least."

"Right," Sloane interrupted with a dramatic sigh. "So shouldn't we actually go *see* the damn snares sometime this moon cycle?"

Choking out a laugh, she nodded and stepped around Wyatt.

"Greta?" he called.

She stopped and looked over her shoulder. Worry lines pulled his face tight "It's okay. I've got this," she assured him, hoping like hell it was the truth.

⟶⟅⟵

They walked the same path she and Wyatt had taken the night before, but Greta was glad for the morning's light to see by.

"Oh, look. There's a Teela bush," she said to Sloane.

"What's that?"

She bent over and plucked a few hearty needles from the thin black branches. She held them out for him to smell. "It's an herb.

Tastes a lot like sage…I think." She honestly couldn't remember what sage smelled or tasted like, but she knew the Mylean version was safe and edible. Luke had taught her that, and they'd used it often as a seasoning in food.

"Cool." He plucked more of the needles and stuffed them in a small pouch. "Wyatt won't let us pick anything he isn't sure about."

"Good policy." She shuddered at the thought of anyone eating from the wrong plant. "Um, stay away from that one, then. Okay?"

He followed her pointing finger to a prickly thing with red-tipped leaves. "Poison?"

"Big time."

"I'll remember that." She could see him filing the information away. So far, he'd inhaled everything she said like he couldn't ever get enough knowledge. It was humbling, especially considering how much she'd always grumbled during Luke's botany lessons. She had much preferred the weapons training. But, like everything else he'd taught her, there'd been a point to the lessons. Maybe he'd known there would come a time when he wasn't around and Greta would have to fend for herself in this hostile environment.

She and Sloane kept moving. Every once in a while she was able to show him something else that could be eaten. They even found three tiny tubers, practically a miracle since nothing grew abundantly or very big when the ground was always frozen, and what did grow in the wild was usually picked over by the animals before anyone else had a chance at it.

The first snare they found was empty, but it had been tripped so Greta showed Sloane how to re-set it about two to three inches above the ground in the narrow, sheltered areas of the brush. She taught him an easy slipknot and showed him how she held the noose open with a few well-placed, thin twigs stuck in the ground.

He took over then and set one by himself. She grinned when he looked up at her for approval. "That's perfect."

But neither of them were smiling when they re-entered camp a little while later, even though they carried two large hares for the pot.

They would have had a third carcass to skin for stew, but the animal caught in the last snare had not resembled anything worth eating. Already lost to the pull of the coming eclipse, the formerly squirrel-like beast had been caked in dried blood and dirt. Its fur was matted and patchy, dead eyes wide as its dead mouth froze in a silent, saw-toothed snarl—teeth the creature didn't normally possess.

There might not be as much time left as she'd believed. The power of the eclipse was strong. How many normally clear-headed Mylean creatures had already turned and were roaming around, wild, hungry, and desperate? How many more would there be once night fell? And then tomorrow?

Greta brought Wyatt up to speed on what they'd found and Sloane handed their catch over to Niall and Carter. It wasn't difficult to see that every single person knew their place in the group, and went about their jobs without complaint. While Niall and Carter were apparently in charge of meals, Jack and Charlie collected wood. Leo fetched water, cleaned up debris, and kept little Jacob out of trouble.

She was ushered to a seat by the fire while the boys tackled their various chores like a well-oiled machine. Her offer to help was brushed aside, so instead she watched. Niall, who was thirteen, and Carter, twelve, argued over what was to be done with their morning's catch.

"You always want to make stew. Well, forget it." Carter's hair fell past his chin as he made a face at Niall. Yesterday she hadn't noticed just how blond he was because he'd been wearing a hood that covered all of it, but today with the sun shining down, he reminded her of Drew. Her brother's hair had been pale blond like that. "I'm sick of it," he said. "Your stew is nothing but boiled water and dirt, and it tastes like it, too."

"Curing the meat is going to take too long." Niall's voice rose in indignation. He was the opposite of Carter, dark skinned with dark hair. And it looked like someone had had a go at cutting it with a flat bladed knife. His hair stuck up around his head in chunky, uneven sections.

"And how do you expect me to make it taste any better when there's nothing else to put in the pot but water and dirt?"

"You could at least try—"

"Relax, jerkwads," Sloane interrupted. He stepped between them, dangling the little pouch of needles and herbs they had gathered together in the forest. "Try some of this stuff. Greta says it's edible, and it'll make the food taste…maybe like actual food."

Niall was quicker than Carter, jerking the bag out of Sloane's hand and throwing the other boy a smug look of triumph. Carter jabbed him in the shoulder, but then they huddled together, each trying to peek inside the bag.

Carter looked up at her and the expression of wonder on his face made Greta blush. "Oh, this smells good. If only we had some potatoes too, we could make a real stew!"

"You should have seen this kid when he first got to Mylena. Talk about chunky monkey. I think he misses his mama's cooking more than he misses *her*."

Greta winced at Sloane's crass insensitivity. He laughed, but then he also ruffled Carter's hair and put an arm around his shoulder like a kid tormenting his annoying little brother.

Greta remembered the tubers, and stood so she could dig them out of her pockets. She handed them over to Carter. "Here, these should help."

Both Carter and Niall started talking a mile a minute and Greta somehow ended up promising to take them out with her next time she went into the forest.

After a quick morning meal, with the hares simmering nicely in a pot over a very low fire, Ray wasted no time pulling everyone together to tell them about his plan to infiltrate Agramon's fortress and rescue the other humans. Greta stood silently behind the small group, leaning against a thick tree trunk.

"Nobody's going to be left behind," he said. "But everyone will have to work really hard if we have any hope of doing this." His eyes reflected a cold determination. Greta would have thought him the very picture of a ruthless military commander if he didn't have Jacob's tiny hand engulfed in his own.

Jack and Charlie murmured fearfully and she didn't blame them one bit. They were only nine years old and being asked to make a life or death decision.

Wyatt stepped forward and the whispers stopped cold. There was absolute silence as they all waited for him to speak.

Their respect for him was obvious. While Ray was the big brother, Wyatt—only two years older—had become the father figure they otherwise lacked. They worshipped him. For his strength. For his wise guidance. For keeping them alive, giving them hope. He would be the final word on any plan to take them out of the cozy shelter they'd worked so hard to build. Greta didn't envy him that responsibility.

"Listen," he started, meeting each one of their wide-eyed

gazes with calm reassurance. "I know Ray wants to do this, and I'm not saying I like the idea of anyone being left in those dungeons to suffer, but it would be crazy dangerous."

Nobody could argue with that.

"The truth is, whatever we decide is going to be dangerous, but this…" He paused. "Basically, there are two choices. Each one of them means leaving the protection of the Dugout as soon as possible. It's not going to be safe here once the eclipse is full."

Niall interrupted, "How do we know this eclipse thing is really going to happen, and how do we know everyone's going to go moon phase because of it? Sloane has been here for three years and he never heard of it before."

"That's because I was locked up in a dungeon, you dumbass," he threw in. "I didn't know that the demented shit going on all around me had anything to do with the moons. But I actually do remember that there was a time when it seemed worse." He grimaced and shook his head. "A lot worse. The ones who weren't locked behind bars died."

"Greta tells me it's coming," Wyatt continued. "She's lived through two of these, and I believe her when she says it's going to be bad." He waited to see if anyone else would pipe in. "So, we either try to find another place, somewhere more secure to hide out until it blows over. Or…"

She knew he didn't want to say it. He didn't want to make them choose. Not when the choice was between their own lives and the lives of others just like them who would be left at the mercy of Agramon's minions while the world devolved into chaos.

Ray didn't have the same conflict of conscience. He didn't seem to have a problem forcing them to take ownership for those lives. "Or what?" he snapped. "How can we keep hiding in the bushes when kids are being worked to death in those dark caves as we speak? When the eclipse comes, it's only going to be worse for them. What if it were us? How can we sit back and only think of ourselves when we have a chance to save the others and finally go home?"

Sloane stood up and glared at Ray. "And how the hell are we supposed to do that?" he said. "You're asking a bunch of kids to go up against a legion of gnomes and ogres, and the baddest demon this side of hell—armed with what? Sticks and stones? And since when have any of us ever stumbled across a portal back to earth? If going home had actually been a freaking option all this time, someone forgot to mention it to the rest of us."

She liked his choice of words. Maybe if she'd put it as bluntly last night, Ray would have listened when she said he was out of his mind.

A few of the other boys nodded in agreement and glared at Ray.

"Listen to me," he repeated. "We may not know where the portal is yet, but we know the creature who brought us here wasn't the only one of its kind. All we have to do is find the other Lamia. We have a solid lead that they're somewhere in the mountains. But," he continued, raising his voice over the muttered complaints and objections, "Wyatt is right. With the eclipse coming, we have to relocate. Once we've freed the others, we head for the mountains and ride out the storm." His voice turned pleading. "We've got to at least try. It's high time we took our destiny into our own hands, don't you think?"

Like a slick politician, he made it sound so easy, as if they were all going for a stroll through the park on a slightly rainy day. They might get a little wet, but nothing a nice wide umbrella wouldn't make better.

She understood. Ray's desperation warred with his sense of responsibility. It wasn't that he couldn't see the risks. As she watched him glance down at little Jacob, Greta knew he understood them perfectly, but his anger was obviously stronger than his fear or his guilt.

Wyatt stepped back in to calm them all down. There was a long silence as they absorbed the ramifications of what Ray was asking. Finally, Carter looked up at Wyatt with big eyes that glistened with so much hope. "Is there really a chance we could all go home?"

Her heart lurched. She sensed rather than saw Wyatt's hesitation, and wondered if he was going to give it to them straight, or try to influence their decision in his role as protector. He looked at her over their heads for a split second, but there was no way she could help him with this. She lifted her shoulders and pursed her lips together. He glanced back down, meeting Carter's expectant expression dead on with all seriousness.

"If we try this rescue thing now, it's going to be very dangerous. It's going to take every one of us working together, and even so, we might not make it. Not all of us." His gaze moved to rest on each of the boys in turn. "So tell me now that you don't want to do it, and we'll just pack what we need and find a safe place to wait out the eclipse. I won't let anything happen to you boys, and I promise we'll still make a plan to free the others and look for a way home once it's safe again—safer, anyway."

Ray opened his mouth to object, but Wyatt grabbed his arm tight. They argued silently for a long moment but Ray finally nodded. There would be no guilt trips allowed.

Charlie was the first to respond. "I think we have to give it a try. This eclipse is going to hit everyone in Mylena, right? Sloane thinks it will affect the guards in Agramon's fortress too, right? So we can't leave the others there. Who knows how many would die?"

Jack, Carter, Leo, and finally Niall agreed as well.

Ray turned to Sloane, but the younger boy spun around and looked at *her*. "Are you going to stay and help us?"

Wyatt cleared his throat. "Sloane—"

"No. If we're really contemplating this, we need all the help we can get, don't we?"

Both Wyatt and Ray had deftly kept any part she might play out of the discussion up until this point, but now the rest of the boys turned to face her, too.

Luke would have told her not to make a decision based on emotion. Her heart pounded. She wanted to say no. How could she look into their eyes and agree to lead them all to slaughter?

How could she let them go on their own?

She groaned and swore. A day ago, even hours ago, she would have. But now…"I'll do what I can."

Sloane nodded. "Then I guess we better make some plans."

After they'd agreed on a course of action for the day, Sloane came around and sat beside her. She was still shaking inside, wondering how she'd gotten herself into this mess. He was quiet for a few minutes, but finally blurted out, "So, I'm guessing you know how to use that thing?"

She followed his gaze and smiled. He'd been eyeing her sword every other minute, so she had an idea where he was going with this. "I was lucky. For some reason, the sprite who found me when I came over decided to keep me alive and teach me." She laughed, but the memory of Luke still hurt too much. "God, I hated him at first. He drilled me constantly. Self-defense, weapons training, and all that stuff about Mylena. I don't think I got a full night's sleep for two whole years."

"Why not?"

"He would attack me while I slept. I never knew when it would happen. Sometimes it wasn't for a week, and then maybe he'd get me three nights in a row, so I was always on guard." She shrugged. "But I guess that was the point."

"How many of the Lost have you taken down?"

She hesitated. "Enough to know that you don't want to come up against them if you don't have to."

"Do you think we're going to have to?"

An image of the twisted, monstrous looking squirrel came to mind and she realized that wasn't even the tip of the iceberg of what was to come. It was a snowflake on the tip of the iceberg. "Yeah, I do."

With that, Wyatt called everyone together and gave her the floor. She spent the rest of the day channeling her inner Lucius and drilling every one of them as hard and unmercifully as he would have.

To her surprise, the boys were already pros at stringing their own makeshift bows. They'd learned to use the softer, springy branches of a Yew-like tree, and had been chipping the thin shale rock laying around all over the place into pointed heads that could be tied to lightweight shafts. They'd even been saving the feathers from whatever wild fowl they'd been able to catch, to fix to the end of the arrows.

Carter was their best shot. He hit the bulls eye—a piece of cloth pinned to a tree trunk about sixty feet away—nine times out of ten, but then he started to slip.

"What's going on?" she asked after watching him miss the last three shots, stopping a safe distance behind him as he huffed and swore.

He shifted, holding the bow and arrow in one hand while he shook out his draw hand. "It's nothing."

She recognized the problem right away. "You need a guard to protect your fingers and your arm from the bow string. It's sharp when pulled tight, and that snap-back is awful."

"I'm not a baby," he said, getting defensive. "I can handle it."

"This isn't about how tough you are," she said quickly. "You're the best shot in the group, so we're going to get you the equipment you need to make sure you're dead-on accurate when we need you to be."

He blushed and nodded, calling out to Ray who, it turned out, was the one responsible for putting together the tents and making sure all their clothes didn't fall apart.

"Sure, I can get that made for you tonight." Ray grinned. "Hey, maybe that means you'll be able to catch us some more of those squawky little things that look like overgrown pigeons. Now that we know what herbs are safe to use, they might taste better."

The look he turned on her was still snarly, as usual, but maybe a little less so. Greta decided it was time to put him to work.

"Are you ready?"

"Bring it on, hunter." His smile was a little too confident.

So she used him as her punching bag for the next few hours, to provide examples of her fighting techniques to the others. That surly look was gone in no time after he'd spent a good portion of the afternoon flat on his back with the wind knocked out of him.

It was actually kind of fun to have someone to spar with. She grinned as they circled each other. She bounced lightly on the balls of her feet, the blood rushing hard and fast through her veins.

This was good for her, too. It sharpened her senses. And Ray was no lightweight. He didn't go down easy. He was eager to learn and caught on quickly, and when she moved on to train the next person, he helped the other boys who needed direction.

It was near the end of the day when Wyatt finally stepped up. He'd been in and out, working with a small group to pack up camp while she trained the others, and then switching them out.

A hush moved through the small circle that had formed around her. She had Ray in a chokehold and when he stiffened in her arms, she looked up and grinned when she saw Wyatt with a sword in his hand. "Where'd you get that?" she asked.

He smiled. "I'm good at slipping around unnoticed and, um… *liberating* people of things."

She laughed. "Don't I know it. You ready to take me on?"

"Only if you're done beating on him."

She shrugged and let go of Ray, giving him a gentle push. He stumbled a few steps and threw a disgruntled scowl over his shoulder at her, but even he seemed eager for the matchup.

"Sloane, give me my sword." He'd been covertly manhandling her weapon whenever she wasn't putting him through his paces and she knew he'd get a kick out of being the one to draw it from its sheath.

She held out her hand and caught Sloane's gentle, straight toss. With a few swift twists of the blade, she stepped back and made room for Wyatt to come closer.

They started circling one another. The boys shuffled back to give them more room. Wyatt removed his coat and threw it to little Jacob. Greta had lost hers hours ago.

She sized him up, wondering what his strength was. She already knew he was stealthy and quick. "Are you sure you can handle that thing?" She nodded to the heavy looking weapon in his hand.

He grinned. "Wouldn't you like to know?"

With a quick glance around, she examined the rapt faces watching them. How far to go with this particular lesson? She didn't want to eviscerate the guy in front of everyone and risk damaging their confidence in his ability to take care of them. But he needed to be challenged and improve if he was going to have any chance of protecting these kids when the time came.

"Okay." She motioned him forward with one hand. "Come get me."

To his credit, he didn't rush her, but continued to move slowly. The ground in the circle was mucky and black after an afternoon of training, and their feet were covered in it.

She could tell he was studying her the same way she'd done to him. After a long moment, he glanced past her and nodded so slightly she might have thought she'd imagined it if Ray hadn't cleared his throat at that moment.

Even as her body shifted instinctively to glance over her shoulder to see what was going on, she realized she'd been duped. She veered out of the way just in time to avoid Wyatt's swinging blade.

"Oh, so you're a *dirty* fighter," she said with a grin, dancing out of reach as he pushed forward and swung again.

"And proud of it." He cross-stepped to the side and hefted the sword up. She was impressed with his moves, but sadly, he would soon realize that any chance he had to take her off guard was gone.

With an agile feint, she went on the offensive, swinging low to high and knocking his weapon up. He barely avoided a blade to the chin as he jerked back and threw her a sharp look.

Serious now, they took turns advancing and retreating. With calculation, she pushed forward, swords clanging over and over again. She forced Wyatt to keep retreating until he realized he was headed right for the line of bodies making up the edge of the circle. With a grunt of exertion, he shoved back to give himself room to maneuver back into the middle of the battle area.

She had to admit, he had her fighting hard. And yet, she *was* going easy on him. He knew it, too. It was in his eyes, filling with a determined steel. "Come on, hunter," he growled. "You can do better than this."

Their swords locked together. He grabbed her arm and dragged her forward to pull her off balance. Suddenly her face was inches away from his, framed between the two blades vibrating from the force of their collision.

Her body tensed. They were both breathing hard and fast, gazing into each other's eyes. His breath caught the same time hers did.

In the frozen moment of stillness, the wind picked up. She felt it ghost across her sweaty skin and the chill brought her back to her senses. She twisted her wrist and slipped her ankle behind his left foot.

He anticipated her move and narrowly avoided being thrown to the ground, but in his attempt at some fancy footwork that would have put him at her unprotected back, he slipped in the mud and went down.

Before he could move, the tip of her sword was at his jugular. Behind him, Sloane turned to Ray with an open hand, who jerked off his nice fur lined gloves and slapped them into Sloane's palm.

They'd been taking bets?

"You're dead." She held out her hand to Wyatt.

He ignored it, getting to his feet without any help before bending back down to grab his sword. He swiped at his muddy pants and wouldn't meet her eyes, bright spots of red staining his cheeks.

Was he upset that she'd beat him? Or was there some other reason for him to feel uncomfortable suddenly? She felt heat rise in her own cheeks at the thought.

"So it seems," he murmured.

Chapter Fourteen

Greta fell onto her pallet late that night feeling many different things. Exhaustion warred with restlessness. Optimism warred with fear.

They hadn't had any more encounters with rabid woodland creatures, but that didn't make her feel much better. The forest had been quiet all day. Too quiet. Deathly quiet.

According to what Isaac had said, the eclipse wasn't due for two more days, but things were already starting to unravel.

They needed more time. As of right now, they weren't even close to being ready. Not ready to move, and definitely not ready to take on a demon the likes of Agramon.

Her anxiety had been mounting all day, despite the relatively uneventful afternoon. More than once, she'd tried convincing Wyatt to ditch this crazy plan, but after the entire group had voted, they were all committed to it.

How could she have agreed to walk them right into Agramon's territory right as the world was about to explode? If only she hadn't felt certain that leaving them here to die instead would have stripped away what was left of her soul.

The old Greta would have weighed the odds and taken the safest path for herself, but so much had changed in a short time. She had changed.

With a sigh, she turned onto her side, hoping to make the whispering in her head shut up. Luke's voice was telling her she'd taken on a duty she wasn't prepared for, heading into danger she didn't comprehend.

There was another voice in her head too, telling her she *could* do it. That she was strong. The voice was telling her she had been made for this and needed to use her skills for something good. It said that these boys were hers now, that she was responsible for them in a way she hadn't been responsible for anything ever before, and she couldn't let them down. It wasn't Luke's voice. It wasn't even her own, or Isaac's.

She thought it might be her father's.

She closed her eyes. Tomorrow would be a new day. One day closer to the eclipse, but also one day closer to the thing she hadn't dared hope for in four years—the possibility that she might be able to go home again.

Why did the thought cause little pinpricks of discomfort behind her eyes?

It wasn't because of Isaac. She couldn't possibly be upset because going home would mean never arguing with him again. Her heart wasn't aching from the idea that she might never see the intense look in his eyes again, or hear his voice. She wasn't going to credit her anxiousness with the idea of leaving him behind. He belonged here and she didn't.

Really?

If Greta didn't belong here, then where? After all this time, could she return home anyway? Did she *deserve* to go home? After what Mylena had made of her, wasn't this *exactly* where she belonged, just like he had tried to tell her?

Fists clenched beneath her cheek, she desperately tried to banish his face, but that only made her more aware of the low noises coming to her through the thin canvas. Small bodies shuffling, snoring, and whispering softly in the tents surrounding hers. Sleep wasn't going to come easily tonight, which was probably more a blessing than a curse.

Deciding to embrace sleeplessness—and thwart Isaac in the process—she rose and loaded up, strapping on her sword and daggers before leaving her tent and stepping out into the chilly night. She might as well make herself useful and relieve Ray and Sloane of sentry duty.

The moons were almost full. By tomorrow night they would be like big pink snowballs in the sky—one slightly larger than the other—and nobody would even notice the cluster of stars glittering around them in fierce, cold glory. How many other worlds were out there, she wondered? Enough to fill that sky?

Circling the outer perimeter of the small group of tents, she found Sloane standing on the edge of the glade with his back against a tree trunk. He wasn't asleep, but he looked pretty close, making her feel a momentary twinge of guilt. She'd worked everyone hard today—except for Jacob, who had excitedly filled the position of water boy/cheering squad. Sloane especially had thrown himself full tilt into her weapons training.

He looked up now as she approached. The weariness in his stance vanished, and he straightened his shoulders and narrowed his eyes to see who was coming.

"Why don't you go on to bed," she said, wrapping her long

woolen scarf around her neck to ward off the chill.

Damn cold. She made fists of her hands and stuffed them under her arms. Sometimes she wanted a pair of thick mittens so bad. They would keep her fingers toasty warm, but the trade-off was not being able to get to her dagger as quickly. She resigned herself to the thin leather gloves with no fingers. "You're going to need some sleep if you intend to survive what I've got planned for tomorrow."

He groaned good-naturedly. "I don't know if I'll be able to move tomorrow, but I'll take whatever you dish out, especially if it means getting to watch you kick Ray's ass again."

She chuckled, having heard Ray's soft step approaching behind her.

"What are you two doing?"

Greta turned around. "I was thinking of taking my turn on the night shift a little early." As much as she'd pushed Ray's buttons since her arrival—intentionally and not so intentionally—Greta had come to respect him for his devotion, loyalty, and sense of honor. The last thing she wanted was to undermine his position as Wyatt's second in command in front of the others. "If that's okay with you."

His smoky breaths floated away like little clouds in the cold air. "Okay by me," he said with an evil smile as he turned to Sloane. "Take advantage of the extra rest buddy, because tomorrow you're my sparring partner."

Sloane looked horrified. "Well, then I guess I'll see you both in the morning."

Greta almost felt sorry for him, but Sloane was going to come up against much worse than Ray in just a few days, and it was her job to make sure he lived through it. No coddling allowed. "Bright and early," she added.

She watched as the brave kid sauntered off in the direction of his tent. Only fourteen years old, she thought, and he was far from the youngest of them.

Dealing with humans was a strange experience. Different from Mylean species, humanity relied deeply on emotion. Greta had almost forgotten that. She'd gotten so used to pushing aside emotion to make way for expedience, practicality, survival. This was a motley little group, each one of them with more guts and strength of character than she could ever hope to match, and they tested her boundaries.

"Why don't I run a quick perimeter check?"

Ray stepped in her path as she made to go by him. "Answer something for me," he said, voice low so as not to disturb anyone's sleep.

She was surprised he wanted to chat. Even if his frosty contempt for her had thawed during the long day spent sparring with one another, they weren't exactly friends. She waited as he seemed to be trying for the right words.

"How have you been able to stand it here so long?"

Greta could taste Ray's anxious desperation. Having lost a brother to this place, he must hate it here more than the others. They all ached to see their families, but at least the younger boys had been blessed to some extent, with forgetfulness. They could also feel confident in the knowledge that their loved ones were safe at home, maybe still waiting for them to return one day. Ray, though, he knew that even if he somehow made it back, his brother would still be lost forever, a casualty of Mylena.

"I guess I didn't have much choice, but I was also very lucky." She sighed, realizing just how true that was...although maybe her luck was finally running out. "I kept my brother from being tossed into that fire, even if I couldn't save myself. And it was luck that I didn't end up a prisoner of Agramon like you. Luck that I found someone willing to protect me and teach me to survive here."

"But you do *want* to leave, don't you?"

Startled by the question, she swallowed hard. "What do you mean?"

"You've built a life here and everything. I just thought maybe you'd given up on going home. Maybe you like it here now, or you don't think there would be anything to go back to anymore."

"I didn't give up." *You so did*. Greta frowned. "I searched. For years, I searched for a portal. But I also owed a debt to the sprite who took me in. I couldn't just leave him." For the first time, that reasoning sounded like an excuse. She shook her head. "Not that it matters now."

"There's nothing holding you to this place, right?"

Glancing from Ray's speculative expression into the dark of the surrounding bushes, she was surprised that the memory of Isaac's glowering face stood in the way of a simple agreement. She clenched her hands into fists at her side. "Why do you ask, Ray?"

"Would you stay? I mean, if we aren't able to pull this off and you knew some of the others would be stuck here, would you still go if you could, or would you…stay?"

Greta thought about her brother Drew, about how she might feel if he'd been dragged through the portal along with her and died here. If the opportunity came, how could she go back to the family they left behind and explain that only one of their children was ever coming home? How would she explain why she had lived and Drew had died? Could she look into her parents' face and be the cause of their horror and disappointment?

Her chest tightened. Ray's young face was shadowed deeply by the night, but she recognized the torment in his glistening eyes.

"That's a hard question. Maybe impossible to answer," she whispered. "I'm not sure anyone could make a decision like that unless the choice was forced on them." She put a hand on his shoulder and squeezed gently. "And you shouldn't have to make that decision now either. Let's take this journey one step at a time, okay?"

"It's just…I was thinking…" He paused. "If it comes down to it and we can't get everyone through the portal, I'm the one who has nobody. Wyatt would be against it because he thinks he has to protect everyone, but I think maybe I should be the one who stays to take care of the boys that don't make it through."

Greta took a leaf from Luke's book, steeling her expression and her tone to show no sympathy, since that wouldn't help anyone. "This was your crazy idea, Ray. Don't you dare fail us before we've even started. We haven't found a portal yet anyway, but if we do, you're damn well going through it." No way was she going to let it go down any other way.

He looked unconvinced and stared back at her for a long moment. Was he searching for assurances in her face? Would she fail him in the end like she had failed Luke?

"Why don't you go on to bed."

He shook his head. "I should—"

"Forget it. Wyatt will be up in another hour. I wouldn't mind some time alone until then."

He considered it and nodded. "Ok, then. I'm actually pretty beat."

Greta didn't doubt it. The boy had taken hit after hit from her all day long. His sigh was much less antagonistic than normal, as if he didn't have the energy to keep hating her just on principle.

He turned to go, but stopped and looked back over his shoulder. "Thanks."

She shook her head and waved him on. She couldn't possibly accept thanks for her pep talk, or anything else she had done in this camp today, not when she knew her words were meaningless, her gestures worthless.

It wasn't going to matter how much they all wanted this plan to succeed, or how much training she gave them in the next twenty-four hours. She had a feeling it was all too little, too late. Odds were, people would die before the dilemma of whether to stay or go even became an issue.

She swallowed against the steel shavings lining her throat. Tears welled up and there wasn't anything she could do to stop them. They ran hot and fast down her cheeks, already cold as they fell off the edge of her chin. She glared into the inky black sky and cursed both God and the Great Mother—and everyone else who might be up there looking down on them.

What the hell happened to the warrior Luke had spent years training? If there was ever a time when she needed to be strong and maintain her stolid detachment, it was now.

"Greta? Are you okay?"

Swiping both hands across her cheeks, she kept her face averted so Wyatt wouldn't see her weeping. "Yeah, I'm fine."

His footsteps crunched in the snow as he came up behind her and turned her around by the shoulders to face him. "You don't look fine. Do you want to talk about it?"

She groaned. "What are you, my counselor now?" His eyes dulled with disappointment and she felt about three inches tall. "I'm sorry. I'm just not used to this, you know?"

"Used to what?"

"All of it. I've faced danger before. The critical, never-going-to-get-out-of-this-one-alive kind. As a human playing at being a bounty hunter, that's just the way it was—the way it *is*. The only way to survive." She sniffed. "But, God. Recently, I… I don't know what's happening to me. I'm falling apart."

His fingers were cold as he took her hand, his touch hesitant and gentle. She blinked up at him through a pathetic sheen of tears. "Maybe you just figured out you still have something to lose. If it were me, I'd probably be scared shitless."

She searched his face, marveling that his features had become so dear to her so quickly. She thought of all the people counting on her suddenly. All of those new connections had the capacity to bring her pain.

One connection in particular came to mind. She didn't want to think Isaac was important enough to hurt her, or admit there was anything between them for her to lose. But it was time to stop lying to herself. He was part of this. Whatever they had was shaky and thin…but it was more than just a dream.

And surprisingly, it was precious to her.

Too bad it was destined to break. If the eclipse didn't do the job, the decisions and promises she'd made today were going to. Her chest ached, like it was something she'd already lost.

She couldn't see Wyatt's face before his lips pressed against her forehead. She felt the rhythmic in and out of his chest as he breathed, and the warmth of his arms coming around her like a wide blanket.

His embrace was almost timid. He didn't crush her to him like Isaac would have. He didn't consume her senses and threaten to swallow her whole. He treated her as if she were made of something treasured and breakable.

Greta opened her eyes and looked up into the smooth chocolate of his gaze. "Wyatt, I don't think —"

"Shh. You think so much," he chided, tapping her temple with the second knuckle of his forefinger.

In his own way, Wyatt had crept up on her with as much stealth and premeditation as Isaac. She was surprised by how twisted-up and confusing her feelings had already gotten. As if one impossible relationship weren't already complicating her life enough.

The moonlight played with the shadows, giving him deeper hollows in his cheeks and hiding his eyes. He dragged his thumb lightly over her bottom lip, continuing up the slope of her jaw. His hand shook a little bit, but his touch made her feel as if she were being welcomed home after a long absence, as if every good memory of being human was wrapped up in him.

Isaac was so different. Fierce and bold and commanding. Daring her to embrace the future and forget about the past. But she reminded herself that half of what she'd felt with him had been *fabricated* — all in her head. And that the part which had been real was also dangerous and self-destructive. *This* was real. Wyatt was real, and he was here with her now in the flesh.

Being with him wasn't a violent explosion attacking all her senses at once, but true intimacy — the kind she could trust — needed time to grow.

Didn't it?

A cough from inside one of the tents brought her to her senses and she jerked back. "I should probably run a patrol."

"Wyatt? Greta?"

Alarmed by the sound of Jacob's call, she turned and raced to the open flap of his tent. He stood there shivering but smiling up at her.

Wyatt followed with considerably less urgency. "What's the matter, Jake?"

Jacob looked up at her and down at the ground, his face a mask of undisguised longing that put all new cracks in Greta's armor. "I…I can't sleep."

Feeling uncertain about her place in what was, in essence, a kind of family, she went down on one knee so they would be at eye level with each other and rubbed her hands briskly up and down his arms to help warm him from the harsh night air.

"I couldn't sleep either," she admitted, glancing up at Wyatt with a raised brow. He nodded, understanding what she was asking. "It's pretty dark, and I think maybe I need some company. Do you want to come and share my tent?"

"Yes. Yeah, sure!"

The young boy grabbed her hand so quickly Wyatt chuckled softly behind her. "Go on then, you sly devil. Tomorrow is a big day and you both need your sleep."

Jacob waved at Wyatt and started dragging her away. "Good night Wyatt."

Greta looked over her shoulder, a rush of warmth flooding her. "Good night Wyatt," she whispered.

Chapter Fifteen

After tucking Jacob into the coverlet beside her, Greta listened to his excited chatter for several minutes. The boy had too much energy for his own good. He seemed to think having Greta all to himself was some kind of treat, and chattered like a little magpie, telling stories about the other boys.

Jack had apparently caught his first hare last week, but Jacob thought it tasted yucky. Once, Charlie and Niall both got sick with ugly red dots all over their faces, and almost died. Ray always gave him all the seeds whenever they found a mocker nut bush. And Sloane cried in his sleep sometimes, but he didn't want anyone to know.

Even when the little motor mouth started to wind down, he refused to close his twinkling eyes, almost as if he were afraid she would be gone when he woke up.

"Oh, and—"

"Magpie, shh," she whispered, testing the baby fine strands of hair at his temples with her fingertip. "Go to sleep now. You can tell me more in the morning, I promise."

As soon as he stopped talking, a huge yawn erupted out of him. He tried to fight it, but another few minutes and his eyes fluttered closed and he was asleep, just like that. Greta lay back, listening as his breathing evened out and his little body slumped bonelessly into the curve of her arm.

After rethinking everything that could go wrong tomorrow and coming up with all new complications but no alternatives, Greta herself fell asleep a long time later, feeling more confused, terrified, and unsettled than ever.

The dream started almost immediately, taking her deep into the dark forest. There was no preamble this time, no muddiness, and Greta wasn't surprised. She'd been expecting him, knew what was happening and exactly where they were—the magical circle near Luke's house.

Although she wasn't the least bit cold, a heavy, wet snow fell softly. Mylena's two moons peeked from behind a layer of clouds. She noticed they were almost in line with one another, proving that she was worrying about the eclipse all the time now, even in her dreams.

He stepped out of the darkness in front of her dressed in black, and Greta couldn't stifle the thrill that shot all the way through her. As soon as their eyes met, she was thinking about that kiss. Pressing her spine hard against the trunk of a tree was the only way she could keep herself from running to him.

A stricken look flashed across his face as he noted her hesitation, but it was gone so quickly she probably imagined it.

"Why are we here?" She crossed her arms in impatience, ignoring the flip-flop of her stomach. "What is it you want from me now?" Her tone was harsher than she'd intended, but it was better this way. Less chance they would end up kissing if both of them were too busy being defensive.

"Tell me where you're hiding, Greta. I've narrowed it down, but I can't find you."

Grateful for small favors, she thought of the tiny body cozied next to her back in the real world, and shook her head. "You know I can't."

"You still don't trust me."

"Should I?"

His lip curled. "If you knew what I've been through to keep Agramon's gnomes and the legion of bounty hunters out of my county and off your trail…"

Greta stepped forward. Truthfully, she did trust him—to a certain extent. And she believed he felt something for her. But as much as she cherished that, she had to consider the lives of Wyatt, Ray, Sloane, Jacob, and the others now.

"Why would you continue to put yourself and your people at risk for me?"

His gaze fell to her mouth. "You know why."

She shoved her trembling hands behind her back. Damn him. This was his dirtiest game yet. A few days ago, she would have given anything to find someone who knew that she was human and still wanted her, but it was too late. Now, even if she survived, she and Isaac could never bridge the gap out there in the real world. They could never have anything between them but this dream. "I'm not one of you. I don't belong here."

"Who says you're not one of us?"

"Please," she said. "I'm human, as much as you may have decided to ignore that fact. You hate humans."

"I haven't ignored anything. I know who and what you are." Exasperation colored his tone. "And I've already told you it doesn't make any difference. Why can't you accept that this is your home?"

Home. No, Greta refused. Damned if she would ever call this frozen wilderness home, even if she lived out the rest of her life here. It was her prison, *not* her home. "If I'm such a perfect fit for Mylena, why is everyone out to kill me?"

"Your gracious personality?"

She gave him the look of death.

His teasing smile faded. "Greta, be reasonable. If you let go of your monumental stubbornness, I can take care of the price on your head. And if you tell me where you are, I can keep you safe through the turbulence of the eclipse."

"Even if I could trust your motives, I don't need your help."

"Just because you don't *want* it, doesn't mean you don't *need* it."

She squared her shoulders. "Did you worm your way into my subconscious just to be an argumentative, overbearing ass? Because I've got better things to spend my time dreaming about—"

"You can't pretend with me. Not anymore." He stopped in front of her with a smoky, purposeful look. "We both know I would be in your dreams whether you had asked me here or not."

Isaac would be the subject of her fantasies for as long as she drew breath into her body, but she would never let him know it. "*Asked?*" she choked. "Shall we revisit the process by which you manipulated your way into the so-called 'invitation'?"

He swung away, throwing his hands in the air before turning back to her with a snarl. "Don't refuse what I can give you. Don't reject my protection. Don't try and force me out. The stakes are too high now."

"I can't do this anymore," she whispered.

His frustration vibrated between them. "Even if I could leave you, should I promise to stay out of your mind when it's the only way I have of knowing you're safe?"

"Since when has my safety become your concern anyway?"

"Around the same time you set yourself on the path of personal destruction." His voice was filled with desperation now, as if he were fighting for his life…or hers.

Was it so obvious she'd taken on a suicide mission?

It hadn't been her humanity that got her through the last four years, but that other part of her—the part which had taken pleasure in every hunt, rocked every kill. The part that was born here in Mylena. She hated that he knew her so well, that he could see the darkness in her.

It had already occurred to her that this quest she was embarking on meant there was a good possibility she wasn't going to see the real Isaac ever again. Something that would have been a blessing just a few days ago now made her heart hurt.

She found herself wishing things were different, that she hadn't met Wyatt and Jacob and Ray. Hadn't learned of the human slaves, and didn't know what horror would befall them if they were left to rot in Agramon's dungeons. All of this would have been so much simpler, her choices easier.

Because the only choice she had now was killing her inside.

"Whatever path I decide to take isn't any of your business. You don't have the right to interfere. I'll find a way to bar you from my dreams even if it means cutting your cursed name from my very soul," she warned. "We're done."

He flinched before his whole body went rigid and the light faded from his eyes. She blinked back the tears before he could see them.

She took a step back. "I'm telling you now, Isaac. You had better stay out of my dreams—and don't bother telling me I don't mean what I say. Don't keep trying to find me either, because you'll only be wasting your time."

Suddenly, his expression narrowed. "Greta, by the Great Mother, what have you gotten yourself into?"

Her stomach clenched. "Just get out. This has nothing to do with you. I won't let you stand in my way."

"Is this about Lucius's death? Revenge is a fool's—"

"This is so far beyond revenge now." She choked on bitter laughter, realizing just how true the words were. "Revenge would be simple."

His jaw tightened. "Whatever it is can't be worth your life."

"You know, you're wrong about that. In fact, this might be the one thing that has made my life mean something, and if I have to give it up to get the job done, then so be it."

His lip curled and the fake forest background around them shimmered. Was he losing control? Had she finally pushed him close to the breaking point? "What's between us is too strong for you to just walk away."

He better be wrong, or they were both in for a world of hurt. "There won't ever be anything between us now."

Greta.

"Liar," he said with a snarl. "I'm impressed you were able to say that to me with a straight face."

Greta...

Her head pounded like someone had started tapping on her temples with a pickaxe.

Please...you have to...

Dizzy, she closed her eyes and shook her head, trying to get rid of the feeling, but it only increased until everything was spinning.

…up…please.

"What is going on?" she asked. "Do you hear—?"

Someone was trying to wake her. On the other side, something was wrong.

Please, Greta. Please wake up.

She snapped her head back. "Isaac, get me out of here."

"Where are you? Who are you with?"

"There's no time for that. Just let me go." Her heart in her throat, she spun around, absently looking for a way out, a tear in the fabric of the dream. Hell, a good old-fashioned door would do the trick—*anything*.

The fake forest, fake trees, fake moons—all of it warped around her like waves on the surface of a deep, black lake. "Isaac! I have to wake up now. *Right* now!"

He grabbed her shoulders, shaking hard. "Tell me where you are."

She shoved at his chest, desperation a crazed thud in her brain telling her to hurry, hurry, hurry.

Glaring into his dark, hard eyes, she tried not to think about anything he could pluck from her mind. Nothing except for the constant thumping refrain of *wake up, wake up, wake up*— "I'm not playing, goblin. Get me out of this dream before I—"

Please, Greta…scared. Please.

Jacob.

Oh, God. She was going to be too late. She cracked. "Isaac, please. I'm begging you. Please let me go." Her fingers curled into his sleeves. Her voice caught on a sob. "They need me."

"The humans," he spat. His gaze cooled as he stood over her, his face turning to stone before her eyes. "Is this your wish?"

"My wish?" Her head snapped back as if she'd been slapped. "You son of a—"

Greta!

She nodded. "Yes, damn you. This is my wish. Just do it. Get me out of here."

Her vision blurred, the sick feeling in the pit of her stomach sucking her down farther and farther into the darkness.

"Fine. Go," he said. "Awake."

Chapter Sixteen

Greta surged upward with a harsh gasp for air, shaking off the tormenting cobwebs of the dream as quickly as she could.

Jacob was on his knees beside her. He jumped back with a breathless shout. She clasped his shoulders and pulled him into her arms. He was shaking badly and she tried to soothe him with a few awkward pats on his narrow back. She felt the warmth of his tears on her neck. "Shh, Jacob. Hey, it's okay."

He shook his head and hiccupped, keeping his nose wedged tight in the crook of her neck. What must he have felt when he tried to wake her and she didn't move?

"What is it? What's happened?"

He swallowed hard, but before he could speak, a sharp cry sliced through the silence outside. Jacob jerked, his fingernails digging into her arms.

"Jacob, I want you to stay here while I'm gone, okay?" It hurt to pull his little arms from around her and set him aside. She reached for her sword and stood to belt it in place around her waist. Since she'd only planned to lie down long enough for Jacob to fall asleep, and then take patrol duty with Wyatt, she hadn't bothered to unstrap her daggers earlier, but quickly checked to make sure they were still secure.

"Greta, I'm scared," the boy whispered. He'd curled up into a tight ball in the center of the pelts. "Are you going to come back?"

She knelt before him and took his hand. Placing a kiss in his palm, she closed his tiny fingers over it. "Of course I'm coming back, magpie. You keep this safe, because I'll want it back, do you hear me?"

He nodded and cradled his hand close to his chest, ducking his head. Another shout, followed by a crack of something loud splintering and breaking made him screech and cry out.

"Shh. Don't be afraid," she said. "You'll be safe as long as you're very quiet and you don't come out of this tent. Not unless one of us comes to get you. I'm going to help Wyatt and Ray now. You wait right in that spot just like I said, okay? That's an order."

She didn't want to leave him, but she told herself Jacob would be the safest of anyone if he stayed inside and stayed quiet. Standing, she forced out a deep breath and willed her heart rate to slow down. She ducked out of the tent and folded the flap tightly over the opening without another look back, knowing if she gave in she wasn't going to be able to go.

Not sure what to expect—more crazed Mylean timber cats?— she paused instead of immediately rushing headlong toward the source of the racket. But the sounds of clashing steel spurred her forward. No timber cat would strike back with a sword.

Sloane was running out of his shelter with a dagger in his hand just as she raced past. Greta pointed behind her. "Go and get Jacob in my tent. Then do what you can to gather the boys together and keep everyone safe."

She couldn't stop to make sure he would listen, but even though he was young, Sloane was smart, strong, and capable. They all were. She had to trust that they had a plan in place for this type of emergency.

As she closed in on the disturbance, she squinted through the darkness, trying to get a bead on the threat. She could make out a pattern of heavy shadows swirling back and forth, with the odd reflection of moonlight off the blade of a sword slashing through the air. An icy block of dread settled in her throat. She had a terrible feeling she knew what was attacking them.

"Wyatt! Ray!"

Please don't let me be too late.

She jumped over the fire pit. It had been stomped out hours ago, but a few embers continued to glow weakly and its heat warmed the backs of her thighs as she landed on the other side between the two engaged figures.

One of them was Wyatt—on her left. The other...

Lazarus.

He had found her again...and from the looks of those dark eyes and long claws, the moons were riding him even harder now than last time. He hadn't turned completely, but the arrival of the eclipse would be just a formality for this guy.

Unnerved by the wave of relief that at least their attacker wasn't Isaac, Greta turned her back to Wyatt and faced the deadly faerie. She blocked his quick thrust with her blade, but the hits didn't stop there. She took a hard shot to the nose when he countered with his fist, snapping Greta's head back so hard she bit her tongue and lost her balance.

"Ah, crap." She winced. The blood started to well in her nasal cavity and she sniffed it back with impatience and a shudder of disgust. Damn it. Why did they always have to go for the face?

She forced herself to stay on her feet, keep her body between Wyatt and Lazarus.

Wyatt tried pulling her behind him. "Greta, what are you doing? Get back!"

She shrugged him off. Lazarus snarled, his sword lifting in a deadly arch over their heads. "Get out of here, Wyatt. Go get the others to safety."

Wyatt jumped forward to stand at her side. "Ray's got it. You need my help."

"Those kids need you more," she cried, kicking out to knock Lazarus back a few steps with a high shot to the chest. "You think if you die here tonight Ray will be able to take care of them on his own?"

"If I die tonight, hopefully it means you'll live," he retorted, his face a mask of ruthless determination. "And I trust you to take care of Ray *and* the kids."

The guy was delusional if he believed they could manage without him, or that she was an acceptable substitute for his compassion and leadership. Greta may have been designated the muscle of this operation, and Ray was most definitely the guts, but Wyatt was its heart and soul, and every boy back there would fall apart without him. The whole group would crumble.

But Greta didn't have time to argue. She kicked out again as Lazarus moved on her, catching him hard in the kneecap. He stumbled and she stayed on the offensive, moving forward right away with a slash of her blade, but he dropped and rolled before coming back on his feet a few steps away.

His roar was filled with such hate and venom she wondered when this hunt had turned personal for him. That's all she needed was to have the most ruthless bounty hunter in Mylena after her blood instead of the money he'd be paid for taking her alive.

Lazarus sprang at her so fast she didn't even get her sword back up. Both his hands closed around her throat. Tightened.

Her mouth opened, but there was no air to scream. She couldn't gasp, couldn't choke, her windpipe collapsing under his iron grip.

"Greta!" Wyatt's cry sounded muffled and far away.

The sword fell from her fingers and she lifted her hands, tearing desperately at the faerie's wrists. She kicked every part of his body her boots would reach, and it did absolutely nothing.

Her strength was failing quickly and every move was slower, like trudging through thick sludge that only pulled her down deeper the harder she fought.

Her vision blurred and darkened. She was going to lose consciousness.

She felt rather than saw Wyatt launching himself at Lazarus with a knife aimed at the faerie's back. She was jerked roughly to the side as Lazarus swung around in an attempt to throw Wyatt off without letting go of her throat. The pain that jolted through her was so extreme, she was afraid her neck had just separated from her spine.

Certain she was done for, she closed her eyes. But the faerie suddenly howled and dropped her into the snow.

Gasping for air, she pulled it into her lungs quickly and deeply even though it hurt like knives tearing at her throat. She dug in her heels and scrambled backward to put space between her and the two combatants. Forcing her fists to unclench, she leaned over her knee and lifted her pant-leg, pulling the long-handled dagger from her boot.

She battled dizziness while the fight continued in front of her. Lazarus growled.

"Come on then, you monster. Let's dance," Wyatt taunted.

Stupid, stupid boy.

She blinked, trying to find him among the shifting shadows. Her vision was still spotty. She got to her feet and managed to stay upright, but couldn't move her neck. *Oh yeah, that's going to be fun tomorrow.*

Lazarus swung his long, sharply-clawed arm at Wyatt with a growl. He ducked to the right and barely missed having his head separated from his body.

"Wyatt, get back!" Her voice came out as a pained, soundless whisper that neither of them heard. Better not to bother. The stubborn idiot wouldn't listen anyway.

She forced her way back into the fight with dagger in hand and a buttload of strength of will—if not strength of body—but even two humans against one massively aggressive faerie was like a couple of bees buzzing annoyingly around a T-Rex. They were just pissing him off. She could feel it in the air, that same gathering of energy, of cold, of power, as the last time.

"We have to run," she croaked, holding her hand out for Wyatt.

"He's turning!" Wyatt called to her in the same moment. He grabbed her arm and they both stumbled a few feet away as the vortex of ice began to form around Lazarus.

Greta knew they wouldn't get far, not if she tried to leave with Wyatt. She could probably stay and stall the faerie long enough for him to take the boys to safety, though. The bounty hunter had been tracking her after all, and might not bother with the others if she wasn't part of the group anymore.

She shoved Wyatt out of the way. "It won't work. Go without

me. You have a responsibility to those boys, not to me…I'll be fine," she lied.

Spotting her sword in the snow, she jumped for it just as Lazarus lunged for the two of them in all his gnarly faced, fangy glory. She dodged his grasp and maneuvered behind him, grabbing his arm as she went and spinning him around until he gave Wyatt his back and the only thing he had to focus on was her.

A bestial cry sounded in the distance. Filled with such monstrous rage everyone paused on hearing it echo toward them through the night.

It was still far out, maybe a couple of miles, but the next thunderous howl confirmed that it was moving fast, getting closer by the second, and whatever it was, it wasn't happy.

Her hopes for getting out of here in one piece plummeted some more. It was also clear that no matter what she said, Wyatt wasn't going anywhere without her. He stubbornly placed himself back at her side as they faced off with Lazarus, who seemed newly invigorated by the prospect of more guests to the party.

Fine. She'd tried. She couldn't be responsible for his death if he wasn't going to let her save him from it.

Swallowing her anger, she focused on the battle. She was doing her best to take the brunt of Lazarus's attack, but she couldn't last much longer. They defended themselves as best they could. She tried not to think about the other creature on its way, looking for a piece of the action, but the furious calls that came every few minutes cut her to the core.

Suddenly, she knew who was coming. Knew what it meant. "Wyatt, you've got to go!"

"Enough." The faerie's voice gurgled with the force of his moon phase. He straightened and glared at her with ice in his eyes.

As she watched, his pupils clouded over and again she felt that stirring of the air. It quickened, imprisoning her suddenly within a circle of smoke. She tried to push through, but touching it was like plunging her hand into the fiercest, coldest ice storm Mylena had ever seen. She'd never felt anything so cold. If she tried to walk through it would probably stop her heart.

He'd just turned their fight into the equivalent of a cage match.

In the distance, as if from miles away, Wyatt called her name. She wondered if he was locked out as much as she was locked in.

Trapped within the maelstrom of Lazarus's power, oxygen was thin and the fog so thick Greta couldn't see her hands in front of her face. She sensed the faerie shifting around her—first in front and suddenly behind—but heard nothing. It was as if all her senses had been fried until she was left flailing about without any of her skills to lean on for balance. Not sight, or sound, or touch.

She took a swipe of Lazarus's claws across her chest and didn't even sense it coming, but she sure as hell felt each one of his razor talons tearing through her clothes and pulling at her skin.

She bit off the cry of pain, refusing to let it pass. He shoved her from behind, blew frigid wind in her face until she couldn't breathe. He bit her shoulder, and his next pass left a deep gash in her thigh. This time Greta couldn't stop the harsh groan that escaped, but she didn't dare move. Holding absolutely motionless, she concentrated on clearing her mind of insecurity, doubt, pain, and crushed all thoughts of Wyatt, Jacob, Isaac, and anything else that could make her weak.

She closed her eyes, which actually helped her focus. When he moved on her again, this time coming up along her left side, Greta was ready.

Her fist shot out and she slugged him in the jaw. His sharp

teeth scraped the skin of her knuckles before he jerked back, but she barely felt it, the satisfaction of having taken him off guard in his own game trumped the pain big time.

"I see you," she murmured. Not with her eyes, but with her other senses. She realized he wasn't as invisible as she'd first thought. Greta just had to reach past his fog and mirrors tricks and listen for him in the spaces between the emptiness.

He roared and lunged at her. She had a bead on him now and was able to slip to the side, but he just turned and came for her again. It became obvious that he could have slit her throat at any moment, but hadn't.

He was *toying* with her.

"I commend your will to fight the inevitable," he growled into the mist.

She was surprised he retained enough control to form basic pronouns, much less actual sentences. Most of the Lost she hunted forfeited that function of civility to answer the pull of the moons.

"Yeah? That's nothing. Let's see what you think of my will when I'm gouging your heart out."

"You stand a much greater chance of keeping your limbs if you give up." His arm suddenly came out of the mist, those deadly claws narrowly missing her as she hissed and jumped back. "But I'm not bringing you in for the bounty, so it doesn't matter to me how damaged you are when I carry you out of here."

She kept looking straight ahead, straining with all her other senses for him to betray his position. "If you don't want the money, what are you doing this for?"

"For the sake of all worlds, you cannot be sacrificed to the demon. You will be brought before Queen Minetta to answer for the crimes of your race."

She frowned, only more confused. *Oh, goody.* Yet another Mylean monarch who wanted a piece of her. And just what crimes was she supposed to have committed now?

"Sorry to disappoint you, but I'm going to have to take a rain check on that one." Her breathing came in rasping coughs, the gashes in her chest pulling painfully with every movement. "It was nice chatting with you, though."

They continued to circle each other. It took a concerted effort to ignore the pain in her chest and the blood trickling down her calf. She was still technically flying blind, but refused to make it easy for Lazarus by standing still like an open invitation, so she took a swing at every whisper of air in front or behind her.

It was obvious she was out of her league. He avoided her all too easily, but at least he couldn't watch for her next shot *and* slice her throat open at the same time.

She began to hear things from the outside—the muffled sounds of another battle. Either Lazarus's strength was weakening and his whirling cage was thinning, or maybe Wyatt had started to make a dent in it.

Greta's shift in focus cost her dearly. Lazarus was suddenly behind her with his arm locked beneath her chin. If he'd wanted her dead, she would have less than a second before he snapped her neck like a fat spring hen's.

Legs bent, she pushed her body backward full into his chest and sent them both careening into the thick haze that continued to keep them trapped together, biting her tongue at the instant flash of ice attacking her. Lazarus's hold on her relaxed as he moved to brace himself. Greta's arm was engulfed within the wall of smoke. She screamed and scuttled back, but her hand was so cold it burned.

Suddenly a shout breached the barrier. It sounded like thunder, the kind that rumbled through the sky and shook the ground, heralding the coming of a drenching that would take up small children and wash them away down the street.

Greta knew it wasn't thunder. She knew it wasn't Wyatt, either. *Isaac.*

Her breath caught and warmth flooded her in deliberate opposition to the icy calm she had been fighting to maintain. She was stupidly glad that he'd found her, and stupidly terrified.

She started to push herself to her feet, but Lazarus was quicker and he threw her hard onto her back before she could regain her balance. His eyes glittered as he came over her. Greta hauled her knee to her chest and kicked him in the face. His head snapped to the side but otherwise her attack made little impression.

She could only hope Wyatt had been smart enough to run, get the boys out of the line of fire and to a safe place where they could ride out the eclipse.

"*Isaac,*" she whispered, wishing she had the strength to send him away to safety, too.

The circle of fog was suddenly falling away, dissipating rapidly.

No doubt because of the large hand reaching through it, wrapping around Lazarus's throat.

The faerie choked, fighting to draw air just as Greta herself had fought not so long ago. She groaned as he was pulled off her and sent flying through the camp. He landed in the remains of the fire, scattering the few glowing embers every which way across the tracked-up snow.

When she dared look up, it was to find Isaac glaring down at her, his face a twisted mask of raw ferocity.

This was no dream lover, or even the infuriating goblin

king who had baited her endlessly. She didn't know *what* he was anymore, but she couldn't look away.

Sprawled flat on the cold earth, she whimpered. He stood over her, their gazes locked together. The power of the eclipse shone from his eyes, but beyond that was something even more compelling. An absolute possession lit his dark gaze, even now when the moons were strong and the instinct for blood should have overridden everything else.

Her emotions numbed by pain, she watched the plumes of wintery air coming from his nostrils. The quick rise and fall of his chest. The clenching of his heavy fists at his sides. Everything about his posture spoke of blood lust and promised death.

Yet it wasn't Greta who bore the brunt of his fury.

When Lazarus got to his feet, Isaac turned away from her and directed all that wildness toward the faerie, his angry cry a clear warning that the hunter's remaining moments were numbered.

She shrank back as Lazarus lurched from Isaac's torturous grip and reached for her again, but Isaac jumped over her and slammed Lazarus to the ground a few feet away.

"Greta!"

Wyatt.

Turning onto her side, she put a leg under her and levered herself to her knees. Wyatt was hunched over a log not far from her. He got to his feet and took a shaky step forward. A long gash crossed his face, blood smeared across his cheek and forehead, and he favored his right side.

Her chest locked with fear. "What are you still doing here?"

"Shut up," he snapped in a sharp whisper. "I wouldn't have left without any one of the others, and I'm not leaving without you. Now get up. We have to go while the two heavyweights are keeping each other busy."

She shook her head. "It's no use. No matter who comes out of it alive, neither one is going to stop. They'll keep coming for me."

"Then we'll just have to go somewhere they can't follow." He reached for her arm. "Come on. They aren't the only ones we have to worry about. Can't you hear it?" He glanced over her head. "The whole forest is shaking. We won't have much time. Have to hurry."

He was right. Even though the eclipse was still at least a day away, its effect was already widespread. She could hear it in the rustling, screeching, snarling echoes coming from all around them.

The world was turning. Greta and Wyatt had no choice now but to run and to hide, or become easy prey.

She found herself looking uneasily at Isaac's intimidating form and winced as he was hit with one of Lazarus's icy tornado blasts. He stumbled backward, giving the faerie an open shot with those deadly claws.

When they tore through Isaac's shoulder and he fell to his knees, her scream was drowned out by his pained shout.

She lurched forward, but Wyatt yanked her back. "Greta, I swear, if I have to throw you over my shoulder and carry you out of here, I'm going to be really pissed."

Lazarus hit Isaac over and over. Greta flinched and bit her tongue, drawing her own blood to keep from screaming. She knew she had to go. She couldn't help him. If she tried, they would all be dead and she'd made a promise to Wyatt, to her own kind. They needed her to get them through this.

"I'm okay," she said. "Go on, I'm with you." She spotted her sword a few feet away and stumbled over to pick it up. She spun around in response to Isaac's roar, but before she could rush to help, Wyatt yanked her back.

"Come on!"

With a firm inward shake, she followed Wyatt without another glance back. A sharp sliver of pain sliced her heart in two as she tried to determine whether she was running toward something… or away from something else.

Chapter Seventeen

Greta and Wyatt dashed out of the glade, but she soon realized they'd just stumbled out of the cauldron and into the fire.

Her gut said it was only Isaac's fearsome presence that had been keeping the other creatures at bay this long, and now that they had walked away from him, the humans were apparently fair game.

What had she done? *Isaac. Oh, God. Isaac. I'm sorry.*

"They're closing in quickly," she called to Wyatt.

Early morning moisture chilled the air, but it was still very dark, too dark to see. That didn't mean they couldn't hear everything. Crunching snow and snapping twigs, and the more ominous snorts, grunts, and growls that came from every direction as more and more of Mylena's inhabitants turned on one another, transforming the forest into a battle zone.

She hoped to God Ray had been able to find a safe place for the boys.

Something close by snarled, and a long, creature-shaped shadow flew out of the bush-shaped shadows off Wyatt's left.

He went down. The thing that landed on top of him was huge and lunged right for his throat.

"Wyatt!"

It was impossible to determine what the animal had been before the moons turned it into a rabid thing, but thankfully, Greta didn't need to know what it was in order to kill it. Ignoring the screaming protest of her injuries, she jumped on its back and drew her dagger across its throat. The creature's howl turned into a choked gurgle.

She threw its dead weight off Wyatt and gave him her hand to help him up.

"Thanks," he muttered.

Wiping the blade on her already grimy pant-leg, she flipped it and handed it over to him. "Take it. I have another."

He nodded and accepted the weapon.

A howl echoed, sounding some distance away, but not far enough.

Not Isaac.

Another beast pitched into their path, eyes glowing yellow. She thought she recognized the animal from the length of the snout, but that's where its resemblance to the Mylean equivalent of a wolf ended. Wyatt stood protecting her back as the beast hunkered down in front of her, but instead of attacking, it launched itself at the dead thing between them, tearing the creature's throat out.

"Move," she whispered, taking a step away from the wolf. It lifted its head, hackles raised, but its attention wasn't on the two of them.

More of them were coming, though. Likely drawn by the scent of blood.

"Follow me," Wyatt said.

They took off again. They weren't followed by the wolf, but Greta kept her eyes and ears open to the sounds of carnage all around them. "Where are we going?" No place would be safe, not from those creatures that had already picked up on their scent.

"We have a back-up place. Ray and the boys all know to run there if something happens in the camp."

A tortured howl echoed in the night. Greta finally looked behind her, the light in Isaac's eyes haunting her.

"Come on!"

She stumbled forward as Wyatt ran ahead. Her vision was blurred by tears and pain and she struggled to keep him in her sights.

She hoped he knew where the hell they were going because Greta quickly became lost. The forest was a maze of white snow and dark shadows that disoriented her. Dizzy and weak, she was failing fast. When they were attacked by yet another pair of crazed wolves, she barely reacted. Wyatt threw her behind him, snatched the sword from her limp hand, and faced off against them both.

Then he was holding her in his arms. The two of them knelt together on the cold ground. Greta blinked at the pair of beasts lying dead a few feet away with surprise. Where had they come from? She didn't recall the blows that killed them.

"What happened? Where are the boys? Did he get them? Are they—" She sobbed, suddenly certain she would never see them again. She would lose Jacob and Ray, Sloane and the others, just like she'd lost everyone else. Her brother. Luke.

Isaac.

"We've got to keep moving." Wyatt tried to push her to her feet, but she shook her head, all the fight bleeding out of her.

Noises hit them from all sides. Growling sounds. Clawing sounds. Chomping sounds. Even the trees shook. The entire forest roared, sending a shiver down her spine.

Something screeched and dropped down on them from above. Wyatt let her go, and both of them slapped furiously at their faces and head. Bats. Hopped up on the eclipse, and with fangs as long as any freaking vampire.

One of them sank those fangs into her wrist. She hissed and waved her arm trying to dislodge it. Wyatt pulled it off and threw it hard against a tree trunk. He wrapped himself around her and tucked her head into his chest, holding on tight until the mad beating of wings scattered.

Had something else scared them off? What would attack them next?

"Come on, get up. We have to keep moving. You can do it. I've got you." He anchored her arm over his shoulder and pulled her upright. She bit back a groan as the raw, torn skin over her chest stretched painfully.

He pulled her along. "It's not far, baby. Just stay with me a little while longer."

She drifted in and out of consciousness as they continued at a much slower pace. She knew this only because every once in a while, she heard Wyatt calling her back to him and felt his hands tighten on her waist and wrist as he hitched her body closer in an attempt to keep her on her feet.

Just as the sky started to lighten and she squinted up at the beginnings of the new day—a day that would only heighten the instability of each and every living thing already hunting them—Wyatt pushed her down in front of an odd reddish stone poking out of the ground. It was shaped like a long cone.

Something moved in the trees behind them. Greta opened her mouth to shout, but she was too slow and weak to do anything about the snarling gnome flying at her from the branches.

An arrow whizzed past her face. It lodged in the gnome's thick chest with a meaty thud, but the thing seemed not to have noticed that the wooden protrusion sticking out of there meant it should fall down. It rocked back on the balls of its feet, screaming and shaking its head. Wyatt stepped in front of Greta with her sword held in his hands.

"Sloane, now!"

Ray's voice called to action a flurry of movement from all sides as Sloane led the charge and four boys attacked the intruder with daggers, rocks and more arrows.

This time the gnome got the picture. Ray put one last arrow into a bloodshot eye for good measure, but it was already falling over dead.

Which would have been peachy if she wasn't falling over herself.

❦

Greta came to suddenly with a crushing feeling weighing down on her chest.

She hadn't dreamed. Not at all.

He's really gone.

Her stomach roiled. She opened her eyes but couldn't see and flung her arm out blindly to grab onto something, anything.

Her hand only scraped against rock on the one side, and nothing on the other.

Her lungs clamped shut. She couldn't breathe.

Shut in.

The eclipse was here and she'd been shut in the darkness once again.

"No," she moaned. "Oh, no." She was aware of the mewling whisper of her sore voice, but only in as much as she was also aware that the damp had seeped into her bones, and the air she tried dragging into her lungs tasted stale and gritty.

They'd brought her under the ground. They'd buried her and left her alone in a tomb of darkness.

I have to get out. Get out. Get out. Outoutout.

Her head thrashed back and forth, fingers clawed at the dirt. Part of her recognized her extreme response as a childish reaction to remembered fear, but it didn't change how she felt. Helpless. Alone. Buried alive.

Her aching muscles protested when she tried to get up, almost as much as her other varied and many shooting pains. She fell back down with a sob.

Out. Out. Out. Get out. "I can't," she mumbled. "I can't stay here. Let me out. Please, let me out."

"She's awake."

She gasped and jerked her head toward the whisper. Pain shot through her chest, but it didn't matter. She recognized that voice. That had been Ray's voice.

Not alone.

The knowledge made it immediately easier to breathe. Greta closed her eyes, focusing on the in and out for a long moment before she turned onto her side and drew her legs to her chest, forehead hitting her knees.

A shuffle. Movement. A hand touched her shoulder. She knew it was Wyatt. She would know his sure, solid touch anywhere. It helped ground her, bring her part of the way back from the scary place in her own mind, even though that little bird continued to flutter desperately against the glass.

"Shh, you're all right," he said.

As the nightmare of her surroundings lessened and she became more aware of reality, she started to soak up the warmth of the other bodies filling the close space with her. How many of them had made it?

"Where are we?" Her voice was hoarse and her throat dry and painful—no doubt a result of getting herself choked almost to death. Once again, she tried struggling into a sitting position, helped on one side by small hands. Carter?

"Greta?" The small voice echoed in the pitch dark. Jacob's palpable fear pierced the veil of her panic. She pulled herself together as much as she could and held out her hand, but the arm she touched was bigger than Jacob's. Wyatt took her fingers and brought them to his lips. She sighed before pulling away gently.

"I'm here, Jacob," she replied with as much calm as possible. "Everything's okay."

Such a horrible liar.

"I can't see you," he whispered. "Can I come sit on your lap?"

"Jacob, not now." Sloane's sharp impatience didn't quite cover his own fear.

Now that she was emerging from the cocoon of self-paralyzing terror, Greta could feel the same emotions coming off everyone. That fear must be more potent for the boys because of her incapacitation. After all, they were relying on Greta the bounty hunter to be the strong one, and so far, she'd done a real bang up job of protecting them, hadn't she?

"It's fine Sloane. Jacob, you can definitely come sit with me. I need someone to help me get warm again."

There was a little bit of shuffling, and then Wyatt handed the small boy over to her. She settled him in her lap and wrapped her arms around him tight, ignoring the pain in her chest and thigh.

She felt his tiny shoulders relax within her embrace and wished it could be that easy for her to find solace, but images of a certain goblin's broken and bleeding face haunted her.

Greta peered over Jacob's head into the darkness where she knew Wyatt sat. Not that she could see him. Not even a faint outline of his shape. If she didn't have Jacob in her arms, she would have thought she was dreaming and the voices were all in her head—obviously not the first time she'd blended fantasy and reality.

"Where are we?" she asked again.

"A very small bunker that we dug into the ground, for just this type of emergency," Ray said.

"We're in the ground?" *In a grave!* "I thought I touched... rock." She shivered again. Jacob reacted to her uneasiness by softly caressing the back of her hand with his tiny one, as if he were petting a skittish kitten.

"Yes, we used the rock to shore up the walls."

That did *not* make her feel better. Now all she could think about was how they would suffocate and die slowly if the walls and roof caved in on them...

She swallowed and took a deep breath. "How big?"

"Not very," Wyatt responded. "Maybe ten by six, shored up every few feet. Enough for us to lay low, but no room to move and no room for provisions. We won't be able to stay long."

Wyatt was all about the understatements. "How well is the entrance protected?"

He didn't answer her right away. "We lowered a pretty solid slab of limestone over the opening, and it's hidden within some dense foliage."

"Oh, God." The close feeling crept back up her throat until she wanted to tear at the walls to get out. The only thing keeping the scream from escaping was the distinct awareness of Jacob's little hand on hers, softly soothing.

Going ballistic in front of these guys wouldn't do anyone any good—although it might not be very long before Greta didn't have a choice in the matter. Her insides were burning with the need for clean air even though she recognized that she technically had no difficulty breathing. "Where is the oxygen coming from?"

Niall piped up this time, from somewhere behind her. "I buried a thick, cored-out log in the ground with us. One end opens up in here and the other on the surface so that we won't run out of air."

"How ingenious," she mumbled.

Wyatt's hand landed on her shoulder again. More than just offering support, this time he was demanding that she keep it together. Greta swallowed and nodded. "So now what?" she asked.

"Well, the good news is that nobody was badly hurt in the raid and we're all here," he replied.

Raid? Is that what that had been? Greta would have called it something else—if there weren't little ears listening intently. "What do we have in terms of weapons?"

"Not much," said Niall. "A couple of knives. Sloane and I have a few arrows left. And we've got your sword."

Greta worried her lip with her teeth, turning the possibilities over in her head. Sadly, no matter how she looked at the situation, she couldn't find an upside. They were in the thick of the eclipse without gear and food.

"Nothing has changed. We were going to leave the camp today anyway. Now we just have to travel more carefully. The plan is still essentially the same." The defensive tone of Ray's voice grated on her nerves.

"The plan was flawed to begin with, Ray," she said, biting her tongue against the more colorful language she knew she shouldn't use in front of the younger boys. "And it was made before we knew the eclipse was going to have such a pronounced effect this early."

She didn't even bother to mention the problem of Lazarus. He could still be out there, still coming for her. That particular doozy was wholly hers to deal with and for as long as she could, Greta was going to try and keep the others out of it.

"We can't stay here for long, so what do you propose we do?" Ray snapped. "You're supposed to be the bounty hunter, renowned far and wide across this goddamn hellhole, and yet all we've done since you showed up is save your ass. Why the hell are you even here if you're not going to be of any use?"

"Ray," Wyatt warned.

"There's a lot more to what I do than being a badass," Greta snapped. "And obviously, it looks like I'm here to be the voice of reason in the face of your reckless, impetuous—"

"Hey, not that I don't find your two disembodied voices going at it highly entertaining and all...but do you really think this is helping the situation right now?" Sloane piped in. "Can we try and focus on something a little more constructive for five minutes?"

"Sorry."

"Sorry."

Both Ray's and Greta's echoed apologies fell flat in the sudden silence that followed.

"All right, then," Sloane continued. "I hereby call this first meeting of the Lost Boys to order."

Greta could sense the grin in his voice and shook her head.

Their presence had made being stuck in the dark…almost bearable. And the discussion had helped keep her from thinking about Isaac. Wondering if he was still out there somewhere, or if…

"We get the point Sloane," Wyatt said with a long-suffering sigh. "But he is right. Greta. Ray. Both of you try putting that energy into helping us come up with a plan that will work."

"This hole isn't going to hold us for very long." Ray let out a huff. "To start, we get out of here, and then we can make a break for Agramon's fortress."

Greta could agree with at least part of that. "Let me go back up," she said. "I'll check things out and make sure it's safe to leave."

"And then what?" Carter cut in, sounding apprehensive. "How are we going to survive with those…things roaming the woods? We'll have a hard enough time keeping ourselves alive. I can't see how we can rescue anyone else."

Good point. Greta hadn't forgotten the kid was only thirteen years old. That they were *all* much too young to even be having this discussion, not to mention too young for everything else that went along with it.

"I think maybe we should focus on one thing at a time," Wyatt said. "I'm not sure it's realistic anymore to think that we can make it to Agramon's castle with all of Mylena baying at the moons."

"We have to try!" Ray's shout caused Jacob to cringe in her lap, but he stifled his cry behind a hand pressed bravely to his mouth and she didn't think anyone else heard it but her.

"No. I'm sorry Ray, but I have a responsibility to everyone here first and foremost, and that means keeping us alive. Once the eclipse has passed—"

"Once the eclipse has passed half of the others will be dead and it will be too late, don't you see that?"

"And if we try to go in there now, then we're all dead!"

Greta put her hand out to stop the two of them from arguing before she remembered that they couldn't see her. "I'll go."

"What?"

"Not a chance," Wyatt said.

"I know of a place where you and the boys can hunker down for the next few days. Once I get you there safely, I'll trek out to this fortress of Agramon's and take a look around. I can't promise I'll be able to rescue anybody, but if it looks like I can…I will."

"Then I'm going with her."

There was absolutely *no way* she was bringing Ray along. She refused to have a loose cannon on her hands on top of everything else.

Luckily, Wyatt was of the same mind. "Forget it," he said. "I don't want either of you out there in the middle of this craziness."

"Honestly, it's better this way." She sighed. "I'll have slightly less suicidal odds of staying off everyone else's radar if I'm not dragging all of you with me. And Ray's right about one thing: If we leave the rest of the kids to rot in there during the eclipse, they're going to be sitting ducks. At least if I'm able to get them out into the forest we all have a fighting chance."

Wyatt was silent for a long time, but Greta knew he was going to agree. "How much time do you need?" he asked.

"Tell me where this place is again?"

"North. The fortress is built into the mountains and its levels go deep into the rock," Ray said. "But you don't need to know, because I'll show you the way."

"No, you won't." Wyatt's voice took on a hard edge that defied the young man to keep arguing. "Let Greta do her job, Ray. I trust that when she gets there, if she sees an opportunity to rescue the others, she'll take it. What I don't trust is that you will use the same reasonable judgment, and I can't risk losing you to something so reckless. I need you too much."

Ray didn't reply. Greta hoped he would be able to see the wisdom of Wyatt's decision, but the hostility coming from his general area of the darkness was palpable.

Everyone else was very quiet as Greta and Wyatt continued to make plans. "It will take three hours to make the trek to Luke's place, and that's if we hoof it. Once there, you should be able to find enough food and blankets to bring down with you."

"Down where?"

"Underneath the cottage. It's kind of like a bomb shelter, with a real steel door that you can bolt from the inside." She didn't mention that it could also be bolted from the *outside*, like Luke had done when he locked her into it. "It kept me safe the last time Mylena went through an eclipse." She swallowed. "But it's easily big enough for all of you if you don't mind close quarters for a couple of days."

They hashed out a few more of the details, making sure everyone knew what their job was so there would be no confusion once they pushed the stone off the top of the crypt. Greta took a few moments to work the tension out of her muscles. She felt stiff and sore, as if she were made of machined parts that had rusted up on her, but she was used to working through the pain.

Finally, it was time. Wyatt and Ray stood and shoved at the heavy stone slab until the light started to filter in and they could see one another for the first time in hours. Greta let out a long, relieved breath.

Everyone was grimy and tired looking, but nobody seemed to have been injured—

Turning toward Wyatt, she gasped. How could she have forgotten that he'd been hurt last night? "Ah crap. Wyatt, why didn't you say anything?"

"I'm fine," he argued. Two ragged lines marked his face, cutting through his eyebrow and down his cheek, having just missed being deep enough to gouge out his eye. The other eye hadn't fared any better, it was swollen and had already turned a deep shade of purple.

"What happened?"

"Crazed goblin." He stopped and gazed at her with a hooded look, then shook his head. "It doesn't matter now. Come on, let's get a move on."

When Greta hesitated, he urged her onward with impatience. "Go. We aren't going to have a lot of time."

She looked over Wyatt's shoulder at Ray. He nodded and moved forward, notching a handmade arrow in his short bow. "I'll return in five minutes," she said, "and if I don't, that rock goes right back over the hole with everyone inside."

Chapter Eighteen

When Greta returned to the others, she was sporting a new gash in her forearm and breathing hard.

The woods were not safe. Not by a long shot. And getting everyone to Lucius's bunker wasn't going to be easy...not that anything was *ever* easy in Mylena.

"We good to go?" Ray stepped out from behind the dense brush in front of the hideaway.

She nodded. "But it's got to be now, and we have to be fast."

Both of them knelt on either side of the large stone they'd replaced over the entrance to the hole earlier. Ray tapped the top five times in quick succession, waited until Wyatt started to push from inside, and then all three of them moved the slab away as quickly as possible.

"Hurry," she whispered, helping Jacob up out of the hole and then passing him back over to Sloane, who was to be responsible for the little one along the way.

Greta took the lead. As they walked, she remained on guard. The first twenty minutes of absolute silence might have given her a false sense of security if she hadn't sensed the unrest lurking just beyond her sight.

The skies were dark with clouds covering both suns and any evidence of the eclipse's progress, but she could see the needles that had been shaken from the trees and scattered across the snow. She could see the broken remains of smaller animals—too many of them—littering the path she'd chosen.

At her side, Ray jumped. "What was that?"

She shook her head and urged him to continue. "It doesn't matter. No matter what you hear…to stop is worse. Keep going."

Worry was making her edgier the longer they were out in the open.

She tensed at a crunching sound in the bushes on her right, then her left. Her heart pounded hard and fast. The night teemed with sounds, all of them terrifying.

She glanced behind her. Wyatt and Sloane had Jacob sandwiched between them. Wyatt's face was a determined mask of shadowed angles. Sloane couldn't hide his fear. He winced and started at every hiss and crack.

Someone behind her stumbled and let out a sharp grunt.

She spun around with a gasp. Niall was helping Jack back onto his feet. "He just tripped."

"Are you okay?" She asked, glancing over Jack's shoulder. Her tone stayed composed, but inside she was screaming at them all to hurry.

Jack nodded and wiped the snow from his pant legs. "I'm good, let's move," he said.

Something huge lunged from the writhing foliage. It knocked Niall over like a bowling pin and landed right on Jack, propelling them both off the path into the bushes. Covered in matted black fur, there was no telling what it might have been before the eclipse, but now, like everything else, it sported a set of extra long teeth and claws that it was already using to tear Jack apart.

The other boys' screams rang out as Greta swore and sprinted forward. She jabbed the creature with her blade and shoved it as hard as she could. It fell back and snarled up at her. Jack's blood coated its chin, and its eyes glowed red as it lunged for her.

Greta's back hit the ground and she dropped her sword as she tried to hold its violently snapping jaws away from her face. Her arms trembled with the strain. Those teeth were less than an inch from her nose.

Wyatt was there in an instant. He grabbed up her weapon and stuck the creature again, just as one of Carter's arrows lodged in the side of its head.

It slumped over her. She pushed the dead body aside, ignoring the blood staining her arms and her clothes. She got up, heart in her throat. "Jack. Is he—?"

Niall held the crying Jacob, and the other boys had all gathered around Jack's body. Greta went cold when Sloane turned his tear-streaked face up to her and shook his face.

Wyatt was trying to calm them down, but Greta looked down. She couldn't take her eyes from the lifeless body.

Another sharp noise rebounded out of the thick forest.

There was no time to issue a warning. She grabbed Niall and Jacob, shoving them behind her just as a gnome lurched from the trees. It had turned, topping her height by at least two feet when it normally would have reached her shoulders. Its bulbous, deformed head was squished between massive, hunched shoulders. Its long arms bulged with muscle the likes of which no gnome could hold on his short, stocky frame without the added impetus of the eclipse.

Its knuckles dragged the ground until it saw the group, and then it raised its fists into the air and roared.

Wyatt, Ray, and Sloane corralled the younger boys into a small circle as per the emergency plan. She'd debated the wisdom of telling them to bolt, but ultimately decided that if they ran into trouble, it wouldn't do any good to separate, in case the boys ended up in more—or bigger—trouble.

The gnome snarled and swung for the boys. She jumped between them and leveled her sword, but it hesitated. Looking at her, it gave what she was certain was supposed to be a grin. It mumbled something underneath its breath that sounded a lot like "*Kill. Kill. Kill.*"

"The feeling's mutual," she muttered before charging, just to make it stop torturing her with its lame attempt at speech. But it was just warming up and as she launched a roundhouse kick to the thing's sternum, she realized "kill" wasn't what the thing was saying at all.

The gnome reached for her. "Key. Key. Key. Master want. Master need."

Key?

The gnome was freaking her out now. She'd dealt with the Lost long enough that the snapping and snarling didn't faze her at all… but the idea that this creature was able to retain some shadow of premeditation in the face of an eclipse that was turning everything into mindless monsters hinted at a motivation more persuasive than nature, something more powerful than the moons.

Agramon. The gnome was one of the demon's creatures.

It came for her, but its tactics had changed noticeably. It no longer swung wildly, intent on destruction, but was actually trying to grab her.

Greta gave no quarter. She didn't need to know what the hell the key was and what made her so damn important this creature would try to override its own powerful, raw instincts. There wasn't time for an inquisition, only death. Swift and absolute.

Wyatt tossed her sword, and she grabbed it and swung at the gnome's reaching hand in one smooth movement. Before the gnarled appendage struck the snow, she'd stabbed it in the chest and the creature expelled a final breath, the rest of its body crumpling to the ground as well.

The entire encounter was disturbing, and the kill ultimately all too easy, but everything else had been hard enough that coming out of one battle without shedding anymore of her own blood was a blessing.

So why was she terrified?

She turned to find Wyatt watching her. "We have to get out of here before the blood draws any more of them," he said, glancing down at Jack's body. There was a catch in his throat, but his voice was stern with command.

Everyone protested. Wyatt was right, but Greta couldn't move her feet, couldn't look away from that young face covered in blood, sightless eyes staring up at her. Jack had trusted her. All these boys trusted her, and she was failing. People were dying. And she couldn't guarantee that there wouldn't be more deaths before this was over.

"Greta." Wyatt grabbed her arm and shook her. "Snap out of it. We need you."

She forced her gaze away, and nodded at Wyatt, taking a deep breath. Nobody wanted to leave Jack, but the noises were escalating, getting closer. More creatures were approaching. There was no choice in the matter. "Hurry," she said, finally pushing ahead. Ray fell in behind her and Wyatt took the rear.

Before the group reached the boundary of Luke's property, Greta fought two more gnomes—neither of which were particularly chatty—and they were attacked by a trio of bear-like creatures. She and Wyatt stood side by side against them while Ray and Carter kept their arrows at the ready.

Luckily, they suffered no other major injuries—or losses. By the time they approached the cottage, everyone was quiet, tired, and shell-shocked.

Greta was the first up the porch steps so she could go in and make sure nothing had taken up residence since she'd been gone. She opened the door and stopped, peering inside but seeing nothing.

Wyatt met her there, his hand landing firmly on her arm, expressing both support and a gentle urgency.

She looked up at his strained expression, aware that her own face showed him each raw, painful memory she'd been trying to ignore for the last week, but she couldn't keep it in anymore.

A week. God, had it been that long already? Had it *only* been that long?

"I don't think I can go in there. The last time I was here…" She shook her head. "All the blood, Wyatt. It's all still there," she whispered.

He lifted his hand to her cheek and leaned forward. Shying away, she glanced meaningfully over her shoulder at the boys.

"Do you want me to go inside first?"

Greta shook her head. "No, it's okay. We don't have time for me to be a wimp." She looked back into the house. "If nothing has been here to ransack the place since…well, there should be a store of non-perishables and some salted boar in the cupboards, and you can grab as many blankets and whatever else you'll need to stay as comfortable as possible while I'm gone," she said.

As they walked inside, she forced herself to keep her eyes open and see everything.

The house was as it had always been. Sparse, but neat and… clean.

"What the…?" When she'd last walked out this door with Isaac, thinking it would be for the last time, it had been a disaster. Now it was as if the violence that took place here had all been her imagination.

The broken furniture had been removed, the floor had been cleaned up. Greta rushed through the cottage to the door of Luke's bedroom. It was gone. All of it. All the blood had been washed away and no matter how closely she looked, she couldn't see a stain in the newly refinished floor.

"Isaac," she whispered. Swallowing the lump in her throat, she pressed her hand to her chest. He had to have arranged this.

"Is everything okay?"

She opened her mouth but couldn't speak so she just nodded and took a step back. Wyatt looked as if he wanted to ask, but didn't. Only his eyes spoke, expressing concern and understanding, and something darker…like resignation.

"I'm all right," she said, finally. "I'm just going to grab a few things. The trap door to the shelter is beneath the big table in front of the stove. Go ahead and open it up. I'll be right there."

Wyatt's mouth tightened before he turned and left her alone in Luke's room. Greta tried not to think of that as she hurried to get the blankets the boys would need, and she tried not to look at the wall where Luke's blood had splattered. Although the stain had been washed away completely, in her mind she could still see the pattern it had made.

Ten minutes later, they were ready—as ready as they would ever be, anyway.

She fingered the handle on the trap door. "You can keep this locked from the inside," she said.

"We'll be fine," Wyatt reassured her, obviously reading the strain in her face. "All of us have been in worse places than this. The eclipse is full this afternoon, so it's only two days, three at most—if we assume it'll take as long for everything to settle down again as it did to get started."

"I'm sorry." Greta shivered. "You know…that it isn't more—"

"If it keeps us safe, then that's all we can ask." He looked stoic and had already told Greta not to worry; the dark wouldn't bother him or the boys in the least. She had a feeling it was the memories of the one who didn't make it that would torture them all.

She marvelled at his strength. Even if he was lying to her, she'd never know it. No matter what his real feelings about being shut in an underground tomb with no light for two days, he projected nothing but calm competence in front of the others, and she admired that about him so much.

"Greta."

She jerked her head up. "Sorry."

"Go."

Yes. She should go. She'd already loaded up with more weapons, changed her clothes, and tended her wounds. Her leg and chest burned from the cuts left by Lazarus's claws, but once the blood was cleaned away, she'd been relieved to see they weren't as deep as she first thought.

There was nothing more she could do here and she needed to make good time while there was still light.

Taking a deep breath, she pushed back her coat and shoved her hand in her pocket.

"What are you doing?"

Her fingers closed around the walnut. She pulled it out and gave it to Wyatt, and then reached up and unclasped the chain from her neck, handing him the locket as well.

"What is this?" he asked, lifting a brow and rolling the walnut around in his hand. Greta couldn't see it, but she'd memorized every smooth contour of the nut and knew the feel of its raised grooves by heart. It had been in her pocket when she went through the portal. Drew had found it and given it to her that day before running off toward the witch's cave.

"Nothing, really." She shrugged.

He caught the chain with his finger and lifted it high before clasping the locket in his hand and opening it up to look at the picture inside.

"Why are you giving these to me?"

"If I don't make it…"

"Don't talk like that," he snapped, dropping the locket into his fist and holding it out to her.

Greta shook her head, refusing to take it. "These are the two things I have from home. I want you to keep them safe for me."

Wyatt glared at her, as if he was seeing what she herself would not admit. "Ray, get the boys down into the shelter," he ordered. "I need a minute with Greta before she leaves."

Carter had his arms around Niall. They were both crying softly. In fact, all the boys looked like they had reached the limit of their tolerance for pain, death, and heartache.

She hated to leave them.

Jacob ran to her and threw his arms around her legs. "Don't

go," he cried.

"I'm sorry, magpie. I have to. But you'll be safe here with Wyatt, and I'll come back as soon as I can," she promised, leaning down to return his hug.

"Sloane said Jack isn't coming back," he whispered with a choked gulp, his face pressed hard into her belly. "What if they get you like they got him?"

She swallowed, seeing Jack's bloodied body in her mind, hearing the screams. "I'll be careful, I promise."

He turned tear-filled eyes up. "I'll miss you. Will you forget about me?"

"How could I ever forget about you?"

His fingers clutched at the folds of her coat like he was afraid to let go. "There are lots of things I can't remember since I came here, and if you don't come back I'm afraid I'll forget you, too."

Her heart tightened painfully and she glanced up at Wyatt, whose eyes were still stormy and dark. He'd clenched his fists at his sides.

Looking back at Jacob, she said, "I won't be gone long enough for you to forget me." God, she hoped it was true. "And in the meantime, I need you to be strong and brave, okay?"

He nodded and hiccupped, hugging her again.

Ray took Jacob's hand and tugged him away gently. His voice was hoarse and thick with emotion, but she was impressed by how well he was holding it together. "Come on, big guy. Get your butt down there. Sloane is going to need your help organizing the supplies."

Jacob's teary smile made her heart melt. "Come back soon, okay?"

Greta stood and looked at all of them. Sloane nodded. Charlie stood a little closer to Niall and Carter. All of them looked terrified.

Finally, Wyatt took her arm and walked with her to the doorway. "This isn't goodbye," he growled. "So don't you dare tell them goodbye."

She stiffened. "Wyatt, be realistic—"

"I should be going with you. Or you should be staying here."

"I have to go. Ray's right. Those kids in Agramon's fortress deserve a fighting chance." She sighed and pointed back inside. "And someone has to protect them. I can't bring everyone with me and keep them alive at the same time. They'll be safe here, but they need you."

"Just make sure you come back, because they need *you,* too." He paused, his gaze somber and penetrating. "*I* need you."

Her mouth fell open in shock.

He nervously shoved his hands in the pockets of his chinos. "I know it's complicated, but I can't stop thinking about you."

"Only because I'm the first girl you've seen in years," she insisted, drawing back.

He took her hand. "It's more than that. And I think you feel it, too."

"Wyatt, I don't think now is—"

He pulled her closer and leaned in. She knew what was coming and drew in a sharp breath. His lips touched the corner of her mouth, warm and soft.

And real.

He was tentative at first, and she could almost convince herself it was just a platonic, come-back-safe-and-sound sort of kiss. But then he shifted, covering her mouth completely, and there was no longer any doubt what he meant.

Her hand shook until she finally rested her fingers on his arm.

She tried not to compare him with Isaac, but it was so hard not to.

Isaac had been pushy, infuriating, and confident. Real or not, his explosive kiss had churned up the already turbulent feelings raging between them, whereas Wyatt was sweet and gentle and a little awkward. He made her want to burrow into him and let him take her away from everything.

She knew if she stopped him right now, that would be the end of it. He would respect her boundaries and never make another move unless she took the first step. But she didn't stop him, and he gripped her waist, his kiss deepening as he gained confidence. He pressed his body and his lips to hers as if he wanted to make sure she wouldn't forget he was going to be waiting for her to return.

The kiss was a promise Greta wasn't sure she could ever accept, even if they both made it to the other side of this eclipse alive.

She twisted away with a gasp, pressing her fingers to her lips. He watched her for a long minute before nodding and moving back to lean against the doorframe of the cottage.

She gathered herself together. "I should go."

"Before you do, I need to ask," he said slowly. "Who was that goblin…to you?"

"What?" she stammered, fingers fluttering at her throat. "I don't know what you mean."

"The goblin," he repeated. "He showed up in our camp out of nowhere, looking for blood. He was ready to take mine. I thought I was dead—until he heard you scream. And then he dropped me like a bad habit to get to you. You want to tell me why?"

She flinched as her gaze flicked to the thin red marks tearing across his face. "No. Actually, I don't."

"What's between the two of you?"

She glanced away. Her mouth opened and closed but nothing came out.

"I saw the way he looked at you, Greta. It went beyond the eclipse. He looked at you as if he would defy the law, the moons, and the Great Mother herself to—"

"That's ridiculous," she cut him off. "How could you have possibly seen all that? It was pitch dark, for one thing, and—"

"I saw it because I feel the same way. And because I knew even before he showed up that there was something you weren't telling me."

Her chest squeezed. "You're right, I haven't told you everything about me. But where does it say I'm required to open a vein for someone I just met?"

He glared down at her. "That's not fair."

"Probably not," she agreed, "but a lot of things aren't. I don't have time for this now, Wyatt."

"No, I suppose you don't. Just tell me he isn't still following you, and I'll try to believe it."

"He's not coming for me, not after that fight." Greta glanced down, swallowing hard. "And even if he is…he's Lost now. Which means if he crosses my path, I deal with him like I deal with all the rest."

He swore. "Come back, do you hear me?"

"Sure. What could happen?" She pasted a cocky smile on her face, but it wasn't fooling anyone.

His expression turned so dismal, she immediately felt guilty for her glib response. "Listen, you were right about one thing. I have something to lose now, so I'll be back," she whispered. "You're going to see my face again…whether you like it or not."

"Good."

She made it a dozen paces before she had to turn back again. He was still standing there watching her and she waved, committing his face to memory.

With each step that took her further away, she was more certain she should have said goodbye.

Chapter Nineteen

Greta was still near the edge of Luke's lands when she stopped and turned around.

"Ray, show yourself or I swear I'm going to kick your morbidly stupid ass all the way back to the damn cottage."

He stepped out, not an ounce of regret showing on his face, but a heck of a lot of attitude.

"Why aren't you back there helping Wyatt protect the others?"

He shrugged. "Wyatt doesn't need me. But you do."

Greta laughed. "Like hell."

"I'm only a year younger than you," he pointed out.

She lifted a brow. "True enough, but I still don't want you with me."

"Well, I'm not going back, so you either take me along or you bear the burden of being responsible for my death at the hands of fairytale creatures gone wild."

"That's not fair to Wyatt. He's going to have kittens when he realizes you're gone."

"Just what kind of irresponsible jerk do you take me for? I

wouldn't leave without telling him, and I wouldn't leave without being certain he could handle himself. He knows where I'm going…and he also knows he can't make me stay."

She shook her head. "He has more tolerance for idiots than I do."

"That goes without saying." The way he looked her up and down let her know she could easily be lumped in with that group.

Without another word, she turned away and continued walking.

"So I can come with you?" Behind her, he rushed to keep up.

She spun back around and pointed a finger in his face as he slid to a halt in front of her. "So long as you understand that *you* are not my priority. I know what's going through your head, Ray, but I'm not going to feed your insanity. You're lucky our ultimate goals happen to mesh for the moment, but know this, if your agenda and mine diverge at any point in time, you're on your own."

Greta hated the wounded look he tried to hide behind righteous anger, but she refused to coddle him. She reminded herself that he was not a child, and she *would* leave him if he got in her way or jeopardized their lives with his irresponsible behavior.

"Fine. At least I know where I stand," he snapped, tightlipped.

"Good, I'm glad we got that straight," she muttered. "So why don't you lead the way?" She held her arm out for him to precede her.

At first, they traveled slowly, carefully. But soon she ramped up the pace and they were slipping through the forest at a steady running clip. She had to stop once to check the bandage on her leg again, but it seemed to be holding up.

For the next few hours, she and Ray managed a relatively cooperative coexistence, and if neither of them were particularly talkative, that was so much the better.

Greta had to give him credit, he was more than capable with a bow when the situation called for it—which it did every so often—and even better at the stealthy stuff than she was.

They came close to running right through a pack of ogres that had devolved into little more than giants snarling at each other over the bloody carcass of a large male goblin. Ray veered silently around them but Greta halted in her tracks like a deer trapped in a pair of headlights, unable to move until she'd convinced herself it wasn't Isaac's body being torn to pieces.

By the time she snapped out of it and moved to follow Ray, he'd vanished. She looked up and down the path they'd been travelling, but found no sign of him. When he suddenly showed up at her side a few meters away, she jumped.

"I told you I could take care of myself," he said with a grin.

She punched him in the shoulder, but from that moment forward, she didn't say anything about him slowing her down again.

It was mid-morning when they approached the mountain pass. Ray knelt in the snow behind a tall rock formation, waiting for her. "This is where things are going to get really difficult."

"Oh goody," Greta mumbled, shoving her gloved hands in her armpits with a deep shiver. Why did the temperature always plummet when she was nowhere near a roaring fire? Just more proof that this place had it in for her. "Where are we going?"

She peered around the small wall toward the tiny path that led into the mountain.

Ray shook his head and pointed.

Up.

"We have to go there."

"*What?*" Her mouth dropped open as she lifted her gaze up the rock wall in front of them. She could feel a tic starting to hammer away in her left eyelid. "Isn't there another way in?"

"Sure. If you want to walk through the front door and be mobbed by everything Agramon's got. Otherwise, we climb. About five hundred feet up there's a small opening in the rock. I don't think anybody knows about it—"

"How can you be sure?"

He shrugged. "Last time I was here it was easy enough to get in and out from up there."

"And when was that?"

"About one moon cycle ago."

Greta shook her head. "So what happens if they've found this second entrance since then and now it's being monitored?"

"I guess we're shit out of luck and we'll probably get slaughtered."

"Shouldn't we have a plan B?"

"If you've got another option, I'm happy to hear it."

Greta rubbed her temples and groaned. She looked up, noting the near alignment of the suns and moons. The full eclipse was close, so close. It might even happen within the hour now. If they made it up that cliff face and inside, they were headed into a war zone either way.

"Okay, so we're climbing." She had to laugh. If she didn't, the entire situation would be too much to handle. "Get a move on. You're going first."

"Don't worry." Ray started forward, inching around the rock. "They're just gnomes. Nasty looking bastards, but I'm sure you can handle them."

She snorted, following close behind, eyeing the steeply

sloping path upward. She didn't bother to mention that besides dark, enclosed spaces, heights were her least favorite thing. He might figure it out soon enough though, because if he so much as breathed on her while he made her climb this thing, they were going to have serious problems.

She watched as he scaled ten feet of sheer rock face in less than ten seconds flat. He made it look easy, but she knew it was going to be hell.

"Oh, sure. It's not that high up," she muttered, brushing the snow off a tiny ledge before gripping it with her already frozen fingers. "And hey, just a couple of gnomes. No big deal."

Finding a corresponding ledge for her boot, she lifted and then paused, already stumped as to where to reach or step next. She looked up. "How many of them are in there, again?"

Ray looked down. "You going to turn back?"

"Does it look like I'm turning back?" she shot up at him.

"It looks like you're having trouble keeping up. There's a spot about eight inches above your head. Grab that with your left hand and then bring your right boot straight up about two feet. There's a narrow ridge that should work. Yeah, like that. Now keep your body flush with the rock and pull yourself up. That's good."

Even though she was probably only about seven feet off the ground, it was already impossible to look down. Instead, she glared up at the space between Ray's shoulder blades and wondered whether her bones would shatter if she fell from this height. "Shouldn't we have a rope or something, in case one of us—?"

A startled shout was torn from her as her leg was suddenly seized from below. Panic caused her stomach to heave and her throat to close. She held onto the tiny jutting protrusions in the cliff for all she was worth and looked down.

Right into Isaac's twisted features. So full of anger, hunger, madness.

He's alive!

Was she imagining that there was recognition in his face? That he hadn't lost himself completely to the eclipse? Even as he growled up at her, she could still see his soul in those glowing eyes.

"Greta, hold on!" Snow dropped on her shoulders and into her face as Ray kept climbing.

Below her, Isaac stood with his long arm outstretched, claws penetrating the thin leather of her boot and digging painfully into her ankle—he'd just been able to reach her. If she had been less worried about falling, and quicker up the wall…

"*Greta.*" Nothing more than a growl, his voice made her heart lurch.

He pulled on her leg. Her knee buckled, but she recovered and scrabbled to hold on.

His nails went deeper. She screamed. The savagery in his eyes cut her, made her ache all over with fear and regret. She couldn't bear to see him like this; reduced to a vessel for all of nature's violence and rage.

She kicked, trying to make him let her go and catching him in the face with the heel of her boot. He only held on tighter.

"Isaac, don't do this. Please," she begged, pressing her cheek to the frozen rock. He yanked hard. Her grip slipped. She cried out and curled her fingers deeper into the outcropping of rock, but one more good pull and she'd tumble to the ground at his feet.

Something whistled over her head and an arrow lodged itself high in his chest—just above his heart. She screamed. "No! Isaac!"

His hold on her leg loosened before he let go with a chilling roar of fury and pain. She looked up to see Ray standing on the edge of a narrow shelf high above her. He'd already notched another arrow. Getting ready to fire again, he pointed the thing at Isaac's heart. "Ray, stop," she cried out. "Don't shoot him."

Reaching over her head, she grabbed another protrusion in the rock and pulled herself up the wall. Desperation gave her speed, but she wasn't fast enough to reach Ray before he let another of his arrows off.

"Eat tail feathers, asshole."

"Ray, no!"

She reached the ledge and hauled herself onto it. Jumping forward, she shoved his bow aside and stood in front of him.

"What are you doing?" he snapped.

Spinning around, she looked back down, but there was no Isaac. No dead goblin lying at the foot of the cliff, and no furious goblin surging up the rock after them.

"Oh, God. That can't be good. Where did he go?" Looking out into the woods, she didn't know what bothered her more—the idea of a moon-mad Isaac lurking in wait for them somewhere, or the image of that arrow lodged in his chest.

"Come on. We have to hurry." Ray pulled on her arm. "The eclipse is full now."

That wasn't entirely accurate, but they didn't have a lot of time before it would be true.

So focused on Isaac, she hadn't even noticed that the sky was completely clear for once, as if the falling snow which rarely subsided for anything dared not encroach on this particular event. But it had turned dark now that the moons were almost completely lined up in front of the twin suns.

She let Ray take the lead as they squeezed through a small fissure in the side of the cliff and found themselves in a dank tunnel. Slowly, she drew her sword. "I want you to stay behind me now," she whispered. Even that low-voiced sound carried in the dark tunnel and she looked back and forth, expecting to see Agramon's goons charging toward them from all directions.

Now that Ray had gotten her here, he seemed to have no problem letting her take charge. "Left," he whispered at her back. "About five hundred feet."

She nodded and took a deep breath.

Although it was dark, there were random breaks in the cavern walls, letting in small amounts of light from some source on the other side. Greta realized this area must have been part of a larger chamber, but at some point the ceiling had collapsed and all that remained was this narrow passage.

Her next step landed on nothing but air. She stumbled and would have fallen if Ray hadn't grabbed her arm and sharply hauled her back. "Sorry," he whispered. "I forgot to mention there's a bit of a drop."

She glared back over her shoulder. "Yeah, that would have been good to know."

He only shrugged.

She shook her head. "Where to now?"

"This is where things get a little tricky."

"Wonderful. Because it's all been a walk in the park up to this point." She peered down. "A bit of a drop" was actually a pit of sheer nothingness that went at least a couple hundred feet straight down. She could see the bottom, but only because huge fires blazed from different spots on the ground.

Greta hated to think what was happening down there at this very moment.

"We have to step out there and scale the wall around to the

other side. There's a tunnel leading down to the cells."

She'd had a bad feeling he was going to say something crazy like that.

"You look nervous," he said. "Are you going to be able to do this?"

"I guess I don't have much choice, do I?" Truthfully, she was stupid terrified. The thought of hanging by her fingers and toes above a chasm that would eat her whole and break every bone in her body if she fell was ten times scarier than what she'd felt climbing that wall outside, worse than the prospect of facing any number of the Lost.

She might as well go first. If the rock crumbled beneath her and she fell, at least Ray would feel guilty over her death for the rest of his life.

Inching to the edge, she peered around. There was a narrow but passable shelf running the length of the wall. Without thinking about what she was doing, Greta stepped out onto it and plastered her whole body to the hard surface, refusing to look down.

"Crap. Crap. Crap." The going was slow, and she did it mostly with her eyes clamped shut.

Besides one heart-stopping moment when she lost her footing and scrambled to press her spine to the wall, she finally reached the other side and waited for Ray, trying to make her heart step back down to a halfway normal rhythm.

He joined her in considerably less time, and jumped down beside her with a grin. He wasn't even breathing heavy, the jerk.

Without a word, they made their way through the next corridor, which angled steadily downward in a spiral, heading deeper and deeper into the heart of the mountain. At first, all she could hear was the sound of her own breathing and the soft crunch of their footfalls in the dirt, but soon enough Greta started to hear other things, things that chilled her blood.

Screaming, shouting, and the growls of creatures that could not possibly be human.

Each step brought them closer to that madness, compounding her anxiousness, and making her certain they would be too late to save anyone.

She held her hand up to signal Ray and crowded against the wall. He stopped close behind her, peering around her shoulder.

A few feet ahead of them, the corridor opened up, most likely to the large chamber they had rounded from above. Watching the chaos, it was obvious the eclipse was full and had left no creature unscathed. Fires burned high, but the temperature in there had little to do with the heat, and a lot to do with the gnomes, ogres, and other distorted beings Greta couldn't identify, all trying to murder each other. "Let me guess. We have to go through there."

"The cells are located on the other side," Ray said, "but maybe they'll all be so wrapped up in destroying each other, they won't notice us." An optimistic thought, but she doubted he believed it.

"All right. I want you to head out of here now." Greta stripped off her long coat to streamline her form for fighting, and drew her sword.

Ray just crossed his arms over his chest and waited.

"Damn it." She shook her head and sighed. "Then here's the way it's going to go. We run. You stay close, right behind me. Obviously, we're not going to try and take them all on. Just barrel through anyone who gets too close and hope for the best."

Ray nodded. His bow was ready, his old eyes reflecting acceptance—of his choices and their consequences, maybe of his approaching death. "I'm sorry I dragged you here with me."

It was a gracious lie, but Greta didn't fault him for it. She wanted to tell him they'd get through this. Instead, she gave him the truth. "You didn't drag me, Ray. And don't start writing us off just yet. I'm tired of getting spit on, beaten, and clawed up. I'm in the mood for some payback."

Turning toward the mouth of the writhing chamber, Greta waited a moment until she saw their opening—a small break in the throng right along the side of the room. "Ready?"

She didn't wait for his confirmation, but leapt forward at a dead run, trusting him to stick to the plan.

Maybe because their sudden presence was so unexpected, or maybe Ray had been right and Agramon's minions were caught up in the turmoil of the eclipse and having too much fun pounding on one another, but they made it halfway across the chamber before the first ogre attacked.

And that's where their luck ran out. He was a big one, and the look that came over his face when he spotted them made her feel like the Christmas turkey for a starving man—a turkey that still needed to be plucked.

Greta didn't stop. Instead, she ran faster and ducked her head at the last minute, hitting the ogre with her shoulder, using as much momentum as possible. As it staggered backward, Ray lodged an arrow in its left eye.

Neither of them paused, just kept on moving—but their very slight advantage of surprise was gone. One after another, snarling heads stopped and turned. Bodies lunged toward them. Greta started hacking. There was no finesse in her defensive moves, it was all about survival.

She sliced the throat of a gnome before spinning in a circle to see another barreling down on Ray. "Behind you!"

"Greta!" He lifted his chin over her shoulder and raised his bow.

In a smooth move, they switched places and Greta met the goblin that had been coming for him, while Ray's arrow found its target in the ogre that had been moments from crushing her skull between its huge clubs-for-hands.

"Crap." Looking left and right, she realized she'd lost sight of the direction they'd been heading—not that it mattered when death was coming at them from *all* sides.

Suddenly, Ray went down, slugged in the face by a gnome with glowing, beady little eyes and a toothy, wide-mouthed grin. Before she could do anything to help, Greta's braid was yanked viciously and her head snapped back.

Her sword clattered to the ground. Thick fingers closed around her throat, and she felt the creature's hot breath on her cheek. From the size of the body at her back, she was being held by an ogre—an ogre about to take a bite out of her.

She kicked back, elbowed, and clawed at him—all the while watching helplessly as Ray was pummeled in the ribs and stomach.

Another gnome joined the fray, looking to get himself a piece of the human on the ground, and the two turned on each other, buying Greta a fraction of a second. But the ogre wasn't letting up no matter what she tried, and the pressure on her throat was steadily choking the strength out of her. They weren't going to make it.

Through the muffled thudding in her ears, she heard a commotion from across the chamber. Their attackers noticed it at the same time. Greta didn't care what the hell was going on, she only knew it was a distraction she could make the most of and nailed the ogre hard in the shin. Her fingers scrabbled for the dagger at her waist. She pulled it and stabbed backward into the ogre's thick thigh muscle. It finally let her go.

Spinning fast, she ignored its enraged cries, adjusting her grip and swinging the short blade in a high arc across the creature's jugular.

Without waiting to see if he would fall over, she immediately went for her sword and then threw herself at the gnomes on top of Ray, slashing and hacking until she reached his side.

He was curled up into a tight ball, unmoving. Blood disguised the extent of the injuries to his face, but when she reached out her hand to check his pulse, he jerked and snarled at her. Good. At least he was still alive.

"It's me, Ray. I've got you," she said. He settled down and tried cracking open his swollen eyes. "Come on," she urged. "It's just a little farther. We can make it, no problem."

"Liar," he croaked, but he pushed himself to his feet. She handed him her dagger, since his bow lay in three broken pieces across the dirt floor.

Greta pushed forward once again, slower this time so Ray could keep up. It forced her into direct combat with more of Agramon's minions, but surprisingly, they weren't overwhelmed. Whatever other disturbance had invaded this chamber, Greta was glad for it because it had divided the creatures' attentions.

Then again, whatever it was, she and Ray were headed right for it.

"Greta!"

With a hard thrust, she finished off the gnome in front of her and turned to fight off the two coming up behind them.

Her strength was flagging. The gashes in her chest and thigh pulled, her throat was on fire, and her overworked muscles screamed as she parried and blocked, but there was still no relief in sight. For all the bodies littering the ground in their wake, it seemed as if Greta hadn't even made a dent in the throng. They kept coming, so many of them she could see no way of leaving this room alive.

A gnome went for her face and she ducked in time, only to have her legs kicked out from under her. She went down hard, the breath whooshing out of her and her teeth coming together with a hard *crack*. Before she could bring up her hands in defense, the gnome was on top of her.

Ray shouted. It sounded so far away, and she felt a rush of panic that he was unprotected. It gave her a surge of adrenaline and she thrust her arms between her and the gnome before it tore out her throat. Two rows of jagged teeth snapped and snarled an inch from her face. Blood coated its lips and chin, and foam dripped from the corners of its mouth like a rabid dog.

Just when she was sure she couldn't hold on any longer, the creature was lifted off her and thrown sideways like a bowling ball into the oncoming horde.

Greta forced the pain aside and jumped to her feet with sword in hand, looking wildly back and forth. Ray was at her side and she pulled him close, reeling around to find herself only inches away from a huge goblin.

Isaac.

Whether it was the eclipse, the fury of battle, Ray shooting at him outside—or a combination of all three—the goblin king had fully turned.

Huge. Angry. Skin almost black. Teeth made for ripping. Hands curled into thick fists. Eyes lit by a fierce, wild light.

She lifted her blade between them, heart hollow and empty.

She hadn't wanted it to come to this.

Chapter Twenty

"Isaac," she whispered. Even like this, she couldn't think of him as a monster. The real Isaac must still be in there somewhere.

Her throat constricted. Now it seemed so natural to say his name, so right. What had once been anathema was now a plea, her last link to the boy who'd invaded her carefully guarded heart and dared her to accept herself for the person this world had made of her.

"*Greta.*" His voice rumbled over her like steel wrapped in velvet, startling in its controlled clarity. "Come."

She could sense the pull in him—between beast and man—and was amazed by the blunt power of his will.

Greta made the decision to put her trust in Isaac's strength. "Ray, let's go," she yelled. When he hesitated, she grabbed his arm and pulled him with her. "He won't hurt us," she promised.

Isaac made short work of any who dared get in their way. When they reached the other side of the chamber and passed through the wide doorway carved out of the rock, he stayed back so nobody could follow them through.

Ray sprinted ahead down a dark corridor. "We have to go this way!"

"Wait," she called, turning back. "Isaac, hurry! I'm not going without you."

He slugged a gnome and sent it flying back before growling at her over his shoulder, but then he stepped over the threshold, looking up and down at the loose rock strewn across the ground. His gaze stopped on a particularly large piece. She knew what he was going to try to do.

She held her breath as he lifted the massive boulder over his shoulders with a great roar. He surged upward and pushed it out of his hands and into the stone above the entrance to the chamber, releasing a cascade of rock that tumbled downward and blocked the way.

It also started a rumbling throughout the mountain that echoed all around them.

Greta grabbed his clawed hand and pulled him with her as she ran toward Ray. "Where are the cells?" she asked.

He pointed down a narrow corridor. "That way."

Isaac gripped her arm. When she turned to him, he shook his head. "No."

"No, what?"

"Leave now." He started to pull her in the opposite direction.

She yanked her hand back. "I can't," she said. "Not without the others."

He glowered, looking fierce and wild as if her refusal just might push him over the edge into total madness. "Agramon needs you," he bit out. "To complete his circle and give his spell the power to open a portal. Can't let him."

"What spell? What are you talking about?"

"He's a prisoner here. Wants to tear open the gate, escape this world."

"Why doesn't he just make the Lamia open it for him?"

"Witch's magick…not powerful enough to break the spell keeping him imprisoned."

"We can make Agramon use his own spell to send all of us humans back home," Ray said.

Isaac snarled at the boy, taking a menacing step forward. Greta held him back. When he turned to her, she could see he was fighting to contain the fury of the eclipse.

"Let me guess," she said. "The spell Agramon has concocted requires human participation to make it work, doesn't it?"

Isaac nodded. "Human blood."

Of course it did.

"If all that's true," Ray said, "if Agramon needs human blood to fuel his magic, why has he put us to work as slaves? Why doesn't he just do it already?"

Without the fires of the chamber to give them some light, Greta couldn't see more than Isaac's great hulking shadow…and the glow of his eyes. He paid little attention to Ray now, his focus wholly on her. "Have to be special." A low grumble. "Humans descendant from a particular bloodline. The rest were used to build the…altar."

She'd been clenching her hands so hard her fingertips were numb. So were her lips, her legs, and feet. She felt disassociated from her own body—everything but her heart. That hurt so bad she couldn't breathe. It felt like a mortal wound, as if her blood should be pouring out onto the floor in front of her.

"*You knew.*" She took a step back, not wanting him to see that he was killing her with every word. "You knew all about this from the beginning. When Luke died and I asked you…you lied. When I found out about the contract on my head…you lied. And in my dream when I asked you again… You told me you had no idea Agramon was holding humans prisoner, and you didn't know what he wanted them for."

When did it end with him? The lies, the tricks, the games? She thought she'd finally begun to see the true Isaac, but now she wondered if there was any such thing. Had anything he'd shown her ever been real, or only delusions of her mind — all of it a dream she couldn't wake up from?

The guilt in his face was the last straw. Greta's blood chilled until there was nothing left but the unfeeling skill of the ice-cold bounty hunter rushing through her veins. "Why are you here now? How did you get in?"

Would he deny it still, or finally tell her the truth?

"You're actually in league with him, aren't you? With the demon. What do you do, return the humans lucky enough to escape his clutches? Do you watch them being tortured, maybe you like to wield the whip yourself every once in a while?"

Isaac came forward, but Greta took another step back, and another. "Ray, go on ahead and get the boys." She didn't look at him, didn't dare break eye contact with Isaac. "I'll hold off the goblin and any others."

"Are you sure?"

"Just do it. Before it's too late."

Isaac didn't even blink when Ray turned and ran. She'd known he wouldn't bother with him, because he hadn't come here for just any human. Not today.

He'd come for her. Only her.

"Return with me, Greta."

She gripped the hilt of her sword tighter, finding little comfort in its familiar weight. "Not going to happen. Now…or ever again."

"No time to explain."

As if he could. "You don't have to explain, I get it. Anything's fair for you, isn't it? You'd betray your own mother—"

Both his hands snaked out and grabbed her arms. She sputtered with outrage as he dragged her close, trapping her sword arm between their bodies. He glowered down into her face, and she was surprised by how controlled he seemed. Was it because he was still young enough, the moons didn't overtake him completely? His skin had almost returned to normal, if not the length of his teeth and claws. Could it be that his fury in that chamber had come not from the eclipse, but from within—maybe even out of fear? *For her*?

She couldn't bear to be so close to him. So close his scent teased, his eyes mesmerized, his touch…

Damn him. "Let me go."

"You must understand."

"I understand perfectly." She twisted and writhed, but that only brought home to her just how seriously outmatched she was.

"You do *not*. You have no idea what this monster has done to my world."

"And I don't care!"

At that, he shoved her away from him in disgust and swatted her sword. It went flying from her hand. "No. You don't care about Mylena or its people, do you? I don't think you care about anything at all." Looking down his nose, he said, "*But I do*. And after centuries of suffering, when the leaders from all the counties finally forced Agramon's evil underground, believe me, it was worth the price. A price my father paid, and a price I was expected to pay when I assumed leadership over the goblin territories."

"What price?"

"The faerie magick keeping him here wasn't made to last. When I took the throne—*for you*," he reminded her with a harsh look, "I learned that my ancestors had agreed to help Agramon find the humans he requires to open the gate, in return for his promise that he would finally leave Mylena once and for all."

Greta felt the wave of vehemence radiating off him, the utter conviction that he'd done nothing wrong. "So you all made a deal with the devil. All the counties," she whispered. The light dawned. "That's where the moon madness comes from, doesn't it? All those stories about humans bringing on the curse of the moons, the eternal winter…it was all a lie to hide the truth—you brought it on yourselves. You broke the laws of nature by aligning yourselves with Agramon's evil, and the Great Mother is punishing you for it."

His face contorted in a snarl. "*Humans* brought Agramon here and we have suffered the consequences. But we finally had the chance to banish his poison from our world. Don't tell me you would not have done the same."

As much as Greta wanted to deny it, could she say for certain she wouldn't have paid a similar price for something that was important to her…like the chance to go home? "Thankfully, I don't have to answer that question."

"I was not so lucky. The burden was set upon me whether I wanted it or not."

"So screwing with my dreams was just an extra thrill before it came time to hand me over?"

"I won't apologize for doing what I thought was necessary to undo the damage humans have wrought on my land. But I never agreed...it was never about that between us—"

"How do you know it was humans?" she yelled up at him, punctuating the words with a hard shove to his chest, trying desperately to push all her rage into him. "How exactly did humans bring a demon to your world?" she yelled. "Well? Give me the details. Show me some—" *Shove.* "Damn—" *Shove.* "Proof!" *Shove.*

He grabbed both her shoulders again, baring his teeth. Her breathing ragged and painful, Greta had a moment before he shook her to notice that her goblin—no, not hers, never hers—looked almost completely normal now, but for the impatient curl of his lips.

It was Greta who felt like a raging beast without any control.

"*You* are all the proof I need. Your blood will prove it!" With glowing eyes and a muttered curse, he clasped her head in his trembling hands and crushed his mouth to hers in a hard kiss that proved just how strong Isaac's control had been until now, how tight a leash he had kept on his true emotions.

She shivered and clutched his shoulders.

Real.

The tips of his claws grazed the back of her neck.

Real.

His pointed incisors nipped the soft flesh of her lips, and his body was rock solid against her.

Real.

This was no dream. It was more real than anything she'd ever felt.

More real...and more devastating.

She'd convinced herself that their kiss two nights ago had only been as intense as she remembered because it had been a dream. She'd convinced herself that the reality couldn't possibly compare. She'd steeled herself for disappointment. And yet, as her senses reeled and her body bloomed with heat, the opposite was true. In his kiss, she felt what she'd never completely experienced before—the melding of Isaac who plagued her dreams, and Isaac who tormented her waking hours.

And nothing had ever felt so vivid, so consuming, so amazing.

When he drew back, it was with a whisper of her name against her forehead in a hoarse and broken voice.

A harsh cry of protest escaped her throat. She didn't want to let him go yet. His thunderous gaze met hers and he groaned in defeat at whatever he found looking up at him, finding her lips once more as the thing that had been building between them refused to be denied any longer, sweeping them both up in its fiery storm.

There was no mistaking his frustration and anger, even his pain. It came off him like a fever, engulfing her with a blast of terrible heat, but she still felt safe, protected. It may only last for as long as he held her, but for now that was enough.

His tongue slid past her lips and she gasped with shock and excitement. A deep shiver ran through her as claimed her, harder and deeper with every thundering beat of their hearts.

His hands were on her waist now, gripping her, holding her to him. Her head spun, she was spiraling out of control, and couldn't let that happen. Not here, not now.

Finally, she pulled away, gulping air deep into her lungs. Guilt overtook passion. Had Ray found the others? Was he even now calling for her help?

The grip on her waist tightened. She looked up and steeled her expression. "If you're going to give me up to Agramon, then let's get it over with."

"You still believe the worst of me." His tone was flat, but for once, he couldn't hide his true feelings behind his royal mask. Greta shrank from the despairing intensity in his eyes.

"Don't you understand anything?" He shook her. "It never mattered what you are, or what I should have done. Not since the very beginning. I fought my own uncle to keep you safe, I've fought my own people. I have no intention of letting the demon have you now. *You're mine.*" A distinct growl of possession. "Agramon will have to make do with—"

With the blood running fast and hot through her veins, she pounded his chest with her fists. "Don't tell me you could coldly substitute another helpless human in sacrifice to him. Agramon won't *make do* with anyone else. We're getting them all out. Even if you stop me, Ray will succeed."

His hands fell away. "You can't save all of them. Your friend might reach the cells, but he won't find the ones Agramon has kept separate to fuel his spell."

Her chest tightened like a vise around her heart. "Damn it, Isaac." The weight was suffocating her to the breaking point. She felt the cracks travelling, widening, and splitting off in all directions.

I can't keep doing this. She was so tired, and there was still so much to overcome. She felt sure he sensed her bone-deep desperation. Would he use it against her? "I can't leave them."

His punishing stare held her, cut her.

"Please." A murmur. She couldn't manage any more than that.

He knew what she was asking. He knew, too, what she would be forced to do if he refused. She didn't want to fight him anymore.

Finally, he nodded. She let out a long sigh. Even after everything, Greta had hoped he would help her. She should hate him for his betrayal, should hate him for what he would have done to her own kind, should hate him for all the lies.

She didn't. She couldn't.

A month ago, she would have been able to deny how she felt. Even a week ago, she could have tried. Now, Greta understood what it meant to feel a responsibility that went beyond her own needs and desires, and she didn't have room in her to hate Isaac. It would be like hating herself—and she didn't have room for that either.

"Come with me," he said.

They followed a dark corridor. Instead of going deeper into the depths of the mountain, it climbed steadily.

After ten minutes or so, the corridor came to an end, opening into a large chamber illuminated by natural light from the open ceiling, which confirmed that the eclipse was over. Mylena's suns still looked almost completely aligned with one another, glowing as lightly as they ever did, but her twin moons had passed completely in front of them and were beginning to break apart back into their natural orbit.

Greta gasped as she entered the room, stopping before she crossed over the distinct line marking a circle that vibrated with magick. "Oh my God. What is this?"

The area had been divided into a pie of twelve, marked at each outside point by a stone figure. In the center was another, smaller circle, empty except for a tall dais—no, it was an altar.

Isaac didn't respond, but she didn't need him to. Her head thumped with the force of the circle's power, her heart pounding in time with it, so loud that the echo was all she heard.

Approaching one of the figures, she was startled to discover that she was looking at an inanimate statue of a human child. She continued on to the next.

"Why would he build these…?"

The sickening, stomach turning feeling of horror built slowly since it took her a long time to accept the truth of what was right in front of her. And then it took every bit of her will not to fall to the ground and weep.

"These aren't statues. These are…" Walking from one to the other, she glanced over her shoulder at Isaac in a demand for confirmation, but he remained silent.

She stopped again at the fifth figure in its place in the circle.

This time her knees did meet the floor, having lost the ability to hold her weight. She pressed both her fists to her mouth and bit down on her knuckles, but the strangled scream forced its way out anyway.

No. God, please no. It must be some kind of trick.

"Isaac, tell me this isn't what I think—" She looked up as he stopped beside her, but her gaze was drawn immediately back to the silent stone face of one young boy in particular—a boy who, in life, had grinned with irreverent dimples in his chubby cheeks, and blinked up at her with bright blue eyes that could never quite hide his impossible stubborn streak. "There has to be some other explanation." A waver in her voice. "*Please.*"

"They were all real human children." Such finality in those words. "Once."

Boys. All boys. Each one a different age, each frozen with such an expression of terror…including Greta's own brother. She reached out, touching her hand to his cold, gray one. How had this happened? When? The thing she'd been certain of all these years was that Drew was safe. To find out she'd failed in that one thing, the most important thing…

"How is it even possible?"

"This is the Lamia's work." A stony, unfeeling tone that made Greta feel all the more isolated in her anguish. "Agramon knew it would take time to find the number of acceptable humans required to open his gate. The witch he captured to retrieve them was compelled to give him a way of safeguarding the vital components of the spell."

"What do I do to reverse it?" There had to be a way. Greta wouldn't leave here without every one of these boys—even if it meant she didn't leave at all.

"Agramon needs the blood of thirteen humans," Isaac confirmed. "But the final piece is special. Once it's in place the rest will be released from their dormant state to complete the spell and set the demon free."

Her heart pounded as her gaze went to that empty space in the center of the chamber. She somehow knew it had been reserved for her. Could it be because she was female, while all the others were male? Was it *her* specifically he needed, or just one more body—any body—who carried her bloodline, like Isaac had said?

Isaac's shuttered expression warned her that if she did this, chances were she wasn't going to be getting up and walking away from it.

Taking the first step over the boundary of the circle, she could feel the power drumming in her head increase into an earsplitting staccato beat.

A hand on her arm. Like being grounded, the beehive hum was forced to slow, to wait. "Don't do this."

She would not be swayed by anything she saw in his face—even her own fear and longing reflected back at her. "I have to."

"You're going to die."

His chest heaved, his eyes glowed. God, he was so fierce. "I can't do it anymore," she said. "I can't live in this world or any other if it means being responsible for the loss of those innocent lives."

She stole some of the goblin's ferocity for herself and smiled. "But that doesn't mean I'm giving in. I can feel the power of the circle calling to me. I think I can control it and direct it." A pause to breathe through the urgency that had her heart tripping along double-time. "I have to at least try. Hopefully if I do this now, before Agramon shows up, we can all get out of here."

The hard line of his mouth and the creases in his forehead were a dead giveaway of how fiercely he continued to fight the wildness inside. The eclipse was still in his blood, even though its urgency had started to wane.

"I know what it means if I destroy Agramon's only chance for escape and he takes it out on this world. And I do care, Isaac. I cared about Lucius, and I care about Siona, Maidra, and all the rest. I care about Mylena." She squeezed his hand. "Even more importantly, I care about you. More than I thought I could care about anything."

She steeled her heart to continue. "But these are children, and it shouldn't matter if they're only human. One of them is my brother, my family. My *responsibility*. Maybe it makes me as much a monster as Agramon, but I'll sacrifice myself, this world… everything to save him."

Bracing herself for his argument, his physical retaliation, she was surprised when he attempted neither.

"I know." A murmur. An admission that stripped them both in an instant, made them both vulnerable.

She gasped in response to the burn spreading through her. Oh

God, it hurt. The damned goblin had never managed to hurt her as much as right now, in this moment when the bleak shadows in his eyes told her how much he loved her, and there was nothing she could do about it.

"Isaac, I—" What to say, when her own emotions were still so divided and uncertain.

"Later. We'll do this later." A final touch, tracing the hard line of her temple where her pulse beat in an erratic rhythm. He was going to stand with her. Protect her.

For the first time, she had no doubts about his intentions. Isaac was here for *her*. He'd always been here for her. He would give up the only chance his people had to be free. He'd sacrifice himself and his beliefs...all for her. And as selfish as she was, Greta would let him.

"Hurry up, sweet Greta. Time—as always—is not on your side."

Again, she stepped into the circle and was instantly flooded with energy. Each step forward was more and more difficult as she fought an invisible wall like the push of a magnetic field. It left her breathless and weak—until she made the final step into the center. And then it was as if the magnet was reversed and she became the attracting end instead of the opposing end, drawing the same energy in thick currents.

Magic washed over her like the waves of the ocean crashing upon smooth, weathered rocks. Greta didn't buckle and break under the pressure. In fact, it fed her, making her stronger, helping her to see.

"Holy hell," she managed on a shuddering moan. Her eyelids fluttered. The sizzle rushing through her body fired all her nerve endings, sensitizing every inch of skin until her entire body throbbed.

Fighting to pull herself together and focus, she clenched her fists tight, forcing her gaze on the statue of Drew straight ahead of her. Her presence in the circle had definitely started something. With her mind, she reached out for the elusive energy rippling all around her, but it seemed to slither away just beyond her grasp.

And then she realized that the boys were the source of the circle's power, that Greta was the medium that would focus it, like sunshine being narrowed through a magnifying glass. It wasn't a matter of chasing the energy, but letting down her guard enough so it could flow the way it wanted to naturally—right through her. Once she did that, the magick was hers to control, and she could feel it bending to do her will.

One by one, each of the twelve stone figures started to shake off the Lamia's enchantment. She wondered which one of them was Jason, the boy Wyatt had tried to save from the Lamia's fire. Greta held her own breath as the first tiny chest expanded to draw air, and then she kept her gaze on Drew, waiting for his cheeks to turn pink, his eyes to lose the lifeless slate gray color and return to a beautiful blue.

Finally, he blinked up at her, his child's face reflecting confusion and fear. She wanted to call out and reassure him, but it took all her concentration to keep the magick sharply focused.

As each of the boys awakened in turn, she sensed the power passing through her increasing exponentially with their consciousness. When the twelfth and final little boy drew his first breath, she tried to shut it all down and step out of the circle's center—and couldn't move.

She'd popped the cork off this genie's bottle, and it would no longer fit back in the small mouth from which the magick was a free-flowing cascade. The power kept growing, filling every nook and cranny of her body, mixing with her blood and twining around her soul until she and it were the same.

Ahead of her, a ripple was forming in the air, and she saw Drew as if through a sheet of running water. The aperture grew slowly but steadily, and Greta realized that she was somehow opening a portal.

Hope warred with fear as the slice in space spread, about two feet tall already.

All the boys in the circle had awakened, looking from one to the other with matching expressions of terror.

From the corner of her eye, Greta saw Ray rush into the chamber. She wanted to call out to him to stay back, but the words disintegrated from her lips. Maintaining control over the magick took every bit of her concentration.

"Holy Mother of God," he muttered, grinding to a halt as he took in the circus show.

Isaac stepped in front of him, blocking him from getting to her. She worried that human and goblin were about to face off against each other, and managed to lift her hand as if to stop them, but only a fraction of an inch, and they didn't even notice.

At that moment, their party had one last joiner and Greta didn't need an introduction to know who it was.

Agramon was everything she'd feared and nothing she could have imagined. Years hunting down Mylena's biggest and baddest had taught her to expect horns and claws, dangerous oozing fluids, and ripping teeth in her adversaries, but the demon looked nothing like any Mylean creature…although that actually made sense considering, like her, he wasn't from Mylena at all.

In fact, besides his huge size—which rivaled even Isaac—and

the glowing whorls that traced every inch of his naked torso, the dreaded Agramon looked…human. He had black hair and his cheeks were razor sharp slashes that highlighted his crazy wide grin. But the difference was in his red eyes. One look in those eyes and it was more than obvious that he was not only evil and powerful, he was wicked insane.

"You started without me." He didn't sound overly worried or disappointed. In fact, he sounded excited.

He stared at her over Isaac's shoulder, those intense, bloody eyes boring into her with cold purpose. Greta's blood would have run to ice if it wasn't infused with all the fire of the circle's power. Trapped in its steel-gripped riptide, she could do nothing but watch in horror as Isaac held his ground, honoring his promise to protect her.

Agramon waved a hand for him to move out of his way. "I wondered whether the new goblin king would fulfill his obligations and follow in the footsteps of his successors. I'm impressed. You've brought me the last—most important—component of my spell."

Isaac growled, hands clenched into tight fists. "You can't have her."

Agramon's brow lifted in surprise. "You can't save her. Why would you even want to? She is the key to my freedom…and yours."

Isaac didn't move aside. "I won't let you sacrifice her. Mylena will find some other way to get rid of you and break its curse."

His selfless devotion broke her heart. She tried to blink away the tears that blurred her vision, but it was impossible to control even that much of her body, and she felt the wetness slide down her cheeks.

Agramon only laughed. "It's too late, anyway. The human has

conveniently set everything into motion and now nothing will keep me from her."

He glanced over his shoulder at Greta with a smile so filled with evil and a dark possessiveness, she felt it like a snake slithering over her skin. Isaac must have taken exception to that look, because he lunged forward with a roar. Agramon met him eagerly, anticipation apparent in his stance as they crashed together.

As the goblin and the demon traded violent blows that would have destroyed lesser beings, Ray inched to the outer edges of the circle, his battered face filled with determination.

"*Ray*." She gritted her teeth, slowly lifting her hand and pointing to the rift. "*Portal. Go.*"

Hands fell on his shoulders, and Ray was thrown with such strength he went flying into the wall. Greta heard the crack of his head smashing against the rock. *No!*

Agramon stepped toward her. What had he done to Isaac? She fought against the magick still flowing from the children into her, knowing she had to cut it off and get everyone through that portal before—

The grinding pain of a hand clamping hard on her wrist, squeezing until it felt as if her bones would shatter, crashed through her. A strangled scream was ripped from her throat. He had her. He was in the circle.

Immediately, she felt the shift as the demon's touch connected him to the magick, re-directing it through her—and into him.

His shout of triumph surrounded her as he pulled more and more power. She could feel its essence darkening as his will tainted it, turned it into a thick sludge in her veins, before it was dragged from her, leaving her weaker and weaker.

She finally understood.

Like fuel in an engine, the boys provided the power, while she was the key to getting it all started…and Agramon was the bastard siphoning gas for his own car. Nothing but a dirty thief.

Beside her, the demon roared. "*Yes!*"

In front of them both, the portal widened. There was something on the other side. Through a blurry film like rippling water, she was sure she could see the dirt floor of a cave and even beyond, it opened up to the familiar sight of blue sky.

She could move more freely, probably because she was now only the conduit for the spell's magick, not its focal point. She fought to turn her head, grateful to see Ray moving, getting to his feet. She couldn't see Isaac.

Agramon's grip on her wrist tightened until she thought he might break her bones and dragged her closer. It was impossible to pull out of his cement-like grip. She was his link to the spell and he wouldn't be giving her up before he was damn good and ready.

One of the boys locked in the circle screamed. She twisted to look behind her just as he crumpled to the ground, blood trickling from his eyes, ears, nose, and mouth.

"What are you doing?" she yelled, frantic. Her voice came out as a struggling whisper. "You've got what you wanted, the portal is open. Now let them go!"

The red light in Agramon's eyes glowed brightly as he glanced down at her. His mouth clenched in a firm line, as if the power he was stealing was almost too much for even him to hold onto. "Sorry. Not going to happen, little girl."

The next boy cried out and went down, his small hand flung toward her.

"Stop it!" she pulled as hard as she could, trying to sever the connection, desperately counting the number of bodies between that poor child and her brother. Five.

"Be still!" Agramon shifted and shoved her to her knees, holding her arm high as he reveled in the rush of power feeding him. "It isn't getting the portal open that's the trick." He grinned down at her. "I have waited an eternity for this moment, and all of you *will* give your lives—and your blood—to *keep* the thing open so I can pass through. So I can pass into *any world* I choose."

Agramon's voice was drowned out by the choked cry of the next child. The power he now wielded was immense, and continued to grow. She could feel it like a massive river of lava that burned everything it touched. She swiveled to see the mouth of the portal, but there was only a dense, endless darkness on the other side now.

Drew looked so scared, so young. Four years wasn't very long, but she'd changed so much in that time. He probably didn't even recognize her.

Yanking up her pant leg with one arm, she slipped her only remaining weapon from the sheath at her ankle. She struggled back to her feet, determined that the next body to fall would *not* be his.

Drawing the dagger back, she twisted and aimed for Agramon's heart. He saw it coming, but Greta's desperation made her faster, and the blade penetrated his thick skin.

With her hilt protruding from his chest, the demon roared and turned on her, but still refused to let go—until a fist landed on the hand clasped around her wrist and pried it off.

Her gaze whipped up. Isaac's face was a brutal mask of rage, having again fallen prey to his raw form. It was also apparent that crossing the circle had been no easy matter. His shoulders were tight and his jaw clenched from the effort he expended to withstand the maelstrom.

She stumbled and fell to her knees as the goblin tore Agramon off the altar. He spared her a quick glance before he turned away with an animal roar, after his adversary. Agramon took hit after hit. Isaac pounded on him like he got a sick pleasure from it, but Greta knew it wouldn't be enough. The demon wasn't going to stay down for long.

"Ray!" Her voice croaked. She could already feel the spell returning to her control, but without all of the boys fueling it, the magick was starting to fade. Glancing up, the view through the portal showed her that beautiful slice of blue sky once more and she let out a relieved breath. "Hurry and get the rest of them through."

Ray nodded. He disappeared out of the chamber. When he returned, he was ushering in a group of children, directing them to the circle. Ten, then twenty, then thirty boys quickly passed through the portal before the only ones left were the children from the circle. Ray ran, pulling each of them from their pedestal and hoarding them together at the mouth of the rift.

Each time a spot was vacated, Greta felt the ebb of her power, and struggled to hold onto as much of it as possible.

She had to keep that door open just a little while longer. But she knew she wouldn't be the one walking through it. Even though she would be sending Drew back...Greta had to stay.

When Ray pushed her brother through, she bit her tongue hard, fighting the tears, fighting against the need to call him back for one last look and to at least say goodbye—but the portal was already starting to close, no matter how hard she tried to keep it stable.

Ray paused, looking back at her.

"Go!" she cried. "Ray, you have to go through that door right now!"

He shook his head. "What about you? Wyatt? The others?"

"Take care of my brother like he was your own, Ray." She needed his promise. "I'll find another way for the rest of them. You don't have to worry."

Still he hesitated, looking back into the depths of the rapidly disappearing rift. "It should be me," she heard him whisper.

"There isn't any more time! Get out of here!"

Mouth parted, he glanced back up to tell her something, but the words died and his eyes widened. With the last tendrils of the spell slipping from her grasp, Greta turned, her chest aching with fear of what she might see. But it wasn't a triumphant Agramon charging her. It was Isaac.

Bloody.

Bruised.

Broken.

A black-skinned, barrel-chested, fully turned goblin with smoke coming from his nostrils and fury rolling off shoulders wide as a house. He was coming for her.

And Greta wasn't afraid.

She glanced back at Ray, opening her mouth to urge him to hurry through the portal. But he shouted her name, rushing toward her instead.

"Ray, don't. Don't touch me," she warned.

When he grabbed her, his whole body stiffened and he gasped. She tried, but couldn't keep the magick from funneling into him. When it did, she felt the forces shift again. Ray gritted his teeth tightly and looked into her eyes. "I should. Be. The one. To stay," he bit out.

"No Ray, don't!"

He pushed her into the portal.

As soon as she fell through, she knew something had happened—both here and out there. She was alone. There was no cave, no blue sky. Instead, she found herself surrounded by nothingness, and spun around to look back out. Out there, Agramon was up again. She screamed to warn Isaac and Ray, but no sound came from her mouth. He wasn't going for them anyway; his gaze was glued to the doorway, glued to her.

She watched as Isaac tried to stop him, but he was right in front of her, coming through the portal…and then he disappeared.

The portal fractured, branched apart. Wherever the children had gone—God please let it be home—she was somewhere else, and Agramon must have been sent to another place entirely.

No. No. No. She started screaming again, pushing through the darkness back to the doorway, but couldn't seem to get any closer to it.

She had to get out. But, oh God, it was too late.

The doorway was almost closed and she was going to be stuck here.

In the dark.

Watching through the slim slice of portal still open to Agramon's fortress, she saw Ray being tossed by Isaac across the room like a sack of feed before he lunged forward with a roar. He reached through the rift, grasped hold of her arm.

His eyes. She didn't want to lose sight of those eyes. They held her for a long moment as his claws dug into the flesh of her forearm.

His furious face was hazy, as if a thin barrier of smoke had formed between them. She whispered his name. If he didn't let her go, would she be caught here in limbo, somewhere in the middle of the worlds, for eternity?

With a final squeeze, he pulled and yanked her forward. She screamed as the portal tried to suck her back in, not wanting to give her up.

"I won't let you go." The low rumble of sound penetrated the slight opening, through her aching chest, and took up residence in her bleeding heart. A voice she would never forget.

The portal slammed shut.

Chapter Twenty-One

The sensations rushed to make themselves known to her all at once, but she hesitated to blink her eyes open. She could feel the warmth of the fire in the hearth, heard it crackling away. Her fingers dug deeply into the furs covering her. A bed, but whose?

Then again, did it matter where she was, what she would see when she opened her eyes? Could she trust any of it? She didn't know any more if she was dreaming or not. The dreams had become her whole world, her only world, and it felt like she'd been locked inside them forever.

No, not dreams, nightmares. Filled with darkness and despair. Of moons dripping blood, glowing eyes brimming with anger and betrayal, and the pain-filled screams of children.

Through it all, *his* voice called to her, reminding her of their bond, of his claim on her soul.

She alternated between joy and terror. Anticipation and despair. He was the devil at her back. So close, always at her heels, but never catching her. No matter how often she tried, she hadn't been able to turn, to look over her shoulder, to stop running and let him catch her.

Until now.

"Isaac," she whispered.

"He isn't here."

Greta forced her eyes open and blinked at Siona. She lounged in the same chair Isaac had been sitting in the last time Greta woke up in this room.

Sunshine filtered in through the open window above her, making her hair gleam and her pale skin look like porcelain.

It wasn't fair that the first thing she saw was Siona's blinding beauty when there was no doubt Greta looked like she'd been to hell and back. In fact, based on the way she felt, she might still be in hell.

Struggling to sit proved a waste of time, and she gave up after the shooting pain in her head forced a groan from her lips. "You're getting a kick out of this, aren't you?" Greta muttered. "Well, it isn't a free show, so get off your butt and help me."

With an evil grin, Siona stood and finally sauntered over to the bed. She looked a little stiff and limped slightly, but that seemed to be the only remaining evidence of her own battle with Lazarus. She sat beside Greta and put an arm around her shoulders to help her sit up.

"Where is he?" Greta asked after she'd caught her breath, wincing at the croak in her voice.

Siona frowned. "He's been working night and day to bring some order to the territory after the devastation Agramon's army left behind."

Greta winced. That had been her fault.

"Which is made more difficult because of his position."

"He's the king. What could be hard about that?"

"Yes, but he's a young king who has yet to prove himself to his people. They know he didn't want the position in the first place, and now they are suspicious of his priorities."

Also her fault. "He can just order them to fall in line, can't he?" That sounded weak, even to her, and from the dry look Siona gave her, the goblin was of the same opinion. "So, then, what happens now?"

"Yesterday he went before the council, to answer charges of public endangerment."

She swallowed, trying to get some moisture into her dry throat. "I don't understand."

"Leander accused him of harboring a gang of humans in the goblin forest." She winced again. Another thing that was her fault. "Of course, the gnome king also named you as their leader. If Leander makes a good enough case, who knows what—"

Greta knew he was there before Siona had stopped speaking. She looked up and saw him standing in the doorway.

The wave of relief might have knocked her to her knees if she'd been standing. He looked whole, healthy, and back to his non-feral self. She started to smile, but the shuttered look on his face as he looked her up and down made her lips wobble with uncertainty.

He'd heard what they were talking about, she could see it in the tightness of his mouth. Was he angry? Worried? Should she be worried?

Did he have regrets already, based on the trouble he was now in because of her? Should she plan to be on her feet and out of here before dark?

Siona got up from the bed with an exasperated sigh. Propping her hands on her hips, she narrowed her gaze on them both. "Stop it."

Greta gasped, and Isaac lifted an imperious brow in his cousin's direction. "Stop what?"

"All the doubt hovering in the air between you," she said. "It's so palpable, I can practically see steam coming off you both. Let go of it, and see the truth."

The truth.

Greta took in Isaac's rigid pose. He remained standing stiff and tall just inside the door. He wasn't wearing his cloak, only a white lawn shirt, sleeves rolled up to his elbows. For the first time, there was a bit of scruff shadowing his jaw and cheeks, and he had dark circles under his eyes, which watched her carefully. Her stomach twisted as she realized it might not be regret that darkened his face, but wariness.

In their tumultuous back and forth, he had always let down his guard first—and she'd always thrown it back at him, using her anger and mistrust as an excuse to keep hiding from what he made her feel.

She let the smile she'd been holding back break across her face, determined to take the first step toward accepting her new life in Mylena…her new life with him.

His expression cleared, but she still sensed hesitation in him as he crossed the plank wood floor with solid thudding steps, taking Siona's position beside her on the bed.

Siona gave them a satisfied nod. "I will assume this means I'm not needed here any longer."

Before Siona could turn to leave, Greta held out her hand. "Thank you."

The female goblin lifted a sculpted brow. "What for?"

"For watching over me. For being"—she cleared her throat—

"my friend."

Siona gave her a baleful grin. "Don't thank me yet, human. We're both going to need to get back in shape. You might change your mind about being my friend when we start sparring together. I have every intention of paying you back for that situation with the faerie."

She chuckled, despite the scratch in her throat. "I look forward to it…and Siona?"

When she turned back around Greta grinned. "I wouldn't get your hopes up," she said. "Your only chance of kicking my butt was when I was unconscious. As long as I can stand, you know I'll wipe the floor with you any day of the week."

"We shall see about that," Siona said as she passed out of the room with a turn of her hip.

Isaac took her hand. His touch was firm. Real. "I am glad that you're awake." He sounded so formal.

"What happened with the counsel?" she asked.

His eyebrows drew together. "I don't know," he admitted with a worried frown. "I hope I succeeded in convincing them that humans are no longer a threat to Mylena now that Agramon has been banished. At least, they haven't posted a writ for the capture of you or your…friends." He choked out the last word as if it caught in his throat like the splintered bone of a wild gallo, and sent her a guarded look.

"What about your people? Will they still follow you, accept you as their king?"

He raked a hand through his hair. "Now that I've betrayed them by falling in love with a human, you mean?"

She gasped at the word "love." Nobody had said that word to her in so long, her memory of it might only be a dream. But for once, *this* was no dream.

His expression had frozen as he anticipated her response. She glanced down at her hands twisting in her lap. "It might help if we can get Siona to spread the word that the human owns a sword and isn't afraid to use it."

"I suppose we'll find out."

She bit her lip, then took a deep breath."I still don't understand how you knew *I* was the key to Agramon's spell."

He sighed. "I *didn't* know, but Agramon was certain of it. He insisted it was about your blood, something to do with your ancestors."

"But how could my ancestors have had anything to do—"

He jerked his chin up. "It doesn't matter. I'm only glad that you're safe now. When that portal was closing, I thought you would be lost to me forever. And even though I pulled you out in time, it was as if some part of you remained trapped on the other side. You've been unconscious ever since. I couldn't even reach you in dreams."

He'd been there, she remembered him. He was the reason she made it back. She plucked at a snag in the thick blanket covering her legs. "How long was I out?"

She squeezed her eyes shut, remembering the darkness of that place. "The others, did they get through the portal?"

Oddly enough, she felt in her bones that they were safe. Drew was safe. She only wished there'd been more time. Time to tell him how sorry she was for everything. Time to hug him just once, and maybe give him a message for their parents. But no, it was better that they never know what had become of her.

"All but the one who pushed you made it through."

"Ray. What did you do to him?"

"I should have killed him, but he was gone before I'd even pulled you back."

"Oh, thank the Great Mother," she whispered. Her breath leaked out in a long sigh of relief. Ray would find his way to Wyatt and the boys. She only hoped they had been safe at Luke's place throughout the eclipse. Had they returned to the Dugout, she wondered, or maybe headed to the mountains in search of the Lamia?

Isaac dropped her hand. Startled, she looked up in time to see the flash of hurt cross his face before his eyes darkened. "You would still choose them over me, wouldn't you?" he asked. "If you thought it was possible, you would have left with them."

She shook her head. "No—"

"Even now, you're thinking about the ones who are still out there hiding in *my* forest. You're wondering when you can go to them."

At her hesitation, he shot up from the bed. She called him back, but he paced back and forth across the room. "After everything I sacrificed for you—"

"Isaac."

"Everything we've been through together…"

"Isaac!"

He rounded on her with molten, glowing eyes and a guttural snarl. Surprised by how quickly he'd started to turn, she gasped as the dark emotions rolled off him in waves, but there was no hesitation when she clasped his hand and tugged him back to her.

"I made promises," she said. "I have a responsibility to them. But that doesn't mean I can't still be with you."

He took several deep breaths and fought to regain control. She put her hand on his chest, conscious of its fast, heavy rhythm.

"I'm glad you brought me back."

His jaw clenched. "You're mine, Greta. I would bring you back from death itself if I had to."

She smiled, curling her fingers in his shirt, tugging him closer. "Let's hope that won't be necessary."

Acknowledgments

This book is a big deal to me. Huge. The whole process, from start to finish, took a lot out of me. From fleshing out the idea, to writing the first chapters, getting feedback from my brilliant critique partners, finishing and polishing the manuscript, submitting it for publication, and then going through the editing process. By the end of it I felt like I'd been stripped raw from the inside out...but it was completely worth it, and there were so many people holding my hand and helping me through it that I know I won't be able to thank them all, but I'm going to give it a shot.

First and foremost, I must thank my husband and my son. If writing and publishing is the deep dark lake in which I find myself swimming, then they are the solid slab of bedrock I jumped in from, always there for me to climb back out of the water to rest whenever I get tired and fearful of drowning. And I love that this particular rock always has clean laundry.

I have to thank the rest of my family, too. My mom and dad, brother and sister, and both of my grandmothers (in their eighties and reading my books!) have all been more supportive than I could ever have imagined. No matter what I write, they never turn down their nose at it and are proud of me.

I can never thank my critique partner enough for everything she's done to help me get where I am today. Christine is not only smart and funny, talented, and experienced in the ways of the Force, she talks me down from that jittery, neurotic place I go to every once in a while. She has the most amazing gift for plotting I've ever seen. At the drop of a hat, she'll take an idea and run with it until we have a steampunk romance with aliens coming down from the sky to torture medieval werewolves…and it all works brilliantly! As a critique partner, she balances my shortcomings perfectly. I can't say enough about how wonderful she is except to send her a…*Snoopy Dance!!*

Other critique partners and beta readers I need to send out a shout out to are Paula W, Amy R, Kimber C. Also, the fantastic Teen authors at Entangled Publishing have been a blast to get to know and are so supportive it'll make you cry, including Melissa West, Rachel Harris, Tara Fuller, Lisa Burstein, Lea Nolan, and Cindi Madsen. These are all super-charged writers and wonderful women whose friendship means a great deal to me. I'm so thankful for their support and encouragement.

Mucho love goes out to publicist Heather Riccio, who is a goddess. The work she's done to get this book into the hands of reviewers and readers has been massive. I am in awe of her powers of organization. As everything started to snowball towards release date, no matter what question I had or what request I made, she was always completely on top of it. If not for her, I might have fallen apart a hundred times, but she's so amazing that I always find myself smiling instead. I could not have done anything without her and I may never let her go.

I also want to thank Deborah Cooke (also known as Claire Delacroix), Michelle Rowen (also known as Morgan Rhodes), Kelley Armstrong, and Rachel Harris, who are all epically awesome authors. Their support of my work has been immeasurably generous, and their kindnesses made me cry hot, messy, destroy-your-makeup tears!

Along the way to publication, there have been so many other people who have been patient with my absences or distractions, supportive of my delusions, enabling of my obsessions, and who are great friends. Some of those people are Stacey O'Neale, Shannon Duffy, Lori Leduc, Yvonne Blackmore, Laurie Pescod, Lisa DeGooyer, Claire Veitch, Gordon Robson, Kait Batte, Colleen Dyck, Adrienne Dwyer, Jenny Schwartz, PG Forte, Stacy Gail, Tiffany Clare, Elyssa Patrick, and Maggie Robinson. Thank you all!

Finally, and most importantly, thank you to Liz Pelletier and the Entangled Publishing Team. Special thanks to Tahra and Jessica, and especially my editor, Heather Howland, who has so much skill and talent for what she does, it makes me breathless with wonder. I'm still in awe that she was able to look at the flawed story I sent her and see beyond it to the beautiful book it eventually became. She saw the tale I was trying to tell better than I did, and she understood my vision for it. She was sharp and brutal and brilliant, and she helped me become a better writer... all with a thousand and eighty other things on the go at the same time.

Before I go, let me thank YOU—dear Reader—in advance. I hope you enjoy the book!

Get tangled up in our Entangled Teen titles...

The Marked Son by **Shea Berkley**

When Dylan Kennedy sees a girl in white in the woods behind his grandparents' farm, he knows he's seen her before…in his dreams. Only he can save her world from an evil lord. Where they're going is full of creatures he's only read about in horror stories. Worse, the human blood in his veins has Dylan marked for death…

Ward Against Death by **Melanie Card**

Ward de Ath expected this to be a simple job to launch his fledgling career as a necromancer. But when he wakes the beautiful Celia Carlyle, Ward gets more than he bargained for. If he could just convince his heart to give up on the infuriating beauty, he might get out of this alive...

Inbetween by **Tara Fuller**

It's not easy being dead, especially for a reaper in love with Emma, a girl fate has put on his list not once, but twice. Finn will protect the girl he loves from the evil he accidentally unleashed, even if it means sacrificing the only thing he has left…his soul.

Get tangled up in our Entangled Teen titles...

Gravity by Melissa West

In the future, only one rule will matter: Don't. Ever. Peek. Ari Alexander just broke that rule and saw the last person she expected hovering above her bed — arrogant Jackson Locke. Jackson issues a challenge: help him, or everyone on Earth will die. Giving Jackson the information he needs will betray her father and her country, but keeping silent will start a war.

My Super Sweet Sixteenth Century by Rachel Harris

The last thing Cat Crawford wants for her sixteenth birthday is an extravagant trip to Florence, Italy. But when her curiosity leads her to a gypsy tent, she exits . . . right into Renaissance Firenze. Cat joins up with her ancestors and soon falls for the gorgeous Lorenzo. Can she find her way back to modern times before her Italian adventure turns into an Italian forever?

Onyx by Jennifer L. Armentrout

Thanks to his alien mojo, Daemon's determined to prove what he feels for me is more than a product of our bizarro connection. Against all common sense, I'm falling for Daemon. Hard. *No one is who they seem. And not everyone will survive the lies...*

Get tangled up in our Entangled Teen titles...

Conjure by **Lea Nolan**

Sixteen-year-old twins Emma and Jack Guthrie hope for a little summer adventure when they find an eighteenth-century message in a bottle revealing a hidden pirate treasure. Will they be able to set things right before it's too late?

Chosen Ones by **Tiffany Truitt**

The government, faced with humanity's extinction, created the Chosen Ones. When Tess begins work at a Chosen Ones training facility, she meets James, and the attraction is immediate in its intensity, overwhelming in its danger. Can she stand against her oppressors, even if it means giving up the only happiness in her life?

Toxic by **Jus Accardo**

When a Six saved Kale's life the night of Sumrun, Dez was warned there would be consequences. But she never imagined she'd lose the one thing she'd give anything to keep... Dez will have to lay it all on the line if there's any hope of proving Jade's guilt before they all end up Residents of Denazen. Or worse, dead...